Ellora's Cavemen

Flavors of Ecstasy

Volume 1

Extra Sensual Perception

Debra Glass

ꕥ

When Iris Thompson is asked to use her psychic skills to help solve a string of recent deaths, she's not surprised when her intuition points to a serial killer, all evidence to the contrary. But she *is* surprised that, though there have been only three deaths, she psychically intuits four names.

Even more shocking are her erotic trances featuring the handsome fourth man, known only as Peyton. As the images intensify, Iris has precious little time to discover if her extra-sensual perceptions are leading her to a victim—or the man of her dreams.

French Kiss

Solange Ayre

ꕥ

Amaryllis Gardner, from one of Boston's best families, is engaged to Dr. Brendan Bradford. Although wealthy, Brendan has no social status due to his Irish heritage. Amaryllis wonders whether he's marrying only to achieve social position.

Suspicious of her fiancé's visit to a supper club/brothel, Amaryllis disguises herself as a French prostitute. They engage in a passionate sexual encounter that leaves both of them desperate for more. Amaryllis soon learns exciting new sexual techniques that thrill Brendan. As their craving for each other intensifies, she fears he desires the wanton prostitute more than his prim fiancée.

HUNGRY LIKE A WOLF

Talya Bosco

ꟷ

Twelve months after the crushing heartbreak of being dumped by Ethan, the gorgeous Alpha werewolf who was the love of her life, Amanda is finally picking up the pieces. But the ties that bind the two lovers are strong, stronger than Ethan's resolve to stay away. One sizzling touch, one passionate kiss, is all it takes for the insatiable hunger inside each of them to explode into life.

But Ethan has a determined rival, for Amanda's affection and a whole lot more, and he'll stop at nothing to win it all.

RESISTING REED

Kristin Daniels

Are lustful thoughts of your best friend's son a sinful pleasure or an act of betrayal?

Reed has never hidden from Marilee the decadent passions he wants to share with her. Now that she's free from her cheating ex-husband, she's finally able to let her resistance slip and give in to temptation. But when their relationship is exposed during an afternoon of sensual self-discovery, will Marilee lose a treasured friendship, or will she be able to keep it all, including the man she loves?

HAVING IT ALL

Desiree Holt

ꟹ

When country rock singer Mac Fontana got his big break, he and Daisy Giles celebrated with a long night of fulfilling sex, where they explored each other's bodies and took their intimacy further than ever before. It seemed as if nothing could ever go wrong. Then Mac broke Daisy's heart and it was ten years before they saw each other again. Now, in one long night of erotic sex, Mac must prove to Daisy that she can trust him again and that together, they can have it all.

TRAPPED

Cindy Spencer Pape

ꟹ

Intergalactic bounty hunters Tabrin Jones and Zeyd Vasari, sometime lovers and continual rivals, are trapped for twenty-four hours in a tiny escape pod. To make matters worse, the atmosphere in the pod has the effect of loosening inhibitions. Amid the marathon sexual experience of a lifetime, will Zeyd also be able to convince Tab that they belong together forever?

An Ellora's Cave Romantica Publication

www.ellorascave.com

Ellora's Cavemen: Flavors of Ecstasy I

ISBN 9781419958519

Editorial Team: Raelene Gorlinsky, Sue-Ellen Gower, Kelli Kwiatkowski, Helen Woodall, Denise Powers.
Cover design by Darrell King.

This book printed in the U.S.A. by Jasmine-Jade Enterprises, LLC.

Electronic book Publication March 2009
Trade paperback Publication March 2009

ELLORA'S CAVEMEN: FLAVORS OF ECSTASY I

ℌ

EXTRA SENSUAL PERCEPTION

Debra Glass

ℬ

Dedication

ꕥ

This book is dedicated to the best psychic detective I know, my good friend, Dr. Jeanette F. McClure.

Trademarks Acknowledgement

ꕥ

The author acknowledges the trademarked status and trademark owners of the following wordmarks mentioned in this work of fiction:

BMW: Bayerische Motoren Werke Aktiengesellschaft

Diet Coke: The Coca-Cola Company

Hell's Kitchen: Granada Media Group Limited

The Tennessean: Media West–GSI, Inc.

Chapter One

ဢ

"All you have to do is tell us what you see."

Iris Thompson pulled her oversized sweater closer and stared at Bill, the detective who'd requested her assistance—her *psychic* assistance. Bill's wife was one of Iris' clients and although Bill was clearly skeptical of Iris' abilities, he'd called her at his wife's encouragement to help him solve a recent string of suspicious suicides.

Iris was just as nervous as Bill. She'd never worked with the police before although she'd been psychic all her life. She'd only recently moved to Nashville from Atlanta, where the police hadn't wanted anything to do with her brand of *help*. Her intuition had brought her here and as her gaze scanned Bill's tiny office, she wondered if this was why—this new direction with her psychic ability.

"I suspect foul play." Bill's chair creaked when he leaned back and laced his fingers behind his head. "I have no leads. Nothing to go on. I was wondering if you'd be able to find anything to link these deaths."

"You mean like the murderer?" Iris blurted. She scooted to the edge of her chair. Common sense told her to snatch up her purse and get the hell out of here but something in her intuition niggled at her to stay.

Bill's eyebrow arched. "Precisely." He pursed his lips.

"But why use a psychic? Why me?" she asked. "Haven't you consulted a criminal profiler?" Her gaze dropped to the file on his desk. She could see the corners of the photographs inside peeping out from under the edge of a manila folder.

Bill pushed the file toward her, tempting her to take it. "We've consulted *two* profilers. Nada. Zip. Zilch. They independently and collectively came to the educated conclusion that these were copycat deaths."

Iris swallowed thickly. She brushed her fingertips over the folder. Chills broke out at her wrist and skittered up her arm. She willed her psychic senses to calm. "That's what the papers say—that these men killed themselves."

Tapping his foot on the floor impatiently, Bill stared. "I'm interested in what *you* think."

When she'd read the account of the first man's death in the paper, her gut instinct had told her there was more to the story than the authorities knew. Now that three men had died under suspiciously similar circumstances, she *knew* the deaths were connected. They'd died—one each week—on Friday afternoons, all seemingly by their own hands. Still, there was more. Iris could tell because psychic energy crackled in the area of her solar plexus so fiercely she found it difficult to breathe.

Her gaze found Bill's and clung. "I feel they were murdered." Her heart pounded. She'd never actually worked with the police before. Most of her readings involved her clients' love lives and financial improvement—not matters of life and death.

Bill pushed himself up and adjusted his too-short plaid tie over his paunch. "What if I leave you alone with this file for a little while? Think you can come up with something for me?"

Iris sighed. Her gaze darted from the folder to Bill and back again. It wasn't that she wanted to examine the file. She *had* to. Her need to help others, to get the bad guy, warred for prominence to overcome any objections or anxiety she had about so serious a matter.

"All right," she conceded. "I'll look. But I can't make you any promises."

Bill's moustache twitched as his lips curled into a smile. "Thatta girl." With that, he picked up his empty coffee cup and headed out the door.

As soon as it was closed behind him, Iris snatched the file off the desk. She'd been dying to get a look at the evidence. This case, according to *The Tennessean,* was unlike any other. There had been three deaths—all victims single, successful, powerful businessmen in the prime of their lives. All had left notes. And all had been ruled death by suicide by the Davidson County coroner.

But Iris knew better.

She opened the folder and spread out a series of grisly photographs. She didn't have to look. She only had to touch.

Steeling herself for the psychic images she knew would inundate her, she flexed her fingers and then pressed her palm to the photo of a man who'd hanged himself in an elevator shaft.

Charles Morrison. Iris sucked in a breath. Her throat felt constricted. She coughed and closed her eyes and an image of him slipping the noose over his neck and then stepping into the shaft flooded her thoughts. But it wasn't the image that distressed Iris the most. It was the emotion—or rather, total *lack* of emotion.

It didn't make sense. Wouldn't a man on the verge of taking his own life feel *something*? Fear, despair, terror?

A shudder racked Iris' spine. Other names came to her. *David Dabney. Geoffrey Weakley. Peyton…*

She tried again.

Peyton…

Why no last name? Iris took a deep breath and blew it out. "Give me vibrations of Peyton," she whispered. "Give me his last name."

Nothing.

Mentally, she tallied the names—Charles, David, Geoffrey and Peyton. Bill had told her there were three victims. She'd gotten four names.

Concentrating, she fanned out the photos in the file. Each one was labeled but only Charles, David and Geoffrey were represented.

When Iris' fingers touched a photograph of David's suicide note, extrasensory images slammed her. Her lashes fluttered closed as she spiraled within, feeling as if she were looking out through David's eyes to watch herself write the note. *I have no other choice. I must do this. I must write this note.* Iris felt as if she was in some sort of trance—but this wasn't like any psychic trance she'd ever experienced. This was something else—something David was *made* to do. But how? Why?

Her eyes snapped open and she twisted in her chair to glance at the door. No one had come in. Bill was standing just outside talking to another city employee.

Iris swept her wavy brown hair behind her shoulder and stared at the photos. Three victims. Four names. Who was Peyton and why was he intruding into her visions?

There was only one way to find out but did she really want to go there? She bit her bottom lip. This wasn't like telling someone whether to pursue a relationship or not.

These were grown men who had allegedly taken their own lives. It wouldn't be like anything she'd ever done psychically. These men were already dead. She wouldn't be grasping at images to encourage someone to take a particular job or go on a cruise. But if nothing else, perhaps she could help these men's spirits make the crossing into the Light.

Still, what about Peyton? There was no photo of him in Bill's file. What if this Peyton was still alive?

Iris sat back in her seat and opened her palms upward. Closing her eyes, she breathed deeply and withdrew to that quiet place inside her, that place where she *received*.

"Peyton," she said aloud. "Show me Peyton."

Iris felt an insistent mouth on hers. A tongue teased her bottom lip and she opened to allow it inside. Molten desire oozed downward as big hands slid her panties down just far enough for fingers to find their way through her slippery folds and discover the spot that ached to have them and more inside her.

"You're wet for me," a decidedly sexy male voice murmured against her lips.

The mouth dragged away from hers. Her lashes blinked open and she found herself staring at the hottest man she'd ever laid eyes on.

Peyton? Instinctively, she knew it was.

He sat on a dark leather sofa dressed in a white shirt and dark trousers. With eyes the color of gunmetal accentuated by an abundance of thick, black eyelashes and lips just made for kissing, he was devastatingly gorgeous. His mouth eased into a seductive grin that deepened a darling pair of dimples in his stubble-shadowed cheeks. His copious almost-black hair boasted a wealth of waves any woman would die for and Iris couldn't resist raking her fingers through it.

"Take 'em off." The sound of his raspy voice and the fact that his gaze never left hers made Iris' stomach quiver.

If this was a psychic vision, it was certainly a realistic one. But Iris didn't stop to wonder if Peyton was a spirit—or if she might be experiencing this through the eyes of his killer. Right now, all she could think was *I want this man inside me—now*. She stood and as she stepped out of her black lace panties, he began hastily unbuckling his belt and unfastening his pants.

The sight of his cock took her breath. When he gripped it and slid his hand up and down the shaft, Iris thought she would come on the spot.

All coherent thought fled as she moved between his legs and sank to her knees.

"Touch me," he whispered as he took her hand in his and guided it to his cock. But Iris needed no encouragement.

Heart pounding, she explored the velvety skin contrasting the stark, pulsing hardness underneath. Jutting arrogantly from a pair of taut, down-covered balls, his shaft was thick and long with a rigid, purplish head. Her pussy clenched. How on earth could she ever take it all inside her?

When he lifted her chin with the tip of his index finger, Iris' gaze flew to his. His eyes glittered in the dimly lit room and Iris recognized the look of lust and something else—infatuation. All her life, she had known *the one* was out there somewhere waiting just for her. She'd known she would recognize him immediately and prayed he would have an instant attraction to her as well.

Now it was happening.

He shifted toward her, at the same time drawing her head closer. "Suck my cock, Iris," he drawled.

The sound of his ribald words sent a surge of heat through her body as she intrepidly maintained his gaze and leaned forward, running her tongue under the ridge of his swollen cock head.

He sucked in a sharp breath through his teeth.

She pressed a soft kiss to him and then flicked her tongue over the glistening bead of lubricant that seeped from the tiny slit. The salty-sweet taste made her throb to have him inside her.

"Oh God," he breathed. "I've wanted to do this since the first time I laid eyes on you."

The muscles in his thick thighs tightened to arch his hips upward and then Iris took his cock in her mouth, tonguing him while she sucked, working him with her hand while she dipped lower to lave his scrotum. The scent of him was a sexy combination of masculinity and soap and Iris breathed it in, wishing she could somehow take his *being*, his *soul*, inside her the way she was taking his cock.

His hands trembled as he guided her head and then suddenly, his fingers tightened and he lifted her off him.

Breathless and flushed, he stared. "You're about to make me come."

A thrill rippled through her at his words and she bent once more to bring him to climax but he stopped her. "I want to come—with you."

The thought of him inside her pussy made her pulse riot. She stood, hiking up her silk skirt while he ripped open a condom packet with his teeth, removed the prize within and then hurriedly rolled it over his rock-hard phallus.

Iris couldn't wait to have that monstrous cock inside her and, too impatient to remove the rest of her clothing, she straddled his legs and lowered herself, sighing as it breached her opening and filled her to capacity.

This was so unlike her. She was usually cautious and a lights-off kind of girl when it came to sex—but not with Peyton. With him, she wanted to see and feel and experience this man through her five physical senses instead of her sixth.

His body trembled beneath her as his eyes shone with appreciation and lust. "You're so beautiful."

His voice chased away her thoughts as he caught her face in his hands and drew her mouth to his, kissing her as his hand dropped to cup her breast. Iris moaned into his mouth as his thumb and forefinger locked on her nipple. All her senses were alive with what he was doing and how good his hard thighs felt beneath her, how exquisitely he filled her pussy and how sensuous his body felt as he undulated seductively against her clit.

"I've fantasized about this," he said breathlessly. "But my fantasies couldn't compare to the reality—to you."

Iris stared. "I've wanted you too, Peyton. You don't know—"

He pressed a finger to her lips. "Don't bring that up. Not now." His gaze found hers and heated. His hands slid under her rucked-up skirt and locked around her hips. "Ride me, baby. Ride my cock. I want to make you come and then I want to take you to my bed and take my sweet time with you."

A rush of desire made her channel swell and tighten. She braced her hands on his shoulders and rode him wildly until she threw her head back and heard herself moaning his name while perfect bliss shattered her from the inside out.

The spasms had not yet subsided when he lifted her off him. "Upstairs. I want you in my bed."

Laughing, she took his hand and as he held his trousers up, they dashed into the foyer and started up the stairs. Suddenly, Peyton's hand tightened around Iris' and he dragged her playfully back down the single step she was ahead of him and pulled her body against his.

His mouth sought hers, his tongue teasing her lips apart to intrude and explore inside.

Crazy desire flooded Iris. "I can't wait," she said, nipping at his lips as he slid one hand up her blouse while the other reached around to cup the curve of her bottom. A prying finger worked its way into her slit. "I want you right here," she gasped. "Right now."

With that, he spun her around, yanked up her skirt and bent her over.

Exultant, Iris braced a hand on one of the steps before her and clung to the wrought iron banister with the other as Peyton moved behind her. Desire surged as she felt his cock ride her crevice and then plunge within. His fingers dug into her hips as he pulled and pushed her, thrusting so deeply, and Iris cried out in encouragement. "Oh Peyton! Hard. Fuck me hard!"

The way he filled her was so good, Iris closed her eyes and focused on the sensation of his shaft pummeling her. His body pushed hard against hers with every thrust and Iris could feel herself drawing inward, her pussy bearing down as she felt the hard pull of an orgasm overwhelming her. Iris' knees went weak and she would have fallen had he not been holding her.

"Jesus, Iris, I'm gonna come," he growled. His hands gripped her harder and Iris whimpered as her own bliss built.

"Come with me, Peyton," she begged as the spasms drove her higher and higher still.

And then, with the most seductive moan Iris had ever heard, Peyton rocked his hips tight up against her so that she felt his thick cock pulsing deep inside her pussy.

When he finally pulled out, Iris straightened and glanced back over her shoulder at him with a grin.

Biting his bottom lip, he inhaled deeply and then a slow, sexy grin crept across his handsome face. "Don't look so smug, sweetheart," he said. "I'm nowhere near done with you yet."

Iris gasped as she came fully back to her senses. Her heart raced in her chest as she glanced around Bill's office. She was still in the chair and still alone.

She crossed her legs and realized her vision had been extremely realistic. Her panties were damp with her come and her clit was still throbbing from a bone-melting orgasm.

Blowing out a sigh, she raked her hand through her hair. She had never experienced anything so *real*—in or out of a psychic trance. She'd felt as if she were actually having sex with him.

As wonderful as it was, it hadn't told her anything about what happened to those men. She gnawed her bottom lip.

In fact, her vision had only confused her more. Whoever Peyton was, he was the kind of man who enjoyed the pleasures life had to offer. He didn't seem to be the sort who would off himself.

The door opened and Bill blustered in, carelessly sloshing coffee as he walked. He plopped down in the chair behind his desk. "What'd you get?"

Iris cleared her throat. A hot blush crept into her cheeks. "Their names."

"Their names are in the folder. What'd you get that's *new*?"

She swallowed thickly. "I got the name of a fourth victim." But referring to Peyton as a "victim" made her blood run cold. After the intensity of her psychic vision, she didn't want to consider that he might already be dead.

Bill raised a bushy brown eyebrow.

"Peyton," she said and just uttering the name caused a wave of sweltering heat to roll up her spine and settle uncomfortably in the back of her neck.

"We don't have a vic named Peyton. Is that a first name or a last name?"

"I don't know." She shrugged off her sweater and then tugged at the collar of her blouse, reminding herself that not everyone could read minds. But she'd called him Peyton in the vision. "A first name."

"You sure?"

She nodded. "Pretty sure." Bill didn't know what she was thinking and that was a good thing.

"Did you get anything on the killer?" he asked.

"That's just it. I saw—in my head of course—one of them do it himself."

Bill inhaled sharply and shook his head. "I may be about as psychic as a lump of coal but my gut tells me these guys didn't want to kill themselves."

"I don't think so either." Iris could hear herself carrying on a conversation with Bill but her thoughts were obsessing on Peyton.

"What about blackmail?" Bill asked. "What do you get on that?"

Iris was getting a "no" even as Bill asked the question. She shook her head. "It wasn't blackmail."

Peyton…

She couldn't get him out of her mind and the promise of another psychic-sex-trance experience with him made her impatient to tune in again.

Tingles swept up her limbs as another thought occurred to her.

What if, the next time she opened psychically, she saw his death?

*****

Iris leaned over to switch off the tub faucet and then gave her white cat, Ernie, a pat on the head. For some reason unknown to Iris, Ernie loved to sit on the edge of the tub and watch her bathe. Perhaps he was just fascinated that humans could stand to have water all over them. "Silly kitty," Iris purred as she tied her long hair up with a scrunchie and slipped off her clothes before stepping into the steaming water.

She sighed as she sank down to her neck in the relaxing heat. When she closed her eyes, an image of Peyton looking up from the sofa at her while she stripped off her panties flashed in her mind. She pursed her lips. Peyton was quickly becoming more than a case for the local cops. He was now a full-fledged obsession. She hadn't been able to get him out of her thoughts since she'd left the precinct.

Her body tightened at the memory of her trance—at the memory of his cock filling her pussy to capacity. Her clit throbbed and she slipped her hand between her legs to assuage the aching little bud. How could a man she'd never met arouse her this way?

She blew out a breath, closed her eyes and imagined him as she touched herself, rubbing her hand over her clitoris in a circular motion, dipping lower to tease a fingertip into her slick pussy.

She wanted to come while she fantasized about Peyton. Although she knew just where to touch and just how hard to apply pressure, she wished it were Peyton's fingers, Peyton's tongue, Peyton's cock enticing her toward the ecstasy of climax.

The water sloshed as she spread her legs wide and massaged her pussy. Squeezing her own breast, she pinched her nipple to the point of pain, moaning as sexual energy formed a connection between her nipple and her clit.

Fantasy images of Peyton coercing her onto her knees while he fingered her pussy from behind, coating it with her slick wetness so he could then rim the sensitive aperture of her anus, caused Iris to quicken and rub herself with furious intent.

How would it feel if he slid his finger inside her *there* while he whispered he was readying her to take his big cock in that hole?

Her breaths came in sharp pants and in her mind's eye, she imagined how her pulse would slow to a thick, heavy throb while he braced one hand on her back and stroked the head of his lubed cock against her anus. She'd protest but only because it was taboo, while her body language begged him to fuck her there and then he'd push through the tight muscles at the opening and slide slowly inside…

Iris cried out and arched against her own fingers as she wrested every spasm of orgasm her body had to offer. Pulsing energy surged through her body, emanating from her clit until finally she collapsed against the sloped back of the tub.

She blew out a sigh. She'd had fantasies about actors and musicians before, but never someone like Peyton. And those little interludes had never brought her to a climax as intense as thinking about Peyton fucking her had.

Intrinsically she felt as if she knew him, but whoever Peyton was, the fact remained he was a stranger. This was crazy. She could already tell she was getting too close and if he wasn't already dead, she couldn't bear to know she'd failed to save him.

Then again, for *his* sake she needed to know.

She *wanted* to know.

She took a cleansing breath and allowed herself to fall into a trance…

Intuitively, she knew the key would be under the mat. Iris' heart pounded as she dropped then dug her nails under the edge of the doormat. Panic surged. Where was that damn key? Frantic, she flipped the mat over and found it taped underneath.

Ripping it off, she lunged to her feet and with trembling hands, shoved the key into the lock. It turned and she was inside. "Peyton!" Her feet carried her through the foyer and into the study. It was quiet.

"Peyton, where are you?" she called.

Something awful had happened. She felt it. She knew it.

Breathless, she hurried through the kitchen and then back into the foyer before a shot rang out and echoed through the house. She rushed up the stairs. "Peyton!"

Please don't let him be dead!

The bedroom door was open but Iris stopped at the threshold. "Peyton?" This time her voice was softer and far more uncertain.

A shard of light seeped through the cracked-open bathroom door. Iris bit her bottom lip. Tears welled. She was too late.

Dread settled in the pit of her stomach as her feet carried her mechanically toward the bathroom.

Through the slightly open door, she could see he was lying facedown on the black and white tiles. Blood pooled around his head and next to his hand lay a pistol.

A shriek tore from her throat…

Ernie arched his back and hissed before he bolted off the side of the tub.

Iris hugged her knees. She had actually screamed. Her throat was raw from it. Cold chills skittered down her arms and she shook uncontrollably. She'd seen Peyton dead and for some reason, she felt as if it were her fault. She'd found him too late.

This time, while she was in the trance, she'd felt an overwhelming sense of urgency. She'd desperately wanted to find Peyton alive—because, in the vision, she was in love with him.

Iris sighed.

She couldn't make sense of these visions and the previously much-desired hot bath had suddenly lost its appeal. She stood, took up her towel and then dried off.

After she'd pulled on her favorite pajamas, she padded into the kitchen to pour a glass of wine but even after drinking her usual two glasses, Peyton still weighed heavily on her mind.

She sat at her desk and fired up her computer, but her search of "Peyton" in the Nashville vicinity yielded no results that sent those telltale *hit* chills skittering down her spine. She made a quick call to Bill but the police hadn't found anyone named Peyton either.

Thank God.

She would have been devastated if Bill had told her a man named Peyton had become the fourth victim.

Iris struck her desk with her fist in an uncharacteristic display of frustration. What good was being psychic if she couldn't prevent the unthinkable from happening?

She tapped her fingers on her wooden desktop. What if it had already happened? A wave of nausea welled and she swallowed it back down. Who was Peyton and how could a man she'd never even met sweep her off her feet?

Chapter Two

ഗ

It was nearly two in the morning before Iris fell into a fitful sleep…

"Peyton, how do you feel?" Iris did not recognize the soft, sensuous voice as her own. She seemed to be looking at Peyton through the eyes of a very feminine, very sexy female.

She could see her shapely, crossed legs and a black stiletto heel dangling provocatively from her foot and past that, Peyton sat in a chair across from her. "I'm fine," he muttered and then raised his arms in a languid stretch.

"Excellent," she purred. "You've done well, Peyton," she said as she leaned forward and patted him on the knee.

Through the woman's eyes, Iris watched Peyton's gaze drop to where her well-manicured hand rested on his leg. He shifted uncomfortably. *Is he not attracted to her?*

Looking down once more at the shape and length of the woman's legs and the expensive shoes, Iris assumed any man would be attracted to this woman. She uncrossed and crossed her legs again—à la Sharon Stone.

"I think one more appointment will be necessary and after that…well…" She felt her lips ease into a slow smile. "We'll just have to see, won't we, Peyton?"

Iris bolted upright in the bed. Her heart hammered. She'd broken out in a cold sweat and her pajama top was drenched. Grasping the front, she peeled the sticky fabric off her chest and then raked her hair off her face.

The realization the killer was a female seeped into Iris' skin.

But how was she doing it?

Her mind fled back over the details of the vision. The woman had suggested Peyton return for one more appointment. What kind of appointment? Was the woman a doctor, or some kind of therapist?

Frustration rose. Iris clenched the sheets in her fists. Why did psychic information come to her in tiny bits and pieces she had to put together like a jigsaw puzzle?

She'd seen one of the men kill himself and in her vision of Peyton, the gun had been next to his hand. It didn't make sense that someone was perpetrating these crimes if the men were doing it themselves.

Iris sighed. Ernie meowed indignantly from the foot of the bed and then snuggled his head back between his paws. Iris leaned forward and gave him a reassuring pat before she snatched her phone and punched in Bill's number.

"Hello," a sleepy male voice mumbled.

"Bill?"

He groaned.

"It's Iris. I picked up something else."

"What time is it?"

"It's late—or early, depending on how you look at it," she said excitedly. "Oh, it doesn't matter! I know the killer is a woman! She's a counselor or therapist or some kind of doctor. Could you check that out and see if there's a connection? Perhaps all four men were seeing the same shrink."

"Sure. Tomorrow. First thing."

"Thanks, Bill."

He mumbled something else and then the phone went dead, leaving Iris with a feeling of unease. She'd hoped he'd have enough sense of urgency about him to get on it immediately, and there was no way *she'd* have access to any of the victims' bank or medical records.

Exasperated, she lay back down.

This time, she didn't have a choice. She had to fully open to her psychic ability—even it did mean finding out Peyton was already the fourth victim.

A sense of trepidation settled uncomfortably in the pit of her stomach but three deep breaths relaxed her sufficiently to slip into a trance…

"I thought I said no peeking." Peyton's dimples deepened and Iris felt terribly guilty for spying on him but the smells wafting from his kitchen were too delectable to resist.

"What?" She bit back a smile and tried to keep from blushing but to no avail. Her cheeks were blazing. "Are you like that Chef Ramsay from *Hell's Kitchen*?"

He laughed and the sound of it was so utterly sexy, Iris' knees went weak. "Not no, but *hell* no."

She inched into his kitchen.

"Come on in," he drawled, waving her inside with a spatula.

Some of the tension melted out of her body as she joined him next to the granite countertop. He gestured toward a stool. "Take a seat, princess. I intend to make good on my promise to do the cooking tonight," he said with a wink as he dried his hands and then began to uncork a bottle of California red. "I hope you like Shiraz."

"My favorite," Iris said as she climbed onto the stool. "How'd you know?"

"Do you think you're the only psychic in these parts?" he teased.

Vaguely, she was aware she was seeing all this psychically as if she was—or rather, *was going to be*—a part of it, but she couldn't control the vision.

His gaze found hers and Iris' breath caught as he flashed a very charming and very genuine smile. He was absolutely beguiling with the sleeves of his pale lavender dress shirt rolled up and with that wavy lock of dark hair stealing across his forehead. *I'm so in love with you,* she thought.

And then, as if he could read her mind, he set the cork aside and moved toward her, planting his palms on either side of the countertop to pin her in the middle. With an ever-so-slight shift of his hips, he nudged her thighs apart, causing the thin fabric of her skirt to ride up as he sidled up against her. His arousal was unmistakable and Iris felt a rush of desire dampen her barely there panties.

Peyton's gray gaze dropped to her mouth and then lifted once more to her eyes. "You look *right* in my house, Iris."

She swallowed and wet her suddenly dry lips with the tip of her tongue. Her heart ran wild.

"Do you know what I'm trying to say?" His voice was soft as velvet and a hundred times as rich.

An odd mixture of joy and terror thrummed through her veins. Did she dare hope he might be defining a future for them? "I…I…" she stammered, unable to form a coherent sentence. Normally, she was fully aware of who she was and what her place was in this world but with Peyton—with Peyton she was a crazy amalgamation of love and lust and giddy-little-girl wonder that made her feel like she was on a roller coaster every time their eyes met.

His fingers swept her brown waves behind one ear and then those dove-colored eyes of his flitted to her lips again. He leaned in impossibly closer. His warm breath fanned her cheeks and Iris thought she would die from anticipation. Waiting for his lips to touch hers was the most intense moment she'd ever known in her life.

She trembled as his fingers threaded into the thick hair at her nape, brushing that tiny hollow there that sent tingles down her spine. His mouth grazed hers with maddening slowness and she heard herself whimper.

"I'm falling in love with you, Iris," he murmured. "Promise me I'll see a lot more of you in my house."

Joyous tears threatened to spill from her eyes as she threw her arms around him and took the initiative to fuse her mouth with his. Their tongues mated. His grip tightened on her hair and he tugged gently, pulling her head back so he could deepen their kiss.

Iris was completely at his mercy. His tongue delved into her mouth, exploring, teasing, mimicking motions that promised what was to come later. Her heart pounded from the wild intoxication of love and lust surging through her body.

When he dragged his lips away, Iris was breathless. One hand found the countertop and she braced herself to keep from toppling off the stool.

His face was flushed and his eyes were stormy with passion. A half-smile drew up one corner of his mouth. "Can I take that as a yes?"

She nodded enthusiastically. "A definite yes."

He stared for a steep second, his eyes holding her trapped. "I *am* in love with you, Iris."

She couldn't stop the broad smile that claimed her lips but the truth was evident in his eyes. Wonder and delight sparkled inside her. "I'm in love with you too."

A frisson of tension melted out of his shoulders. Something akin to gratitude flashed in his eyes. "I owe you my life."

She bit her bottom lip and although she was watching this vision through her own eyes, she couldn't grasp the details behind his statement. Inside, she was screaming to ask him what he meant but it was as if she were merely a passenger in her body with no will of her own.

"But it's not that," he said. "In fact, I'm beginning to think fate had a hand in this. If I hadn't gone to—"

"Please don't remind me of that. It was too horrible," she was horrified to hear herself say.

Peyton poured two glasses of dark red wine and then handed one to Iris. "Then we'll never speak of it again. I wouldn't do anything to remind you of it."

She sipped her wine.

"I've never met anyone like you," he said, turning that penetrating gaze on her once more.

She took a deep breath. How could she tell him he was the man for whom she'd waited all her life? He'd think she was nuts. But then he said, "I've known somehow, there was a woman for me out there. You."

"Good things come to those who wait," she managed to say but all she could think about was stripping off her clothes right here and bending over this stool so he could fuck her.

He opened his stainless oven door and took a peek inside. "A half-hour and you'll be eating the best thing you've ever put in your mouth."

Iris laughed and then arched an eyebrow and let her gaze drop provocatively to his crotch. "Oh, I doubt that."

Peyton blew out a sigh. The way his lips puckered made Iris long to kiss him again. "A half-hour, you say?" she asked coquettishly.

He took a swallow of his wine. "A half-hour would give me just enough time to eat your pussy and make you come on my tongue."

Iris sucked in a breath. His ribald speech sent desire unfurling through her body like a lightning bolt. She shifted on the stool as he set his glass aside and moved toward her. Lust blazed in his eyes and Iris gasped when he suddenly lifted her off the stool and set her on the cold granite countertop.

"I've been dying to know if you have panties on under that skirt," he said, taking her former position on the stool before sliding his hand underneath her clothing, going higher and higher until the back of his knuckles brushed against the lace of her thong.

"You're wet," he said as his gaze found hers. He moistened his lips with the tip of his tongue.

Iris swallowed. "*You* make me wet." Anticipation thrummed steadily through her veins while her pulse pounded in her clit.

His eyes held hers while he wriggled his finger underneath the edge of her panties. Her stomach muscles tightened as his fingertip stroked her clitoris and then delved between her nether lips in search of her opening, and when he pushed his finger inside, her breath left her lungs in a ragged rush.

But when he withdrew his finger, disappointment welled—only to be replaced with a surge of desire when he slipped the glistening digit into his mouth and voiced his approval in a long, drawn-out moan.

Iris inhaled. Her clit throbbed and she shifted closer to the edge of the countertop. "I can't wait to have your mouth on me, your tongue on me right here." She took his hand in hers and pressed it to her clit. "Eat me, Peyton," she whispered as she hiked up her skirt. "Eat my pussy."

With a guttural growl, he pulled her thong to the side, spread her thighs wide and buried his face in her essence. Iris trembled and as she seized a handful of his dark hair, she cried out and pulled his face harder against her pussy, lifting her hips to give him full access.

His hand locked around her hip and he pulled her even closer so that she rested her red pumps on his shoulders. Iris took in the sight of him with his face nuzzling her pussy, her thighs sprawled wantonly wide and her feet on his shoulders. It looked as hot as it felt and, coupled with the sound of her little moans and the wet smacking of his ardent kisses, the experience was quickly drawing her to the edge of bliss. His expert lips drew her clit into his mouth and he sucked hard, then softly, drawing back to flick the stiff point of his tongue over the distended bud. Iris' thighs quivered and she drew him harder against her with the heels of her shoes.

Once more, his long index finger worked into her pussy, searching for and finding the little pleasure spot that always—always—made her come.

"I love the taste of your pussy," he murmured against her and buried his face again so that Iris couldn't distinguish between the heat of his breath and mouth and hand, which all vied to enthrall her with pleasure.

Just as he brought her to the brink, he drew back far enough to gaze up into her eyes. Iris stared. Her breaths were quick and shallow. His mouth shimmered with her wetness and his finger slid easily in and out of her pussy in one rhythmic little thrust after another.

Her clit jolted and she whimpered.

His lips eased into a devilish half-smile. "What's the matter, Iris?"

She squeezed her eyes shut but only for a moment. *Eat me. Please put your mouth back on my pussy. Make me come.*

He seemed to be enjoying her torment. "Hmm? What's wrong?"

She sucked her bottom lip between her teeth and writhed on his finger. It felt good but it wasn't enough. She'd been just about to come when he'd decided to tease and torment her. "Please, Peyton…"

"What?" He pushed his finger up to the second knuckle, withdrew it slowly and then added a second finger.

Iris melted. "Don't stop. Suck my clit while you finger me," she said boldly. "Make me come and then I'm going to suck your cock."

The stool grated on the tile floor as he shifted forward and locked his mouth on her swollen bud once more.

Iris groaned and bucked, holding his head and splaying her legs open impossibly wide while his tongue laved her clit and his fingers fucked her pussy.

"Yes," she hissed as she threw back her head and allowed desire to swell over and through her, starting slowly and then building in intensity until she shattered from the inside out.

But Iris' desire was only temporarily sated. It was Peyton's turn and she wanted him to come with the same intensity she'd experienced. She slid off the countertop and he helped her gently to the floor before he dragged her body against his and kissed her.

"Do you taste your sweet come?" he asked, his lips brushing hers, his obvious arousal stiffly prodding her belly.

She voiced her acquiescence and deepened their kiss. He was right. Her come *was* sweet but right now, she was focused on making Peyton explode. Her fingers found his belt buckle and she deftly unfastened it along with his trousers, freeing his cock.

He moaned into her mouth when she took his thick shaft in her hand, sliding her hand downward to cup his balls before gripping his pole harder. "Damn, baby, you know how to touch me," he said as his kisses moved from her mouth to her neck.

Iris tilted her head back to give him better access. He'd found her spot. *God,* had he found her spot. Squeezing her thighs together, she whimpered as tendrils of pleasure emanated through her body from those insistent little kisses at the curve of her neck.

Peyton's hands swept around her body, searching, touching, teasing…finding her hard nipple through her clothes to give it a passionate pinch. Iris wanted him inside her but first she wanted to taste the luscious cock she fondled in her hand. Making eye contact with him, she sank to her knees and nuzzled her face against his rigid phallus.

The muscles in his stomach tightened as she swept her long hair behind her shoulders and then ran her hand up and down his length. He smelled of soap and skin and she couldn't wait to taste him. His hands trembled as he threaded his fingers into her hair and drew her gently toward his cock. Iris engulfed him, filling her mouth with the bulbous, plum-colored head and taking him as far as she could while blazing a path around his cock with her tongue.

"Oh *fuck* that's good," he whispered, arching toward her.

Iris moaned and used her hand to help please him, gripping and using the perfect suction to slip completely off his cock head and then to push him between her lips again. His reaction thrilled her when his legs trembled and she heard his hand slap down on the granite countertop for support.

"I've been thinking about coming in your mouth all day long."

Iris' pussy tightened and she sucked harder and deeper, intent on fulfilling Peyton's fantasies. His harsh breathing deepened and the one hand that still held her head suddenly tightened. "Fuck, I'm coming," he rasped. "Damn, Iris. Goddamn!"

Jubilant, Iris sucked and swallowed every spicy drop…

* * * * *

Trying in vain to suppress a yawn, Iris ushered a client out the door of the office she rented in West End Nashville.

She'd hardly gotten any sleep the night before and after that last psychic trance, she'd had to dig her vibrator out of her lingerie drawer and find a fresh pair of double A batteries. She'd come three more times and had cried Peyton's name during every orgasm.

She heaved a sigh. This was crazy. She was falling in love with a man she'd never met in real life—a man who might be dead.

Wearily, she walked behind her desk and checked her appointment book. Her next psychic reading wasn't scheduled until an hour from now. That would give her just enough time to nab a nap.

After lowering the blinds to block out the bright morning sun, she collapsed on the sofa. Although her office only consisted of one room, she had enough space for the couch, two small chairs for her clients, a desk, her collection of extrasensory-boosting crystals and a fish tank.

Pulling a plush, cranberry-colored throw over her legs, she stretched out on the sofa and closed her eyes.

Sleep, however, eluded her. Instead, she slipped once more into a psychic trance…

"You're speechless, Iris," Peyton said.

Her gaze lifted from the glimmering diamond ring in his hand to the soft gray of his eyes. She had to remind herself to breathe as her heart thudded against her rib cage.

He stared from his kneeling position on the carpeted floor of his living room. "Will you marry me?" He sounded uncertain, as if he didn't know she had dreamed of this moment since they'd first met.

Gripping the leather cushion of his sofa, she swallowed thickly. "Yes, Peyton." Her voice was but a whisper strangled by emotion.

With trembling hand, he braced himself on both knees and slid the ring on her finger. Exultant, Iris scooted forward on the sofa to draw him into her arms.

Joy and desire battled to surge to the forefront and she found herself weeping and kissing Peyton with wild abandon. His palm cupped her breast and he gave it a delicious squeeze before sliding his fingers down her arm to draw her hand to the hardness burgeoning in his pants. She gasped into his mouth and groped him, slipping even farther toward the edge of the cushion and spreading her legs so she could pull his groin to hers.

He tore his mouth from hers. "Dammit, you always do this to me," he said through clenched teeth as he undid his belt and unfastened his trousers. "You make me want you so fucking bad I can't wait long enough to take off my clothes."

Breathless, Iris stared as she hiked up her skirt. "You'll get used to me now that we're going to be married."

A seductive laugh emanated from him. "I seriously doubt that." And then she gasped as he caught her wrists before she could pull her little black thong down. "Not like this. Not this time."

"I..." she began but her voice trailed off when he began buttoning his trousers. He stood and took her hands to draw her to her feet as he did.

"This time," he said, fingering the ring, "I want to take my time with you. I want you in my—*our*—bed."

Overjoyed, Iris searched his eyes and then she cried out when he effortlessly swept her off her feet to carry her upstairs and into the bedroom. As he lowered her to her feet, he dragged her body against his, splaying his hand across the curve of her ass to hold her tightly pressed to his glaringly obvious arousal.

She wiggled her backside playfully and then changed the tempo completely, grinding her hips against the hardness straining against her abdomen.

"You're making this hard for me," he said, his eyes glittering with the cleverness of his double entendre. His gaze swept her face and he brushed a curling brown tendril behind her shoulder. "I love you, Iris. I love that your eyes are as blue as a spring sky and that your hair is the same color of the caramel squares I loved as a child." He leaned in to nuzzle her temple. "I love the way you smell, so soft and feminine and so *you*."

Iris' heart felt as if it were going to burst out of her chest. It was so filled with love for him and her pulse was racing with the promise of what was about to come. No man had ever made her feel this way. Not ever.

She'd been in love with him from their first meeting but nothing in her psychic background had prepared her for the wonderful compatibility they shared. They both loved old movies and drank Diet Coke in the morning instead of coffee. Both wanted future children and loved to lie awake snuggling during a thunderstorm. If Iris had created him herself, he couldn't have been the more perfect man for her.

Peyton's long fingers threaded into her hair and he caressed the back of her scalp while tracing her bottom lip with his thumb. "It's killing me to take my time," he whispered.

Iris was dying too. Heat coiled around her spine and her pussy actually ached to feel him inside her. She'd never wanted him more.

But when he slanted his head down to kiss her, neither he nor Iris could fight their mutual need any longer. As his lips sought hers, he unbuttoned her blouse and then reached inside to possessively cup her breasts.

Iris clung, whimpering in his mouth as he kneaded her nipples through the lace of her bra. Shrugging her shoulders, she sent her red silk blouse whispering down her arms. Peyton voiced his approval and slipped his hands under her bra straps, pushing them down so that her breasts were freed.

He drew back far enough to admire the fullness and the taut, pink nipples before he leaned down to suck each eager tip until it was diamond-hard.

Closing her eyes, Iris burrowed her fingers into his hair and held him there, moaning when he took as much of each breast into his mouth as he could, laving her nipples with his tongue and then suckling until she was squirming to assuage the heady throb and swell of her clit. She knew if he touched it—just once—she would come undone.

When she opened her eyes to watch him, she caught the rainbow reflection of her diamond in the soft light. It was beautiful—but to her, the most beautiful thing about the ring was what it represented. The unending circle, the symbol of their love, the fact he'd laid claim to her as his wife and the promise of their future together.

Fresh desire unfurled within her and when he sated himself of her breasts, Iris took the opportunity to begin unbuttoning his shirt. The crisp, starched cotton rustled as he wriggled out of it and then let it fall to the floor.

His chest was magnificent. Although he was a man who went for his morning run religiously, he wasn't overly muscled and yet tight and smooth in all the right places. Iris ran her palms over the hard planes of his chest, taking wicked pleasure in the way his body felt. Nuzzling her face in the sparse patch of dark wisps between his nipples, she breathed in the spicy scent of his cologne which mingled with his own natural fragrance. His chest expanded as he inhaled.

Iris' gaze found his as she unfastened his pants and then pushed them, along with his boxers, down his thick thighs. Her heart skipped a beat when his luscious cock sprang free. She could feel the tension in his body as she dropped to her knees and brushed her lips across the swollen head.

He shook with need. "Iris, please…"

She curled her hand around the base of his cock and caught sight of her ring once more. The perfect combination of love and lust flooded her and when she took him into her mouth, joy filled her being at the pleasure she knew she was giving him.

While her mouth and hand worked his shaft in tandem, she gently kneaded his balls with her other hand until she felt he was on the verge of coming. She wasn't ready to let him come just yet.

A seductive moan escaped his lips as she pulled away. As she stood, she stepped out of her slinky skirt and thong.

His gaze wandered down to her toes and then lifted once more. The little half-smile that claimed his lips made Iris' heart beat like the wings of a caged, wild bird. She didn't have to be psychic to be able to read the look of love and desire in his eyes.

"You are absolutely beautiful," he said as he guided her to the bed. As she crawled onto the mattress he followed, seizing her around the waist to pull her beneath him.

She laughed jubilantly as he moved over her, positioning himself between her sprawled thighs.

"Iris, I want you to know I will *always* love you and respect you."

She simply stared at him, her love for him making her speechless.

"You've made my dreams come true," he whispered, his voice charged with emotion. "I thought I was the kind of man who would never marry, who'd never take a risk with a woman—but you've changed me. You've changed my heart."

"Peyton..."

He brushed his lips across her forehead and then looked deeply into her eyes. "Promise you'll keep me in your heart for the rest of my life."

She shook her head. "You'll be in my heart for the rest of *my* life."

His mouth claimed hers and, as his tongue slipped through the opening of her lips, the thick head of his cock breached her opening and Iris moaned as it filled her in one long, slow slide.

For a heart-stopping moment he stilled and shuddered. Then, winding one hand under her head and the other under her hip, he began to drive his cock into her.

Mindless, Iris clung and opened her thighs as wide as possible, granting his body complete access to hers. Running her hands over his hard shoulders and down his tapering back, she gripped the firm cheeks of his ass, loving the way his muscles contracted and released with every demanding thrust.

The feel of his cock head lapping the pleasure spot in her pussy made Iris mewl and writhe beneath him. It felt so good and the thought that this would be hers in the future filled her with a sense of wonder and awe—and terror that life was fragile and uncertain.

She'd almost lost him once before.

But there was no time to think about that. Her breath rushed out of her lungs as her body took over. Pleasure uncoiled and cracked like a whip, shooting to the tips of her limbs and then sucking back to wind through her pussy with an intensity that caused her to arch and cry out.

Her nails dug into his ass as she rode the wave, begging him to come with her.

Peyton pushed up on his arms and slammed into her pussy before an animalistic groan tore from his throat and his face contorted in the most beautiful, most male expression of ecstasy Iris had ever witnessed.

Finally, he wilted and buried his face in her hair, cupping her breast in his palm as he undulated sensuously within her.

"God, I love being inside you," he whispered in her ear. "I love making you come."

Smiling mischievously, he moved off her and scooted to the edge of the bed, where he rummaged in his nightstand drawer.

"What are you doing?" Iris asked playfully.

"Just getting your little toy," he said as he produced a bottle of lubricant and Iris' silver, egg-shaped vibrator.

She smiled broadly as he switched the vibe on and it hummed to life. She'd come so hard, she knew the toy would drive her crazy as soon as it touched her pussy. Still, she opened her legs as he moved between them and trailed the little buzzing bullet up one thigh and down the other.

Peyton drew her hand to the vibrator. "You put this where you want it." He began to lube his index finger. "And I'll put this where *I* want it," he said, arching an eyebrow.

Iris' pulse accelerated. She knew what that meant. Her eyes fluttered shut as she pressed the pulsating vibe to her clit while his finger worked its way down the sensitive flesh between her legs to her anus.

"Open your legs wider, Iris."

She whimpered but did as she was told, imagining how good it would feel to have his long, thick finger breaching her there. Right now, he merely circled it, gently prodding, teasing.

Iris arched off the bed and pushed toward his finger but he wouldn't give her what she wanted—not yet.

"I'm going to get you so worked up," he said, "that you'll be begging me to slide my cock in there."

Images of him doing just that flooded her thoughts. She was going to come without his finger inside her if he refused her any longer. "Please, Peyton…"

He had the audacity to chuckle. "Do you want my finger in your ass?"

"Yes," she hissed. The vibration on her clit was hurtling her toward the brink. "Yes! Now!"

His well-lubed finger slid easily into her anus and when she felt his fist pushing against her bottom, she exploded. Stars flashed behind her eyelids and she became vaguely aware of him withdrawing his finger and twisting her over so that she was on her knees.

"I want my cock in there," he growled as she heard the sound of the lube bottle's top popping open. Seconds later, the head of his cock was pushing at her opening.

Iris tensed, spreading her thighs wider to give him the best angle. The eager orifice gave way and his cock head was inside.

"Slowly," she warned. Pain rimmed the edge and she willed herself to relax to admit him. She could feel his hands trembling as he gripped her hips and then slowly, he pushed the full length of his cock into her anus.

Iris' channel clenched over and over. Her clit throbbed. She loved the way he filled her there. Having him embedded to the hilt in her ass wasn't like having him in her pussy but anal sex was equally as pleasurable and, in an odd way, more sensual.

"It's hard to fuck you slowly," he breathed.

"Be still," she whispered. "Let me fuck you."

His grip on her hips loosened as she began to rock back on him, slowly at first and then slightly faster.

"You should see this," he said.

Iris caught a glimpse of him in the dresser mirror. He stared down at the spot where they were connected.

"My cock is in your beautiful ass," he said, his voice husky and low.

His words inflamed her and she moved even faster. Peyton growled and pushed the vibrator back into her hand. "Vibe your clit while I fuck you."

Bracing herself on her shoulder, she pressed the bullet to her bud. At once, spasms racked her body, emanating from the fullness inside her and the intense sensations on her clitoris.

Peyton thrust into her once, twice, and then his moans mingled with hers.

Iris felt heavy as she lay on his bed—*their bed*—while Peyton went into the bathroom to clean up. He returned with a warm washcloth and gently wiped the lube and come from her bottom. He tossed the wet cloth basketball-style into a hamper and crawled back onto the bed.

Iris turned in his arms and rested her head on his chest. The sound of his heart beating reminded her how fragile this existence was and she said a silent prayer that she and Peyton would spend many happy years together.

"Did you know I was going to ask you to marry me?" he inquired as he wound a lock of her hair around his index finger.

Iris chuckled. "No. Being psychic doesn't really work that way."

"You knew…that day… You knew what was about to happen," he said. "I would have died if you hadn't figured it all out and saved me from—"

A knock on the door snapped Iris out of her trance.

Chapter Three

ꟍ

For the first time in her life, Iris ended up having to return a client's money. After that mind-shattering trance, there was no way she could pick up information for someone else.

Tired and confused, she plopped down in her desk chair and rubbed her throbbing temples. Although she'd been psychic all her life, she'd never had visions like the ones she had about Peyton.

That last vision had been far too personal. Leaning back in her desk chair, she rubbed her ring finger. It had seemed so real.

In all her readings, she'd never seen herself as a participant. She'd always viewed them as if watching a movie.

Sick reality knotted her stomach. Her inner voice chided her. *When you lie down with a dream, Iris, you wake up lonely.*

Propping her elbows on the desk, she steepled her fingers while she thought back over the trance.

Peyton had told her she'd saved him.

She swallowed. Hard.

Did that mean he was still alive?

Her heart soared only to come crashing back down around her.

Squeezing her eyes shut, she was assailed with the images from the trance she'd had about discovering him dead on the floor, lying in a pool of his own blood.

Someone was murdering these men and the only clue Iris had to go on was a pair of long, shapely legs and the velvety sound of a femme-fatale voice. But it was as if the killer weren't even present when the men died—as if she were wickedly enjoying it all from a distance.

Flipping open her cell phone, she scrolled through until she found Bill's number and then punched the call button.

"Iris! I was just about to call you," he said. "That lead you gave me panned out. They were all seeing the same dentist."

"Peyton too?"

"Yes. I've got to go. We're on the way to make an arrest right now."

Iris blew out a sigh as she snapped her phone closed. After two more deep breaths, she leaned back in her chair and mentally willed herself to open to the possibility a dentist could somehow be the murderer—but nothing happened.

Frustration welled. She was simply too tired to pick up psychically but Peyton's life could be hanging in the balance.

"Caffeine," she said aloud, as if some sort of insight struck. A Diet Coke and candy bar would give her overused, overtired and oversexed psychic skills a much-needed boost.

After gathering enough change to feed the machines downstairs, Iris grabbed her purse, slipped out of her office and took the elevator to the basement.

A lady was already in the snack room, bending to retrieve her soda from the machine. When she stood, Iris stared, stunned. The woman was absolutely movie-star beautiful, with long black hair, catlike green eyes and the most voluptuous pair of lips Iris had ever seen.

Iris didn't recognize her as someone who rented office space here. Perhaps she was new.

"I'm Iris." She offered her hand.

Although the woman was already several inches taller, she lifted her chin in a gesture Iris deemed as imperious. She looked like a jungle cat that had just picked up the scent of fear and was ready to pounce. "Valerie Thrasher." She gracefully extended her hand. "You're the psychic." It was more of a statement than a question.

Iris swallowed and as she took the proffered hand, Valerie said, "I'm the hypnotist."

When Iris' skin touched Valerie's, something akin to an electric shock shivered through her being.

A violent rush of images inundated her.

Valerie crossing her legs…

Valerie's sultry voice coercing men under her hypnotic spell to kill themselves…

And Peyton…

Peyton sitting across from Valerie…

Iris knew she was staring with her mouth hanging agape but she couldn't stop. Valerie was the killer! She was hypnotizing men to take their own lives.

A terrible chill sank straight to Iris' toes. Bill was wrong. And Peyton was next!

Her mind raced frantically. "You…you haven't been here long."

Valerie pursed her luscious lips in thought. "About a month."

Iris' mind flitted back over Bill's file and the dates of the suicides. There had been one death a week—one death every Friday. Her knees started shaking. This was the fourth week of the month.

Today was also Friday. *Oh God, Peyton…*

Knowing she was stepping out on a dangerous limb, Iris said, "I think one of my friends is a client of yours. Peyton?"

Something flashed in Valerie's green eyes. "I operate under a strict code of confidentiality." She crossed her arms over her ample bosom.

Every fiber of Iris' being told her to run, to find Peyton and rescue him but hell, she didn't even know his last name. But Bill did.

This couldn't be happening. He might be under Valerie's hypnotic influence right this minute.

Iris trembled. *What am I going to do? I have to save him and I don't even know him.* Even if she called Bill and told him the dentist lead was wrong, they'd never find Peyton in time. Never.

A lump welled in her throat.

He might already be dead.

She suddenly realized her visions of Peyton had portended future events—for both of them. All the images—the lust, the love, the promise of marriage, all of it could be swept away in a heartbeat.

"Are you all right?" Valerie arched one thin brow. "You look pale."

Iris stared, her mind racing.

Valerie's eyes darkened.

Iris staggered backward. Her back found the wall behind her and she gaped at Valerie. "Why?"

Valerie's nostrils flared slightly and she caressed her soda can with rhythmic slowness. "When I saw 'intuitive' under your name on your office door, I thought you were just another run-of-the-mill charlatan. It appears I was mistaken."

Iris flinched. "Why are you doing it?" Iris asked. Her heart hammered.

Valerie's full lips drew into a wicked smile. "You're psychic. Don't you ever think about the *power* you have? The control?"

Iris shook her head. She wanted to run but she found herself mesmerized by the glint in those malevolent cat eyes. Iris blinked stupidly. She was suddenly so sleepy she could hardly hold her eyes open.

Valerie moved toward her with the stealthy grace of a panther. "Does it not thrill you to know you're capable of having the world at your feet? Perfectly in control, perfectly knowing anything and obtaining everything in your wildest dreams?" Her eyes held Iris whole while her voice was insidiously hypnotic. "Haven't men abused you? Used you? Lied to you?"

Panic surged as Iris realized she was falling under Valerie's spell.

Peyton…

Iris knew she was his only hope. He would die if she didn't do something. Now.

She closed her eyes and shook loose the web Valerie was spinning. "No!"

Instinctively, she pulled the trash can between them to block Valerie and then Iris ran, scrambling up the steps to get from the basement to the ground floor instead of taking the elevator.

Valerie called after her but Iris refused to allow herself to listen. The woman was some sort of insane Svengali who could weave a spell with the sound of her voice and the glint in her eyes.

Iris rushed into the parking deck and as soon as she was safely in her car, she locked the doors and then whipped out her cell phone. Her fingers shook uncontrollably as she scrolled through her contact list for Bill's phone number.

Holding the phone and trying to back out of the parking spot, she nearly rammed a concrete support beam. She looked over her shoulder and slammed the brakes just in time—and then something slammed the hood of her car.

Iris gasped and twisted her head to find Valerie, hands braced on the hood of the car.

Valerie's eyes blazed as she lunged at the driver's side door and tried to open it. A scream tore from Iris' throat as she hit the gas and sped off, squealing tires as she wheeled out of the parking deck.

"Iris?" Bill asked over the phone.

"Bill! Thank God! You were wrong about the dentist. The killer is a hypnotist! Valerie Thrasher. You've got to tell me Peyton's last name!" She ran a red light to pull onto West End Avenue.

Her pulse rioted as she headed west toward Bellemeade. She didn't know why she'd turned that way. She just had. "Bill?" she asked impatiently as she sailed through another red light. "I need to know *now*!"

"Peyton Hartley," he said.

"Where does he live?"

"4720 Benton Smith Road, just off Harding Place."

She knew she'd turned west for a reason. "I'm headed there now. Send the police and an…and an ambulance."

But after Iris tossed her cell phone in the passenger seat, she felt suddenly empty and terrified. A lump rose in her throat and with it, that image of Peyton lying in a pool of his own blood.

Iris shook her head to chase away the vision. "No! It won't happen. I won't let it happen." But inside, she wasn't so certain.

Nashville traffic on a Friday afternoon was a bitch and when Iris finally turned onto Harding Place, she was thwarted by a long line of slow-moving drivers. Even switching on her hazard lights and honking her horn didn't yield results.

When she ultimately arrived at Benton Smith Road, she turned and raced around the circle until she found the address. The driveway wound downward and when Iris saw a silver BMW in the garage, her heart sank.

The house looked sickeningly familiar. She'd seen it before—in her vision of his death.

Her knees felt as if they'd give way as she climbed out of her own car and raced toward the front door. She rang the bell and then beat on the door. "Peyton!"

But she knew he wasn't coming.

She cupped her hands and peered in the window beside the front door. The house was dark.

Was he already dead? She shook her head. "No. Please, no!" Hopelessness threatened to overwhelm her—until she recalled that in her vision, she'd seen a key taped underneath the doormat.

Squatting, she flipped it over and just as it had been in her vision, there was the key taped to the mat.

Her hands quaked as she ripped it loose and then stuck it in the lock. She twisted it and the door opened. "Peyton!" she called.

She started to dart into the study but then she remembered her vision. He'd been upstairs. There was no time to lose.

She raced up the stairs as fast as her feet would carry her and then ran straight to his bedroom.

The bedroom door was slightly open. A nauseating sense of familiarity swept over her and she trembled as her feet carried her toward the bathroom door.

When she pushed the door open, Peyton stared and blinked.

Iris gasped. In his hand was the pistol she'd seen in her vision.

"Who are you?" he asked, bewildered. His gaze dropped to the gun in his hand. "What am I doing here?"

Relief surged through her being. She wanted to rush to him and take him in her arms but she stopped short, reminding herself he had no idea who she was.

Shaking, he put the gun on the bathroom counter and stepped away from it as if it had scorched him.

Iris took a cautious step closer. "Peyton...are you all right?"

His gaze brushed hers and then riveted once more to the pistol. He was clearly confused. "I don't know. How'd I get here? The last thing I remember, I was sitting in Valerie's office."

Iris nodded. "I know. She hypnotized you—to kill yourself."

He dropped down onto the closed toilet lid and rubbed his face as he looked suspiciously at the gun.

Iris could tell he was filtering through muddled memories.

His gaze lifted to hers and her breath caught at the sight of the same beautiful pair of gray eyes she'd seen in her visions. He swallowed. "How'd you know?"

"I...I work with the police."

Sirens wailed in the distance and Iris knew the house would be swarming with Bill's coworkers any second.

Peyton blinked and shook his head as if he could shake loose the dark spell in his brain. "I was going to her to get over my fear of the dentist."

"I know."

Peyton seemed thoroughly bewildered and Iris resisted the overwhelming urge to go to him and hold him and weave her fingers through those dark waves. This was the man she'd kissed and made passionate love to in her visions—but had that only been a means her spirit guides had used to inspire the urgency in her to save him? Or did she dare hope she'd seen her own future?

Through the intensity of her psychic trances, Iris had fallen head over heels in love with Peyton—and the cruel reality was, it was only a dream.

A bevy of cops burst through the door, with Bill behind them.

* * * * *

While the police had interviewed Peyton, Iris had explained her encounter with Valerie Thrasher to Bill.

Bill had informed Iris the police had arrested Valerie but that she vehemently denied any wrongdoing. At the same time, the dentist had linked the victims to recommendations to Valerie from him for his patients to overcome anxiety about dental work.

Numbly, Iris went down the strikingly familiar stairs where they'd made love in her vision and then out the front door. She walked toward her car, doubting Peyton would be able to remember much of his sessions with Valerie—but hopefully enough to finger her as a killer.

She slipped her fingers under the door handle of her car.

"Wait!" a voice called.

She whirled to find Peyton running out the front door. "Wait!" he called, obviously relieved to see she hadn't yet left. "I'm sorry. I didn't even get an opportunity to thank you."

Iris wiped her palms on the sides of her skirt. She shrugged. "It's what I do."

"You…you saved my life."

He was so handsome with the setting sun glinting off his unruly hair. Iris could only gape at him while her body responded to seeing him in the flesh. Her nipples tightened instinctively. Her tummy warmed and need unfurled downward.

"That detective said you're a psychic."

Iris' lips parted. Unable to find the right words, she simply nodded.

"Is that how you knew?" he asked.

"Yes," she replied, finally finding her voice.

His gaze swept her face and Iris felt a telling blush creep into her cheeks. She bit her bottom lip.

"You're not at all what I've always pictured psychics to look like," he said with a flirtatious arch of his eyebrow.

She smiled. "Did you think we all wore head scarves and big hoop earrings?"

"Um…honestly? Yeah."

She laughed.

He stared and then held out his hand. Iris took it and the spark of electricity that jolted through her body struck her with utter clarity and familiarity. Their touch affected him too. She could see it in his eyes. Her heart fluttered rapidly.

Instead of shaking her hand though, he held it in his. "It's funny…I feel like I know you but the truth is, I don't even know your name," he murmured as he examined their entwined hands.

"Iris."

His gaze flew back to hers. "Like the flower," he said. "My favorite."

The blush in her cheeks heated to a blaze as the desire and love she'd known only in her dreams began to show signs of a promise yet to be fulfilled.

"Iris…would you consider having dinner with me sometime?" he asked. "Sometime very soon?"

She blew out the breath she'd been holding. "I'd love to."

A smile deepened the dimples at the corners of his mouth. "Are you sure we've never met before?"

FRENCH KISS

Solange Ayre

&

Dedication

ꟾ

Dedicated to my friend Belinda, who helped immeasurably with this story.

Trademarks Acknowledgement

The author acknowledges the trademarked status and trademark owners of the following wordmarks mentioned in this work of fiction:

Vassar College: Vassar College

Waldorf: Hilton Hotels Corporation

Chapter One

Boston, Massachusetts
November 1912

ꟗ

Hiding in the ladies' cloakroom for the duration of the Endicotts' ball was simply not a possibility. Yet Amaryllis Gardner knew if she left the safety of the dark alcove, one of her catty friends would pounce and make sly remarks about her fiancé's absence this evening.

Hearing the click of approaching heels, Amaryllis backed into the deepest corner of the room, concealing herself behind a velvet cape. Her nose twitched at the overpowering scent of gardenia perfume.

"I feel sorry for Amaryllis," Laura Lodge said to Maude Winthrop as they entered the cloakroom. Laura delved into a coat pocket. "Good, I *knew* I'd brought my extra hankie." She tucked the handkerchief into her bosom. "How humiliating for her to be sitting with the dowagers when she has a fiancé. Not that *my* parents would have consented to an engagement with such a man—even one as handsome as Dr. Bradford."

Amaryllis' cheeks burned. *Eavesdroppers never hear good of themselves.* She should make her presence known.

Giggling, Maude said, "Perhaps her parents are glad to get Amaryllis out of the house. She's almost twenty-six, isn't she?"

"On the shelf for years. I can scarcely blame her for accepting him. Still, Dr. Bradford is *not our kind.* One can only assume his gold makes up for that clinic in the back slums."

Amaryllis squared her shoulders, steeling herself to charge out and defend her fiancé.

"But what do you suppose he sees in her?" Maude wondered. "She's too plump for fashion and she's never been pretty."

Hearing the facts stated so baldly, Amaryllis shrank back, biting her lip.

"Isn't it obvious? Married to one of the Gardner girls, he'll be accepted by the people who matter." Laura took her friend's arm. "Let's get a glass of punch." The two women left the cloakroom.

On the shelf. Such an unpleasant phrase, as though one were a cheese left too long in a grocery store, spotted with mold.

If only her shyness had permitted, she'd have come out of hiding and told them she was marrying for love, not money. Nor had she been swayed by her fiancé's handsome face. She loved him for his keen intelligence, his concern for the poor and his devotion to his profession.

And he loved her. She was certain of that. Absolutely certain. Brendan Bradford cared nothing for society. He would never marry for mere social acceptance.

As she ventured out of the cloakroom, her mother descended upon her.

"Where have you been?" Beryl Gardner demanded. Her thin nose lifted into the air, making her look like the ultimate Boston Brahmin. Amaryllis' sister Lily liked to call that expression, *Dear Mother detects the odor of horse droppings.* "What *have* you been doing to your hair? Goodness, have rats nested in it? No wonder it took you so long to catch a husband."

Hurt, Amaryllis pushed futilely at the strands escaping from her pompadour.

"Brendan is looking for you," her mother said, adding under her breath, "*Brendan*—such a terrible name."

"It's a perfectly lovely name!"

Her mother gave a delicate shudder. "So...so *Irish.*" She fixed her daughter with a forbidding stare. "Remember, you must tell him tonight about the delay."

Amaryllis gritted her teeth, envisioning the wedding she'd been planning for the last few months. Clinging to her father's arm, she'd float down the staircase, clad in the Worth gown bought during last year's trip to Paris. Brendan, waiting by the parlor fireplace, would look up with a smile. Or would his glance be somber as he contemplated his new duties as her husband? He was a reserved young man with a serious turn of mind.

The thought of him gave her the courage to question her mother. "I still don't understand why Great-Aunt Eugenia's death must delay my wedding."

"We simply cannot entertain on a grand scale while in mourning."

"But Mother, I'm willing to have a small wedding."

"Try to have some sense, you silly goose. We must hold our heads high and carry off the day with flair—*if* you insist upon marrying that Irish upstart."

"Brendan's a wonderful man! I'm lucky to be marrying him!"

"There's nothing wrong with being a respectable spinster. While married life has benefits, there are certain drawbacks as well." With a brusque nod, her mother added, "An unmarried woman need never submit herself to a man's animal desires."

A grin threatened to quirk up the corners of Amaryllis' mouth. She couldn't wait to submit to Brendan's animal desires. The memory of his slow, hot kisses was enough to turn her faint.

A thrill went through her as she caught sight of her fiancé pushing his way through the crowd. Nothing suited Brendan's tall form and broad shoulders better than a black tailcoat. Her distress melted like ice chips on a hot sidewalk. His thick black hair, intent green eyes and lordly nose stirred something deep within her. How she longed for their wedding night, when he would embrace her in the marriage bed.

Heat rose to her cheeks. A well-bred virgin like herself was supposed to know nothing of such matters. But with all her sisters married now, she had gathered a tantalizing amount of information.

"There you are, sweetheart," Brendan said. Ignoring her mother's disapproving frown at the endearment, he hurried to Amaryllis, taking possession of her hands. His touch sent a wave of warmth through her.

Surely the spark of joy in his eyes was real. Surely he cared for her…truly cared, as much as she cared for him.

With a few words of excuse to her mother, he drew Amaryllis away to an uncrowded corner. "I apologize for my late arrival." Lowering his voice, he said, "I was delayed because Mrs. Rafferty delivered tonight. A most difficult procedure."

"How is she?" Serving as a volunteer at the Atlantic Family Clinic twice a week, Amaryllis had met Mrs. Rafferty several times.

"Doing quite well, considering it's her fourteenth birth." Amaryllis fell a little deeper in love with him as a smile lit his eyes. "She had a boy. He's to be named Terrence *Brendan* Rafferty."

"Is this baby number fifty or fifty-one named after you?" she teased. How lucky she was to be engaged to a wonderful man like Brendan.

Yet even now, in this exciting new century, people were prejudiced against the Irish. All her life she'd seen the signs on office and shop windows—"No Irish Need Apply". Signs she'd barely noticed until she met Brendan but that now hurt her with their rejection of her fiancé's people.

Marriage to a Gardner would elevate him in society's eyes, just as Laura had stated. Once again doubt assailed her. Was he truly marrying her for love?

Often at night she lay in her solitary bed, thinking of his laugh, his gentleness, his intense gaze when something interested him. Love for him would swell inside her heart until she sighed with longing. Did he love her as much as that?

And now their wedding was delayed.

The musical quartet struck up "On the Beautiful Blue Danube". Offering his arm, Brendan led her to the dance floor. As she watched their reflection in one of the long mirrors decorating the ballroom, her tall fiancé seemed mismatched with his short, plump partner. The expensive swan-bill corset she wore would never give her torso a fashionable S-curve, nor would all her maid's attention to her hair change its horrible red color.

How could he possibly be in love with her?

When the next dance began, Amaryllis suggested they go downstairs to the library for privacy.

The library in the Endicott home was impressive, lined with deep walnut shelves that reached to the room's high ceilings. Amaryllis seated herself on the velvet couch in front of the marble fireplace. She shivered, wishing she'd brought a shawl.

The fire had burned low. Brendan poked it and added a log. As the flames leapt high, she thought of the first time she'd seen him. He'd come to speak at the First Unitarian Church about the Atlantic Family Clinic, the medical clinic he'd founded for immigrant families. When Mrs. Choate formed a group of ladies to volunteer, Ammie signed up, in spite of her mother's misgivings.

It was the twentieth century now, the age of the "new woman". Even well-bred women were earning their own livings, working as teachers and nurses. A few even studied medicine. Most of Ammie's friends from Vassar College were engaged in good works for the poor. Jane Peters volunteered at Hull House in Chicago, while two of her sorority sisters were involved with the Henry Street Settlement in Manhattan.

After a week of volunteering, Ammie realized that Brendan's eloquence and stirring voice had inspired her even more than her determination to do charitable work. The first time he'd accompanied her home, treating her to ice cream along the way, had seemed like a miracle. They'd been inseparable ever since.

Brendan joined her on the couch, putting his arm around her shoulders. "You're chilly, sweetheart," he said, drawing her close. She inhaled the clean scent of his starched shirt. With a cold feeling in her stomach, she related her mother's decision.

To her gratification, he seemed sincerely dismayed. "Couldn't we have a small wedding? While I'm sure your family misses Great-Aunt Eugenia—"

"We haven't seen her in *years*," Amaryllis told him, her anger rising. "The mourning period is Mother's excuse. She hopes that given more time, we'll break our engagement."

"Not likely." Taking her gloved hand, he unfastened the buttons at the wrist. His thumb stole inside, caressing the bare skin of her palm in leisurely circles. "How long must we wait? An extra month or two?"

"More like half a year." Her heart plummeted at his distressed expression. "I argued with her—truly, I did."

"Then let's elope." The slow movement of his thumb inflamed her. "Six months is unbearable."

"I-I can't. Mother would be angry." She shuddered at the thought.

His hand left hers and moved to her back. His fingers stroked the bare skin above the top of her ball gown, tracing the curve of her spine and lingering at her neck.

Amaryllis' heart pounded. They were rarely alone like this without a chaperone. Would he use this opportunity to take liberties? Would she be able to stop him?

Did she want to stop him?

The log in the grate crackled, shooting sparks upward. Brendan gazed at her. The firelight turned his eyes pine green with attractive flecks of gold. His intent expression enchanted her, leaving her powerless to resist when he drew closer still and his mouth captured hers.

His lips moved softly, encouraging her lips to part. The tip of his tongue traced inside her mouth, then glided sensually over her tongue.

Confused, she broke away—then was immediately sorry. She craved his mouth on hers again.

His long fingers caressed her cheek. "Was that too much?"

She put her arm around his waist, pulling him tightly against her. He felt so big and warm and solid in her embrace. All the years she'd waited for a man of her own were worth it, because she'd found Brendan.

"Kiss me again," she murmured.

He'd never kissed her like this before. His tongue thrust against hers, stroking inside her mouth possessively until she whimpered, aroused and terrified by the sensations his lips and tongue produced. Her senses overloaded with the mint taste of his mouth, the fresh smell of his skin, the tickle of his mustache against her face.

He broke from her long enough to murmur, "Love you, Ammie."

She touched the side of his cheek, entranced with the feel of his skin, so much rougher than hers. "Love you, Bren."

She let her head loll against the back of the couch. He pursued her, his lips fusing to hers. Timidly she stroked the tip of her tongue against his. He groaned deep in his throat. A thrill went through her—she'd pleased him. His tongue played with hers, touching, then darting back, encouraging hers to pursue.

Growing bolder, she thrust into his mouth. His lips captured her tongue and sucked on it. Tremors of excitement raced down her spine.

She was so absorbed that at first she didn't notice his hand on her bodice. His fingers slipped inside and lightly teased her breast, circling over her naked skin. She gasped, overcome by the unexpected delight of his touch.

Was she a wanton woman to allow such goings-on? She wanted to tell him to stop but the pleasure of the caress hypnotized her. Two fingers rubbed her left nipple, filling her with a heated sensation of urgency.

"I've wanted to do this for so long," he breathed.

She'd wanted it too—although she hadn't known it. Now she knew she wanted more.

Goodness, she wanted more.

His palm cupped her breast and squeezed gently. A moan broke from her throat. She couldn't believe she was allowing this. Opening her mouth to tell him to stop, she whispered instead, "Oh, that feels wonderful."

He kissed the exposed tops of her breasts, making shivers of pleasure radiate throughout her body. "That blue dress makes you look like a mermaid," he said.

A mermaid? She imagined a beautiful sea-woman, rising from the waves to lure a mortal man. No chaperone, no mother, no rules…how lovely it sounded.

"When we're married, I'll take your hair down and spread it all around your shoulders," he said. "Then I'll undress you, because mermaids never wear clothing."

"Brendan!" His talk, shocking though it was, gave her a delicious thrill. She was on the verge of something dangerous and wicked.

Inside her bodice, his fingers moved to her other breast. He captured the nipple between his thumb and forefinger, rolling it gently. She jumped, startled by the caress, startled by the sensations jolting through her. Her breasts felt swollen, as if they craved his touch.

She wanted more…more touches, more caresses, more of his hands moving over her body.

She'd never felt like this before. His kisses always gave her a pleasant flutter in the pit of her stomach. But this feeling was different. She was frightened by what he was doing but even more terrified that he'd stop.

"When we're married, I'll look at my mermaid's lovely breasts," he said. "And then I'll suck them."

What would that feel like? She imagined his wet mouth pulling on her nipple and her pulse quickened. "I-I'm sure it's wrong to speak of such things."

"Not when we're engaged. You know what married couples do, don't you, sweetheart? They make love." His mouth moved over the side of her neck. His lips opened and he stroked her neck with his tongue. She twisted her head from side to side, almost unable to bear the enthralling touch of his mouth.

Her breasts tingled. Even more distracting was the heat growing between her legs. Heat and a deep, longing ache.

She craved the press of his hand on the sensitive skin of her inner thighs. It would feel so good if he stroked her there.

She shifted on the couch, letting her legs part slightly. No wonder bad women were called "loose". Everything about her was opening for him, allowing him to do whatever he wanted.

"Ammie, has anyone explained to you about the marital act?"

His voice was kind but she was too embarrassed to look at him. "Mother told me," she murmured.

His expression turned doubtful. Perhaps he didn't believe her mother had explained it correctly. "On our wedding night, we'll lie down together and I'll put my penis inside your vagina." His fingers trailed alongside her neck, making her breath catch. "Does that sound shocking? I assure you, the act of love will be enjoyable for both of us."

This was essentially what she'd been told—although her mother had used more flowery language. "I don't quite understand how everything happens," she said hesitantly.

The corner of his mouth quirked. "When the time comes, I'll teach you." Picking up her hand, he placed it on the fly of his trousers.

She gasped at the feel of something large and hard underneath the fabric. "Bren—what *is* that?"

"That's what happens to a man's penis when he's ready to make love." His voice dropped. "Don't be afraid to touch me, sweetheart."

Tentatively she trailed her fingers along the bulge. Visiting the Louvre last summer, she'd seen pictures and statues of unclothed men. Their penises had looked like soft, small appendages, about the size of her middle finger—not a long, stiff length like this.

"I don't see how this will ever fit inside me," she said.

"Everything will work out quite well, Ammie. Trust me." He gazed into her eyes, the tenderness in his allaying her fears and filling her with happiness. "When we're married, we'll make love every night. I look forward to giving you pleasure."

"But Bren, Mother told me that ladies don't enjoy marital relations. She said on our wedding night, I should lie quite still and think of George Washington."

"George Washington!" Brendan chuckled. "You'll be thinking of *me* and what I'm doing to you." He kissed the side of her neck. "I'll show you that your mother is wrong." His warm mouth moved down the side of her throat, making her pulse leap. "I wish I could make love to you now."

"We can't!" Yet the very thought made her tremble with longing.

"I know. But let me show you something you'll like." He raised his brows, asking permission without words.

Somehow his kisses and touches had prepared her for more. Shyly, she nodded.

He pushed her skirt up slowly, giving her a chance to pull away. But she was too interested in what he was doing.

He grasped her ankle in his hand. His warmth penetrated through her silk stockings.

Another forbidden yet exciting touch. His palm moving up her lower limb gave her a pleasant tickling sensation. The hot longing at the apex of her thighs grew strong.

"Your legs are beautiful, Ammie."

Was he sincere? Or was it just an easy, meaningless compliment?

His chest heaved as he stared at her legs. "Beautiful," he said again, his voice as serious as when he spoke of his patients. Then she knew he meant it.

He stroked her knees while she trembled. His hand moved inside the wide leg of her drawers, trailing a long, circuitous path upward. Caressing her rounded thighs, he finally reached the place where her stockings ended. His fingers explored the naked skin of her upper thighs. The enticing pleasure of his fondling made her feel lightheaded.

A needy fullness centered in her pelvis. She needed something but she wasn't sure what. Gasping, she shifted on the couch, letting her legs move far apart.

"Your skin is soft as a butterfly's wing." His deep voice rumbled through her. She'd always loved his voice. And his kiss. And the touch of his hands.

Brendan had been proud of the iron control he'd kept over himself during the three months of their engagement. Knowing how shy she was, he'd feared to give her passionate kisses. If he frightened her, she might let her selfish, bossy mother persuade her to break their engagement. An unbearable prospect.

In his thirty-three years, he'd never met another woman who stirred him so deeply. He thought of her day and night—especially at night, when he'd stroke his cock while remembering their few stolen kisses. He'd imagine thrusting into her sweet, tight pussy and his cock would lengthen and thicken. He'd picture her raising her hips to meet his quick plunges, begging for more, crying out his name as a climax overtook her.

No matter what he did at night, he always woke in the morning with his rod engorged to steely hardness. Usually after feverish dreams of his Ammie spreading her legs for him.

As she was doing now.

The devil inside him was tempting him to unbutton his trousers and thrust into her right now, right here. To make her his own.

No, that wouldn't be fair. He mustn't take her virginity in a furtive moment in another man's house. When he first made love to her, he would be gentle. He'd calm her fears and teach her, patiently, how to give and receive pleasure.

But the first lesson could commence *now*.

The crotch of her drawers was open, a convenience of ladies' undergarments to facilitate sanitation. She made no protest when he reached inside. His heart swelled. She trusted him enough to let him touch her sensitive, naked skin. He cupped her mound and she shuddered. Good Gad, she was hot and wet. His cock strained against the fly of his trousers.

Carefully he rubbed upward along her labia until he reached her swollen clitoris. When he gently brushed his thumb against it, she moaned, startling them both. To silence her he kissed her more feverishly, thrusting into her mouth with his tongue the way he wanted to thrust inside her with his cock.

He stroked her pussy again and again, pleased when she lifted her hips and pushed against his hand.

"Don't stop," she whispered. He smiled, because he had no intention of stopping until she found her full pleasure. Her face was flushed, her eyes closed tightly. "Oh, Bren! Yes, more of that!"

He quickened his strokes. Hearing her fast, panting breaths gave him more satisfaction than the most beautiful symphony. Ammie's first climax would come from *him*.

"Right there—yes—yes!"

Good Gad, she was beautiful, caught in the delight his fingers were giving her. His own excitement increased.

Rubbing up her soft curls, stroking her labia, he felt the moment when strong tremors began pulsing through her. She cried out, a frantic note in her voice.

A strange feeling rose within him, like a bubble swelling inside his chest. He'd given his beloved a special gift. He'd never loved her more than this moment, when she lay back against the arm of the couch, half stunned by the force of her climax.

After a few moments, she sat up and straightened her skirt, looking down with embarrassment. To set her at ease, he put his arm around her shoulders.

Amaryllis still felt overwhelmed with what he'd done to her. She picked up the hand that had given her so much pleasure and kissed his palm. "I never knew…"

"You've never touched yourself, Ammie?"

She'd never imagined he would ask such a question. But he was going to be her husband. She mustn't ever keep secrets from him.

"One time…years ago," she said haltingly. "Mother came in. It was mortifying. What a scolding! She said…she said only dirty girls and whores would do such a thing."

Brendan kissed her. "Yet another instance of your mother being wrong." She must have looked unconvinced, for he added, "Who's the doctor? Me, or your mother?"

"You, Bren." She squeezed his hand, heartened when he squeezed back.

"She's wrong about delaying the wedding too," he said. "It's so hard to wait for you. I want you to be my wife. If we eloped—"

"I can't. My parents would be furious."

He looked down, releasing her hand. Her heart sank. Was he angry?

Then he straightened and met her eyes. "I'm sorry, Ammie. I'm selfish to suggest it. I know you're looking forward to a fine party."

"Actually, I rather dread being on display. But Mother would be angry if we made a runaway match."

A gong sounded from the dining room at the far end of the hall. The company had been summoned for dinner.

"I'm afraid I can't stay," Brendan said. "I'm meeting a colleague at the Gentleman's Supper Club."

She'd excused his late arrival, knowing that a doctor's time was not his own. But this was too much. "Oh, Bren! I was so looking forward to dining together."

"I promise I'll make it up to you, sweetheart. Dr. Clark is leaving town tonight. I must talk to him about the family clinic before he goes. Will you forgive me?"

She said she did. In her turmoil, she didn't think about his destination until she walked him to the door. The footman handed him his medical bag and umbrella.

She watched him cross the square, the tails of his jacket flapping in the November wind as he headed toward the house of Mrs. Dunne, the notorious widow who ran the supper club.

Brendan had given her unbelievable pleasure. But for him, there'd been nothing except disappointment.

She remembered the hushed discussions about the scandalous supper club. Opened just a few months ago, the serving girls there were rumored to be soiled doves who were "no better than they should be".

A brothel in the middle of Brahmin territory? How terribly shocking! So the whispers went.

Was Brendan truly meeting another doctor? Or was he visiting a woman of ill-repute?

Setting her lips, she stalked to the cloakroom and scrabbled through the coats until she found hers. "Tell my mother I've gone home with a headache," she told the footman at the door. Before he could answer, she set off briskly toward home, one block away.

She wasn't sure what Brendan was doing but she was certainly going to find out.

Chapter Two

ꙮ

An hour later, Amaryllis squared her shoulders and knocked at Mrs. Dunne's front door. The curly black wig, purchased two years ago for a masquerade party, made her scalp itch. She had changed into her plainest skirt and shirtwaist, hoping that if she persuaded Mrs. Dunne with money, the woman would lend her clothing suitable for a woman of the house.

Her heart galloped like a racehorse. She'd never done anything so rash in her entire life. But for Brendan she'd do anything. Suppose she was about to lose him to one of Mrs. Dunne's fast women? She couldn't let that happen.

She loved him enough to pursue him into this house.

The door swung open. The butler's gaze flashed over her. At least she assumed he was the butler, although his broken nose and cauliflower ears made him look more like a prizefighter.

Surveying her with impatient eyes, he said, "You must be Genevieve d'Elsie. What kept you, girl? We've been expecting you since noon." He bustled her inside. "Was your train late? It's good that Madam won't be disappointed. She's been looking for a French girl for months."

Was it her disguise, concealing shy Amaryllis behind the black curls of a Parisian prostitute? Or the admiring glance the butler gave her? Whatever the cause, bold words slipped easily from her lips. "*Oui, monsieur.* I regret to say I missed the early train." She found it easy to fall into a French accent, having studied the language since the age of eight and perfected her skills during a trip to France. "I rejoice to find myself here at last."

"No harm done. You still have forty-five minutes before dinner begins. Run along upstairs and ask for Ruby." He gave her a familiar pat on her backside. She suppressed a gasp. "She'll find you a serving uniform."

Amaryllis hurried up the stairs, clutching the marble banister because her knees were shaking. The butler's crude touch had brought her folly home to her. She was pretending to be a woman of ill-repute—a prostitute—a woman who sold her body for money. No wonder the man had felt free to offer a lecherous caress.

She would help serve at dinner while spying on Brendan. Before anything else could happen, she'd ask to speak privately to Mrs. Dunne, explain why she'd come to the house and mitigate any possible anger on the woman's part with money.

Set on the plan, her spirits rose as she reached the second-floor landing. A bedroom door opened and a young blonde woman came out, clad in a most startling costume. The loose, gauzy blouse was made of material one could see through—her lace-trimmed chemise was clearly visible. Her full skirt was short, exposing her lower limbs.

Was this what the women wore in their bedchambers when entertaining gentlemen? Amaryllis couldn't imagine herself in anything so revealing, even for her fiancé.

Reminding herself that she must not blush if she wanted to be convincing, Amaryllis asked, "Where might I find Mademoiselle Ruby?"

"I'm Ruby," the woman said in a friendly tone. "You the new Frenchy? C'mon, hon, your room's over here." She led Amaryllis to a large bedroom with a view of Chesterfield Square. Although it reminded her of her own bedchamber, at home her walls were *not* hung with paintings of satyrs caressing nymphs' breasts.

"Hon, your face is as naked as a jaybird," Ruby said. "Did you bring your cosmetics?"

"I am waiting for my trunk to arrive."

"Hold on, I'll lend you some kohl for your eyes and rouge. You can't serve dinner like that." With a sudden grin, Ruby added, "Although with that bosom of yours, I doubt the gents will be looking at your *face*."

Amaryllis was still trying to absorb that comment when Ruby paused in the doorway and gestured at the room's large bed. "Get yourself gussied up for dinner. Your serving uniform's laid out yonder. Madam likes to see all us gals lined up five minutes before the gents come in."

"*Oui, mademoiselle.*" Her stomach churning, Amaryllis approached the bed.

Horrified, she stared down at her serving uniform—a gauzy blouse and short red skirt identical to Ruby's.

* * * * *

Gregory Clark leaned in close, grinning in anticipation of his joke's punchline. "So on the second visit, the patient's completely naked. He says, "Doc, am I crazy?" And the doctor answers, 'My good man, I can see your nuts.'"

Brendan chuckled because it was expected, not because he was paying attention. He kept picturing Ammie's disappointed face when he left her alone at the ball.

Damnation. How to make it up to her? Perhaps he'd buy chocolates on his way to the clinic tomorrow and send them around with one of the messenger boys.

Everyone knew that flowers, books and chocolates were the only gifts an unmarried girl could accept from her beau, aside from a ring to mark their engagement. Ammie's mother would never permit the lavish presents he really wanted to bestow upon his beloved. A sapphire necklace to match the sparkle of her blue eyes. Her own carriage and two fine horses to allow her to drive wherever she wanted without her mother's permission. A lacy peignoir she'd wear in bed for him…

He grimaced, wondering why every time he thought of her, his mind veered to the carnal. He loved everything about his fiancée—her kindness to the patients at the family clinic, her quick wit and intelligence, even her shyness. So why was he continually imagining her underneath him in bed, moaning and writhing while he thrust into her sweet channel?

And now their wedding was delayed. Could he withstand the torture of waiting more lonely months until she was his?

How surprisingly responsive she'd been in the library, his shy Amaryllis, moaning when he caressed her nipples. When they beaded under his touch, his cock had swelled in response.

She invaded his thoughts at will, to the extent that he found himself looking for her at the clinic on days she wasn't scheduled. If he saw a short woman with a magnificent figure in the park, his heart skipped a beat—surely it was Ammie. Even tonight, he found himself watching one particular serving girl who slightly resembled his fiancée.

Ammie's form was more pleasing, of course. And he much preferred her lovely copper hair to this young woman's wild black curls.

She had to be a new arrival. He examined Mrs. Dunne's girls every month, charging a nominal fee in the interests of public health. She'd wanted him to take his fee in trade but of course he'd refused. A man engaged to the beautiful Amaryllis Gardner could have no interest in prostitutes.

Nearly stumbling, the new girl carried in a selection of after-dinner alcohol. Her arms shook, making the bottles of wine, brandy, port and whiskey dance against the heavy silver tray. A red-faced, middle-aged man reached out and pinched the girl's right buttock. Squeaking in surprise, she nearly dropped the tray.

She whirled around, glaring at the pincher. The surprised faces of most men in the room and the gasps of the other serving girls showed her she'd offended. Putting the tray down, she dropped a curtsey and spoke in a near-whisper. "*Pardonnez-moi, monsieur.* You startled me."

Brendan bolted upright in his chair. Unable to breathe, he gaped at the girl.

No, it simply wasn't possible.

"I'll excuse you this time, missy," the red-faced man said. "Especially if you make it up to me—later tonight."

"Oh!" The girl swallowed. "Would Monsieur care for a drink?" Almost dropping the bottle, she managed to slosh whiskey into his glass.

Gregory nudged Brendan. "Pretty piece. I prefer blondes though. Are you all right, buddy?"

"Fine," Brendan mumbled, although he felt like the top of his head was exploding.

Their figures were alike…their voices were alike…but surely his beloved would never disguise herself as a female of easy virtue and enter a house such as this one. What possible reason could she have for doing so?

The answer came immediately. *To spy on me. To see if I'm truly having dinner with Gregory Clark.*

Anger jolted through him. Setting his lips, he tried to tamp down its flames. He had to be mistaken. This woman couldn't possibly be Ammie.

He must not give way to his emotions until he was sure.

Mrs. Dunne was dining across the room with Colonel Grayson. Brendan caught her eye and beckoned. With a quick word to the colonel, she made her stately way over to Brendan, smoothing her emerald-green skirts across her ample hips.

"I see you have a new girl tonight," he said. "She's French?"

He watched Mrs. Dunne's face closely, looking for the telltale signs of a liar…the inability to meet his eyes or a slight stutter in the speech.

"Genevieve d'Elsie just arrived today. She wasn't eager to leave New York City but I paid her madam quite a good sum to send her to me. I knew my gentlemen would appreciate a French girl." Mrs. Dunne smiled. "Don't you think she's lovely?"

"It's more important that she is disease-free," Brendan said. Good Gad, he sounded like a prig but he was too upset to speak normally. "Shall I take her upstairs for the usual examination?"

"That would be so kind of you." Mrs. Dunne smiled. "I hesitated to ask while you were occupied with a friend."

"You'll excuse me, Greg?" Brendan asked.

"Go right ahead. I'll sit here and drink my port." Gregory winked. "Enjoy yourself."

Brendan went to the foyer and retrieved his medical bag. If this young woman was truly a French prostitute, she would not object to the procedure. If she was his fiancée, surely she would confess her folly before allowing an intimate examination.

Returning to the wide center hall, he found Genevieve waiting by the stairway, her blue eyes wide and scared in spite of the harsh black makeup surrounding them. Her skin was pale beneath the layers of powder and rouge.

He gave a slight bow. "Miss d'Elsie, we shall go upstairs to your bedroom. I'll wait outside while you disrobe." Was she his Amaryllis? He wasn't sure. The wig and cosmetics hid the woman's true appearance all too well.

If she were his fiancée, now would be the time for her to stop pretending. "Have you any questions before we begin?" He waited.

"Non, monsieur." Who could identify a voice from a breathy whisper?

He followed her up the stairs, watching the swaying movement of her hips and her pert, full buttocks. His cock lengthened, pushing against his trousers.

* * * * *

Aware of Brendan just outside the closed door of her bedroom, Amaryllis pulled off her skirt and blouse. They had seemed so immodest a short time ago. But now she was expected to be completely naked in front of a man. And not just any man—her fiancé. A dizzying mixture of horror, fear and sweet expectation stole through her.

Reluctantly, she unbuttoned the distressingly short chemise and lifted it over her head. Hurrying over to the gaslight, she turned it down to a mere flicker, leaving the room in shadows.

Should she confess to Brendan? She feared his anger. Perhaps he would break their engagement, outraged by her entrance into this house of sin.

She couldn't blame him.

Better to stay quiet and let him do his examination. Once he was gone, she would apologize to Mrs. Dunne and pay her with one of the twenty-dollar gold pieces she'd brought. Afterward she'd never return to this house.

In any case, she was satisfied that Brendan had come here for exactly the reason he'd stated—dinner with another doctor. How could she have mistrusted him? Shame rippled through her.

A peremptory knocking brought her out of her reverie. "Miss d'Elsie, may I enter?"

She dived into the bed and pulled the sheet up to her shoulders. "*Oui, monsieur.*"

The door opened. Brendan paused on the threshold, gazing at her with raised eyebrows. "Your modesty does you credit. Surprising in a woman of your profession." He closed the door. Using the corner washbasin, he scrubbed his hands thoroughly, then approached the bed and opened his medical bag.

"I-I have not been a prostitute for very long." A panicky thought occurred to her. Was he planning to examine her nether regions? Could she forestall that? "I must confess something to you."

He stopped riffling through his bag and looked up sharply. "Yes?"

"*Monsieur,* I am a virgin."

"Is there anything else you'd like to tell me?" He sounded almost...angry. Surely he didn't suspect her? If he did, wouldn't he have questioned her immediately?

"Why, no," she said. "What else would I have to confess?"

Was it disappointment that crossed his face? "How old are you, miss?" He sat on the side of the bed, a flashlight and a wooden tongue depressor in his hand.

She wondered what he would do with the flashlight. She knew policemen used this new invention but had never known that Brendan carried one.

"I am twenty-five years old."

His lips twitched. What had she said to amuse him? Was twenty-five too old to embark on a career of sin?

He turned on the flashlight. "Open your mouth," he ordered. Shining the light into her mouth, he checked her throat then examined her teeth and gums carefully. She wondered why he was concerned with this part of her body. Didn't prostitutes work with their other ends, so to speak? Surely gentlemen didn't *kiss* them, the way they kissed their wives and sweethearts.

His index finger brushed along her lips. "A beautifully healthy mouth," he said. So attuned was she to pleasure at his hands that even this light touch aroused her senses.

"Miss, you must be careful to remove your paint and powder when you sleep. The skin must be allowed to breathe."

"*Oui*," she murmured. Was the examination over?

She didn't want him to leave. Somehow his touch had brought all the strange feelings from the library flooding back. She wanted his fingers touching between her legs again, stroking her until those strong new sensations took over her body.

"Now I will examine your breasts," he said.

Amaryllis would have been shocked. But she was not Amaryllis now. She was Genevieve, the French prostitute.

For just a moment she hesitated. Like waiting on the edge of a bathing pool, she knew once she jumped there could be no turning back.

No matter who she was, she loved Brendan. She must be courageous and play her part.

Boldly she pulled the sheet down, exposing her entire body.

She remembered how he'd caressed her, the wonderful sensations when he rubbed her breasts. To her consternation, the very thought made her nipples harden and deepen in color, as though begging for his attention.

And they received it. He froze, staring as though he'd never seen a woman's body before.

Was it really true that her nakedness had the power to hold him spellbound?

What would a real prostitute do next?

Shocked at herself, she cupped her breasts in her own palms, offering them up to him. "*M'sieur* likes what he sees?" she asked.

His Adam's apple moved as he swallowed. "Very much."

Ever since he'd given her a woman's pleasure in the library, she'd wanted more.

Her school friends and sisters were long married. An elderly virgin, she was closed away from the knowledge of sexual love.

Her wedding was delayed for months.

Now she was undressed, hidden away in a room with the man she loved. A room with a huge, luxurious bed.

Words suddenly poured out of her. "*M'sieur*, perhaps you would consider making love to me? I would like my first time to be with a man young and handsome. And since you are a doctor, perhaps you will be gentle? *Je vous assure*, I have no—how you say?—no social diseases."

"I cannot possibly make love to you." He glared at her, his eyes blazing with anger.

"*Pardonnez-moi*," she said quickly. She blinked, almost overwhelmed by the mixed emotions rushing through her—disappointment that he didn't want what she offered, happiness that he was faithful to his fiancée.

But maybe he wasn't thinking of fidelity. Perhaps he simply didn't find her naked body alluring.

"No doubt I am not enough beautiful for *M'sieur*?" she asked.

"You're very beautiful." He raked his hand through his dark hair. Perspiration glistened on his forehead. "But I am engaged to be married."

"Me, I understand. *M'sieur* will be married in a few weeks' time, no doubt?"

He cleared his throat. "Actually, the wedding has been delayed until next spring."

"And *M'sieur* is expected to restrain his animal urges for months?" Nervous, she wasn't sure where her words were coming from. "Truly, I feel sorry for your bride. You will be like a mad bull when you finally take her to your bed."

His tongue ran quickly over his lips. "Perhaps you have a point."

"I have been a virgin too long." She lowered her voice. "Please—you will show me *l'amour*?"

He gave her an intent look. "Are you *sure* there isn't anything you want to tell me?"

She shook her head, making the springy curls of the wig dance. "Only this—that I desire you." In her heart she added, *And I love you Brendan. Please, let me experience your touch.*

He blinked. His voice was hoarse when he asked, "If I agree—how much will you charge?"

She gulped. She had no idea how much the women in this house charged their visitors. Why hadn't she asked Ruby?

The scarlet women who worked down by the docks, who sometimes came to the family clinic, made no more than a few dollars from each man. But surely the lovely young women at this house earned far more than that. Should she say ten dollars? Twenty?

The answer came to her. "I will not charge you because this is my request."

An eager flame leaped up in his eyes. "Then I had better service you well for the favor."

Anticipation filled her as he strode over to the armchair by the fireplace and shrugged out of his tailcoat.

Now Brendan knew why Ammie had followed him to Mrs. Dunne's house. She hadn't come here to spy on him.

The episode in the library had awakened her curiosity—as well as her womanly passions.

She'd touched his cock through his trousers. Naturally she wanted more—to see it, to stroke it, to feel it thrusting inside her.

She craved the pleasure he'd promised her. *She wanted him.* Exhilaration sped through him, competing with arousal greater than he'd ever known.

Unbuckling his belt, he relived the moment when she'd whipped the sheet away. A grin tugged at his lips. She'd concealed her lovely tresses with that preposterous black wig but she hadn't disguised the light-colored hair of her mons.

He'd never removed his clothing so quickly. Onyx studs went flying as he pulled his shirt over his head. He stepped out of his shoes and jerked his trousers down.

Coming to the bed clad only in his union suit, he paused, gazing down at her lovely body. Lying so still, she was an ivory statue that an artist had decorated with delicate color—the fiery copper splash of her sex, the flushed nipples that were pink like the glorious amaryllis flower she was named for.

Despite the wig, she had the wonderful fragrance of his own dear Ammie. Lemon verbena, a scent he loved because it was hers.

Was it right to claim his bride early? He fumbled with the buttons of his union suit, wondering if either of them would regret this night. It wasn't too late. He should tell her that he'd seen through her disguise. That they must not make love until they were husband and wife.

Stepping out of his union suit, he awaited her reaction.

Her cheeks reddened as she stared at his naked body. If he hadn't already known she was his Ammie, that blush alone would have confirmed his suspicions. She scrutinized the dark hair on his chest. Her gaze moved downward. His rampant cock stood proudly erect, pointing at her, the tip glistening with a pearly drop of fluid.

"Oh!" she said softly. Reaching out, her fingers brushed along his shaft.

The soft touch was electrifying. All hesitation vanished. He joined her on the bed, desperate to possess her.

Amaryllis knew she ought to be embarrassed. She was a wanton girl, lying naked and exposed with a naked man. But instead of embarrassment, she was suffused with happiness.

At last she had Brendan all to herself. When he knelt between her legs, a deep sense of rightness took hold.

They'd chosen each other months ago. She loved him more than anyone else on Earth. This was the culmination of everything she'd ever wanted.

He grasped her breasts in his big hands, squeezing them gently then rubbing his thumbs over the nipples. They puckered under his touch. Her breasts telegraphed a message of arousal to her vagina.

Ready yourself for Brendan's lovemaking.

Her entire pelvis responded with heated longing. Involuntarily she raised her knees. A soft, wet sound came from her vaginal lips as she parted her thighs.

He gazed downward, his expression intent as his hands fondled her breasts.

When we're married, I'll look at my mermaid's lovely breasts. And then I'll suck them.

The sensation of his hot, wet mouth on her left breast gave her pleasure almost too intense to bear. Her breathing quickened as he licked all around the areola. When he closed his lips around the hard nubbin and sucked hard, exquisite jolts of pleasure shot through her. Both breasts tingled as though an electric current flowed through them.

He moved his head to her right breast, his hand squeezing the left. Her vagina clenched when he nibbled gently on her peaking nipple.

She'd never felt anything so wonderful as his hot mouth on her sensitive skin. Lying here with him naked, he could do whatever he wanted to her vulnerable body. The thought of his hands stroking everywhere, his penis surging inside her, made her anticipation rise. She moaned.

He paused as though surprised.

"Don't stop!" she pleaded. She almost said "Bren" and changed it to "*Bien.* Good" in the nick of time. "So good, *m'sieur*. Please, more touching."

Gazing into her eyes, he gave her a wicked grin. "You like my hands on you? And my mouth?"

"*Oui!* Touch me everywhere." She arched her back, raising her breasts in wanton invitation.

This time his mouth was more demanding. He licked and sucked, grazing her skin with his teeth. She whimpered, her head thrashing on the pillow, every inch of her skin feverishly awaiting his next touch.

A day ago, she wouldn't have known what was happening to her, wouldn't have understood what her body craved. Now she knew she needed the rubbing between her legs that had brought her that wonderful burst of pleasure in the library.

Shifting on the bed, Brendan wished he could whisper his beloved's real name. The dark cave of her navel tempted him. He tickled it with his tongue, gratified when she squeaked in surprise.

When had his cock ever been so hard and full before? He couldn't wait to feel the slick, tight walls of her tunnel clenching around him.

He fingered the delicate curls around her sex. She drew her breath in sharply. He murmured, "Shall I stroke your pussy, Genevieve?"

"Pussy?"

He almost laughed. What prostitute didn't know that word? Stroking along her vaginal lips, he said, "Here, pretty girl. This soft part of you. Do you like my fingers here?"

She answered with a sound like a cat's purr. He laughed and she joined in.

How very dear she was. He must be careful to give her pleasure this first time. If she experienced only the pain of losing her hymen, it might affect her sensual reactions for the rest of her life.

Entering her with the tip of his finger, he realized she wasn't ready. No matter how much his cock demanded release, it wasn't yet time.

Moving downward, he spoke softly. "I'm going to do something that will make you eager for love."

She asked with a little gasp, "What, *m'sieur*?"

His only answer was to gaze down at her gleaming pussy. How beautiful it was, like a flower opening in the morning with dew on every petal.

He'd waited forever to look at the flushed, pink folds of her pussy. He'd waited forever to taste her. Slowly, gently, he ran his tongue up her labia. She shuddered in response.

"*M'sieur!* What did you do?"

"I'm going to lick you everywhere, pretty girl. Relax. I promise you'll enjoy this." He brushed his tongue against her in short, light licks, rewarded when she cried out with delight. He teased her labia with the tip of his tongue, tiny and delicate touches. Each time he drew back for a breath, her pussy was wetter, more swollen.

After a while, the gentle strokes were not enough for her. He knew by the way she lifted her hips, pushing her pussy against his tongue. He licked harder and longer, going all the way up her labia. Shivering, she gasped, "Please…please…"

More long licks with the flat of his tongue, ending each time with a quick touch to her clitoris. Her breath came in ragged gasps. While his tongue still lapped her juices, he teased along her entrance with his thumb.

Tremors arced through her and her pussy clenched around the tip of his thumb. Triumph filled him as she cried out incoherently. He'd done this for her—brought his beautiful Ammie to climax. Treated her to another facet of sensual pleasure.

He soothed her with long licks until finally her hips stilled.

Now she was ready for the act that would make her his. Slick and wet, her pussy was open and ready. He got into position. Holding his engorged cock at the base, he rubbed it along her labia. Her breathing hitched.

He pushed inside her tight tunnel with one powerful thrust, feeling the band of her virginity give way. This time she cried out with shock.

He bit the inside of his mouth, forcing himself to hold back from moving. He'd never felt anything so good as the velvety walls of her pussy pressing against his cock.

Stroking her cheek, he asked, "Are you all right?"

"*Mon Dieu!* I feel like a steel rod is inside me. So strange…"

He hated to think he'd hurt her. Tenderly he kissed her, desperate to move and struggling to retain control.

Amaryllis lay still, trying to get used to the feel of Brendan's penis. She wasn't exactly in pain—the momentary twinge had ended quickly—but it felt so odd to have this huge, hard object inside her.

The touching and licking had been wonderful. But this part? She wasn't sure whether she liked it.

I look forward to giving you pleasure, he'd said. How could this ever be pleasurable?

Would it help if she thought about George Washington?

"Pretty girl—" His voice was almost a groan. "I'm sorry. I have to move."

He pulled back. She felt the withdrawal in every nerve. But she was slick and wet inside, so the motion was smooth. It didn't hurt.

He pushed forward, burying his penis deep inside her again. He paused and she felt him tremble. It took her a moment to understand. He was holding back, giving her a chance to get used to this.

He moved carefully in and out, all his muscles taut. Somehow her body began to anticipate his movements.

She breathed slowly in rhythm with his unhurried strokes. The same feeling she'd had in the library overtook her…the sensation that she was relaxing under his attentions, loose and receptive for whatever he chose to do.

She put her arms around him, stroking his back lightly with her fingers. Groaning, he began to move faster. His penis sliding in and out began to excite her, giving her the same feeling of anticipation as when he'd licked her.

Tentatively she lifted her hips to meet his thrusts. The longing, the wanting ache, swiftly overtook her. How could she lie still, when moving with his rhythm felt so satisfying?

Every time he moved, thrills raced through her. She cried out each time he plunged deep. Urgency built with every thrust of his penis.

"You're wonderful," he murmured. "So tight and hot. Perfect…" Her delight grew when he began a faster, harder stroke. The incredible feelings in her core escalated, making her whimper and hope for more. She only needed a little more…just a little more…

His hand pressed against her breast, his thumb moving roughly over the nipple. A climax swept through her like a hurricane. Her hips thrust upward and stilled while pleasure consumed her with dizzying force. Her vagina clenched around his penis.

Brendan groaned. The strong pulsing of her orgasm around his cock brought him to the peak. His seed shot from his cock with the speed of an express train. The force of his release shook his entire body.

You're mine now, sweet Ammie. He regretted he couldn't say the words aloud. But he could never regret that he'd finally possessed her. How could he have waited for this even one more day, much less six months?

He settled beside her, wishing he could fall asleep holding her.

She turned her face toward his. Doubt shook him when he saw tears welling in her eyes. Quickly he put his arms around her and pulled her close. "Are you all right?" he asked.

She nodded, blinking. "I did not expect such feelings. *M'sieur*, I am overwhelmed."

He kissed the corner of her mouth, the tip of her nose, her left eyelid. Finally she smiled.

A loud pounding came at the door. "Brendan? I've got a train to catch." Gregory Clark's voice.

"Damnation," Brendan muttered. Sitting up in bed, he called back, "Give me five minutes."

"Good Lord, man, how long does it take to do a simple gynecological examination? You've been in there over an hour!"

"Five minutes," Brendan called back firmly. Bending down, he kissed his beloved. "I'm sorry, pretty girl. I must go."

She nodded, her lips trembling. His heart misgave him. She'd lost her virginity tonight, a traumatic event for any woman. Leaving her now made him feel like a cad.

Well, he could do one thing for her. He found towels in the washstand. Wetting one, he brought it to her and tenderly cleaned her private parts. She said nothing, her eyes large and trusting as he worked.

He wondered what she'd done to gain Mrs. Dunne's cooperation. How was she going to sneak back into her parents' house? What would she say to him at the clinic, the next time she came to volunteer?

He cleaned himself and dressed quickly. When he went to give her a last kiss, her lips clung to his.

He hadn't meant to say any such thing but the words spilled forth without thought. "May I see you tomorrow? Will you be here in the late afternoon?"

Joy sparkled in her eyes. "Yes, I will be here," she said, her voice eager. "I live here."

He wanted to reproach her for her duplicity. But wasn't he just as bad by playing along?

"You won't have any other gentlemen visitors tonight?" he asked, sudden doubt shafting through him.

"Of course not!" Her voice was filled with indignation. She bounced up from the bed, wrapping her arms tightly around his neck. "Only you—only you!"

Only you, my sweet Ammie. He kissed her again, his mouth lingering on hers until another knock sounded on the door.

Leaving her was like tearing his heart in two. He wished he'd never promised to take Gregory to the train station.

Striving for calm, he said, "Farewell, pretty girl. I'll see you at four o'clock tomorrow." Gathering up his medical bag, he forced himself to leave the room.

Amaryllis watched the door shut, feeling an overwhelming desire to burst into tears.

Emotions warred inside her. She couldn't wait to see him again. And yet she hated the thought of him returning to this house.

She'd chosen to do this, tempting Brendan beyond his ability to resist. And she'd been so seductive, so pleasing, that now he wanted to see her again. The prostitute Genevieve d'Elsie—not Amaryllis.

Her fiancé was unfaithful. And it was her own fault.

The door flew open. Mrs. Dunne stalked into the room, a telegram in her hand. Glaring, she demanded, "Young woman! Who *are* you?"

Chapter Three

ຣ

Quaking, Amaryllis explained who she was and what she was doing in the house. To her relief, Mrs. Dunne accepted it as a good joke.

"Amaryllis Gardner!" she exclaimed. "The shy young woman who can scarcely say boo to a goose? My goodness, when you get your courage up, you go all out!"

"I'd do anything for Brendan," Amaryllis said, raising her chin.

"I can see why," Mrs. Dunne said. "Handsome *and* rich. A rare combination. Although I suppose that snooty mother of yours doesn't like his Irish blood."

"Precisely. That's why she's delayed our wedding."

"Well, dearie, I am a great believer in free love. You're smart to test your fiancé out before the nuptials. If I'd done as much, I wouldn't be in the fix I am today. Perhaps you've heard the story?"

Amaryllis shook her head.

"Mr. Dunne and I married ten years ago. He was never able to have marital relations with me. Six months ago he ran off, leaving me nothing except this house." She tossed her head. "Colonel Grayson suggested I open the Gentleman's Supper Club. It's been most successful, if I do say so myself."

"The girls seem happy," Amaryllis said cautiously. She knew that prostitution was wrong. Yet Ruby and Gloria, the girls who'd helped her get ready for dinner, seemed cheerful and content. And much nicer than any of her old schoolmates.

"Of course they are," Mrs. Dunne said with a smile. "They're all very genteel, sweet girls. I have high hopes that some of them will marry their clients." She waved the telegram she'd carried into the room. "I'm so disappointed that Genevieve d'Elsie has decided to stay in New York City."

"So that's how you knew I wasn't a real prostitute?"

Mrs. Dunne laughed. "Well, when Mr. Carter gave you that little pinch at dinner, I *did* wonder why it upset you so. But I didn't suspect you until I received this telegram." She crumpled it in her hand. "Now I'll have to look for another French girl. *You'd* be a prime favorite with my gentlemen, dearie. Are you sure you don't want to come back tomorrow?" She winked. "It never hurts to have some pin money of your own."

"Actually," Amaryllis said, "I wonder if we can make a financial arrangement?"

* * * * *

Savoring one of the chocolate-covered caramels Brendan had sent, Amaryllis read his note again. *Sweetheart, I'm so sorry I had to leave you last night. Unfortunately my discussion with Dr. Clark was too important to delay. I enjoyed our time together in the library.*

She should never have let him touch her like that. One thing had led to another. A slippery slope indeed. Yesterday a pure virgin, today a wicked woman who'd had sex without the bonds of matrimony.

And enjoyed it. And was going back for more.

At two o'clock in the afternoon, Amaryllis slipped out the servants' entrance of her home, wearing a hooded cloak that concealed her wig. She'd won herself a chunk of time by telling her mother she was walking the three blocks to her sister Poppy's house and would stay for dinner.

She made her way to Mrs. Dunne's and entered through the unlocked back entrance. The cook, hard at work in the downstairs kitchen, had been apprised of Amaryllis' coming.

After greeting her, he pointed her in the direction of the back stairs.

Heart pounding, she went down the hall to "her" room and seated herself at the dressing table. In just a few hours, she'd be in Brendan's arms again. Thinking about it made her nipples tingle. His hands on her breasts, his penis thrusting inside…the strange feeling of heated urgency flashed through her core.

Using the cosmetics Ruby had lent her the night before, she made up her eyes and rouged her cheeks. She peered anxiously into the mirror, hoping Brendan would once again be fooled.

The afternoon sun provided too much illumination. She went to the room's one long window, closed the blinds and pulled the red velvet curtains shut.

Much better. Her features would be hidden in the shadows. Brendan would never suspect that demure Amaryllis was the same person as this house's bold French prostitute.

"Genevieve, is that you?" Ruby's voice. When Amaryllis told her to come in, Ruby entered, yawning.

"What a night!" Ruby's blonde hair was in disarray and there were circles under her eyes. "Three gents—and I reckoned the last one would *never* get out of the saddle. Lord have mercy!"

Three? Amaryllis' eyes widened in horror. She couldn't imagine having *three* gentlemen do what Brendan had done to her last night.

She had to be careful not to give herself away. She and Mrs. Dunne had agreed to keep their arrangement between themselves.

"Did you make a lot of money?" she asked cautiously.

"You bet! Mr. Carter tipped me an extra five dollars too." Ruby looked pleased. "Say, all the gals are talking about you and Doc Bradford. He's never stayed with any of us before."

"Truly?" Happiness rippled through her. So Brendan *had* been faithful.

Up until now.

Ruby nodded. "Do you think he'll be back?"

"He's visiting me this afternoon," Amaryllis said, a touch smugly.

"Peachy! Do something special to keep him coming around. Did you suck his cock last night?"

Eyes widening, Amaryllis shook her head.

"C'mon, girl! You've got to do that. Nothing keeps the gents happy like a good sucking." She gestured at the pitcher and basin in the corner. "I always give 'em a wash first."

Amaryllis couldn't help asking, "They don't mind?"

Ruby shook her head. "I make a big fuss over it while I scrub. 'Oh, sir! What a beautiful peter! I've never seen such a big one in my life! Please, please be gentle when you put that huge thing in my poor little cunny!'" She rolled her eyes. "You know the drill."

"Yes, certainly," Amaryllis said, trying to sound like she knew what she was talking about. "Do you say that to all the gentlemen? Even if their cocks are small?"

"*Especially* if it's a dinky one. Say, how's the doc? Pretty good size?"

Unable to believe she was having this conversation, she measured off a distance with her hands.

Ruby tilted her head. "Hmm. Rich, handsome and a nice cock. Sounds like a keeper."

Nothing keeps the gents happy like a good sucking. How did that work? Did Ruby mean actually put her *mouth* around his *penis*?

A sudden image popped into her mind. Her legs spread wide, while Brendan licked the most sensitive part of her body. How incredible his tongue had felt. The thought made her vagina pulse with heat.

He'd done that for her. Perhaps...perhaps she could reciprocate.

*****

Entering Mrs. Dunne's house, Brendan wished he'd made a much earlier appointment with Am—with *Genevieve*. He'd been nearly useless at the clinic, his mind on his lover instead of his patients.

"Go on up, sir," the butler said, waving at the staircase. "Early, aren't you? Plenty of time for a good fucking, then back downstairs before dinner ends."

"Exactly so," Brendan said coldly. Why had he ever told Amaryllis he would come back today? Why was he continuing this charade?

But by the time he was hurrying up the stairs, his qualms had disappeared. He couldn't wait to see her again.

Had she made it home safely? Had she received the box of chocolates and his note, apologizing for leaving the ball early? He'd written, *I enjoyed our time together in the library.* That was innocuous enough, even if her mother snooped.

Making love to you last night was the most beautiful experience of my life, darling Amaryllis. That's what he'd really wanted to write.

How wonderful it had been, initiating her into the mysteries of sensuality. What would he teach her today? His mind dwelt pleasantly on the range of possibilities.

When he knocked at her door she flung it open immediately. Her eyes were bright with anticipation. "*Bonsoir*, Dr. Bradford! I am most joyous to see you today."

For a moment he simply stared at her, overwhelmed at how beautiful she looked in a blue satin wrapper with a low neckline. Her uncorseted figure was breathtaking. Her full breasts stood firm and high.

The maidenly garb she usually wore had never affected him like this. When they were married, he would ensure that *all* her gowns displayed her lovely bosom.

Good Gad, he couldn't wait to have her naked underneath him again, moaning, her hips rising to meet the deep, impassioned thrusts of his cock.

He pulled her into his arms and kissed her, pleased at how readily her lips opened under his. Her tongue stroked the inside of his mouth. Immediately his cock leapt up, eager to begin the afternoon's activities.

"I missed you," he said. Stepping inside, he shut the door. The room was so dim, it was hard to make out her dear features. "I thought about you all day, pretty girl."

"I missed you too, *m'sieur*."

"Call me Bren."

She looked up at him, eyes flashing. Too late he realized his mistake. Only Ammie called him that. Now he'd given "another woman" permission to use her private name for him.

She looked down quickly. "*Merci.* Thank you," she murmured. "Bren, would you care for a glass of champagne?" She gestured at the bottles on the table. "Or wine? What would you like?"

"I'll tell you what I'd like." Bending, he kissed the fragrant valley between her breasts. "I'd like to see you naked. On all fours." His hands dropped to her buttocks, caressing and molding them through the thin fabric of her wrapper. Ignoring her squeak of surprise, he squeezed the lush cheeks of her bottom while pressing his pelvis into hers.

He wasn't sure whether she liked the caress until her breath caught. She let her head fall back and moaned.

"Can you feel my cock?" he murmured into her ear. "It's never been so hard before." He rubbed his length against her soft, yielding pelvis.

"Bren, let's make love." She blushed but he loved hearing the words.

"Undress me," he said.

She gave him one swift, shy look. *Pure Ammie,* he thought, his heart filling with happiness.

She reached up, sliding his coat off his shoulders. "That's right, darling," he said softly, encouragingly. "You want to see me naked, don't you? You want to see my cock again."

She took a deep breath—gathering her courage? "I want your cock inside me." Her bold statement thrilled him.

When she unbuttoned his shirt and the union suit underneath it, her eager fingers made him tremble. As soon as his chest was bare, she ran her palms over it. He sucked in his breath. His engorged cock pushed against his trousers. His pelvis tightened, his balls drawing up painfully.

Good Gad, he had to take her soon. Desperately wanting to speed up the process, he shrugged out of his shirt, stepped out of his shoes and yanked his trousers and union suit down.

"Please sit, Bren," she said, grabbing his hand and leading him to the velvet chair near the bed. Puzzled as to what she had in mind, he did as she asked.

She knelt at his feet. He enjoyed the view of her lush breasts. Naked in the chair, he waited, wondering what she had in mind.

She took his rod in her hand, holding it firmly at the base.

"Good heavens, Genevieve," he groaned. "Touch me."

Her blush spread along her cheek and down her neck. "Ruby told me about this," she half whispered. "If you don't like it, I'll stop." His eyes widened with disbelief as she lowered her head and took his rod in her wet, clinging mouth.

The warm rush of pleasure almost stunned him. He gripped the arms of the chair, letting his head fall back. Her mouth encased his length, then moved back slowly, her tongue rippling along the sensitive underside of his cock. He stared at her, enthralled with the sight of his engorged rod between her plump red lips.

"That's incredible," he murmured.

She took her mouth away, her hand continuing to pump up and down. "I'm so glad you like it. I practiced all afternoon."

"Practiced *how*?" he demanded.

"On a banana."

He sighed with relief. She took him in her mouth again. Her tongue swirled around the head of his cock, teasing the slit.

"Suck me, pretty girl," he groaned. "Suck my cock. That's good. Yes, that's right." Good Gad, he wanted to climax.

But all day he'd thought about taking her from behind. Putting his hands on her shoulders to hold her back, he said, "I want to fuck you now."

Her eyes widened at his language. "*M'sieur!*"

Amaryllis knew what the word meant but was shocked to hear it on Brendan's lips.

"I wanted to fuck you all day," he went on. "All I can think about is your pussy tightening around my cock."

Why did the longing inside her grow when he talked like that? She felt heavy and slick, ready for the thrusts of his long shaft.

"Get down on all fours," he said.

"Here?" she asked.

"Here. *Now*," he said.

She knelt on the thick carpet, then dropped onto her elbows. Instantly he was behind her, pushing aside the wrapper, exposing her bare buttocks.

His fingers stroked her labia, teasing up and down. She shuddered with the pure pleasure of his touch.

Something hard rubbed up and down along her slit. She sighed with happiness at the feel of his cock. Ripples of delight went through her.

"Tell me, pretty girl. Tell me what you need."

He wanted her to say the words. "Give me your cock," she said.

He pushed it against her. She cried out, welcoming his hard length against her slick entrance.

"Do you want me to fuck you?" he asked. "Tell me."

Heat rose to her cheeks. He really wanted her to say that word? She moaned, anticipating his first thrust.

"What should I do to you?" he asked. His cock teased her without plunging inside.

The wicked words poured from her lips. "Fuck me! Please fuck me!"

He thrust inside her pussy, impaling her with his long, thick cock. Goodness, being filled like this was even better than she remembered.

He pulled back, then rammed in hard. His hands squeezed her buttocks, heightening her excitement.

"Yes, Bren! Fuck me!" She *liked* saying the word. He thrust again and she pushed back against him, finding it increased her delight.

"Good Gad!" he groaned. He moved relentlessly. Each deep plunge of his cock made her shriek. Pleasure spiraled higher and higher.

Her climax was overwhelming, as though every nerve in her body had exploded. She pulsed around his cock. With a shout of pure satisfaction, he released deep inside her.

* * * * *

Eyes closed, he felt her looming over him.

"Bren, are you sleeping?"

"Mmmm...maybe," he muttered.

He was overcome with the sweetest exhaustion he'd ever known. After all these months of celibacy, three incredible bouts of fucking had worn him out.

Her voice was urgent. "You cannot sleep here tonight. Mrs. Dunne will not be pleased."

Opening his eyes, he found himself greeted by the sight of her rose-tipped, naked breasts. Mesmerized by their beauty, he pulled her on top of him, burying his face in her soft skin. "I don't want to leave."

His cock stirred. Was it time for round four?

"You must go," she said firmly.

He sighed. He'd almost forgotten—of course she had to get back to her parents' house.

Resolutely he sat up, holding her in his lap. "I need to spend more time with you. But not here. I can't keep returning to this house."

"No?" She sounded surprised. He hid a smile. How often did she believe *she* could come here? He had to protect her reputation. He hated to think of the scandal, if their meetings came to light.

"Let's go away for the weekend. We'll take the train to New York City on Friday." He tilted her chin up. "Say yes, pretty girl. We'll have a wonderful time. I'll take you to restaurants—dancing—buy you gowns and jewelry." He couldn't wait to see a sapphire necklace resting on the smooth skin above her breasts.

"I-I am not sure what to say." She bit her lip.

The idea of spending the entire weekend between her lush thighs galvanized him into action. Giving her a kiss, he released her and climbed out of bed. "We'll get a suite at the Waldorf," he went on.

"It *is* a wonderful plan." The sparkle in her eyes showed she was tempted. "But I don't know—"

"I *do* know." Picking up his trousers, he found his wallet and took out two twenty-dollar gold pieces. Laying it on the dresser, he said, "This money should keep Mrs. Dunne happy. Meet me at the station at half past two on Friday—I'll come directly from the clinic. We'll catch the three o'clock train to New York City."

Her eyes seemed to blaze as she looked at him. "I will be there. I promise."

"And Genevieve?"

"Yes?"

"Be sure to pack that blue wrapper."

*****

Arriving for her Thursday afternoon work at the Atlantic Family Clinic, Amaryllis was torn. Should she challenge Brendan about his love affair? Or keep her mouth shut and go on the trip as Genevieve? The weekend he'd described sounded like so much fun.

For the last few years, her life had been as dull as ditchwater. Good works, lectures at the First Unitarian Church, a deadly round of receiving and returning calls at her mother's side. Her school friends and sisters, married with children, had little time for a spinster.

Brendan had brought the joy of loving and being loved into her life…and now, incredible pleasure as well. But the thought of him frequenting a house of ill-repute was devastating. Did she truly want to marry a man who would do such a thing?

Amaryllis hung up her coat and quietly told the secretary that she would be in the back office.

The secretary nodded. "Shall I tell Dr. Bradford you're here?" he asked.

"It's not necessary." He knew she usually worked on Thursday. He could search her out...*if* he was still interested in his prim fiancée.

She was copying Brendan's scrawled notes into a patient file when he appeared in the doorway. "Sweetheart, I've been watching for you all day. Why didn't you stop in and greet me?"

Laying her pen down, she said, "I wanted to get to work right away."

He strode into the room and took her hand. "You look so serious. Are you pondering my suggestion to elope?"

"Certainly not," she said, her voice icy. How could he talk about eloping when he was running off for the weekend with another woman?

"Are you still angry about the ball? Did you get my note?"

She nodded. "Thank you for the chocolates."

"Don't I get a kiss?" He squeezed her hand.

Anger overtook her as she remembered how he'd kissed Genevieve the day before. No matter that Genevieve was herself—*he* believed she was a different woman.

Rising to her feet abruptly, she gave him a quick peck on the mouth, not at all the type of kiss she'd been giving him for the last few weeks.

"Something's wrong," he concluded, grasping her other hand. How could he look at her like that, as though he was troubled, as though he was concerned about her? "What is it, sweetheart?"

Oh, nothing. Absolutely nothing. Except for your torrid love affair with a loose woman named Genevieve d'Elsie!

"Are you coming over for Sunday lunch, as usual?" she asked.

His gaze avoided hers. "Well...I'm afraid not. I'm going away for a medical conference this weekend."

"A medical conference." She repeated the words with scorn. "Are you sure you're not leaving town with another woman?" Would he confess? Perhaps if he did, she could bring herself to forgive him.

"Whatever would make you think that?" The coolness of his tone spurred her anger. How could he lie to her so easily?

"You went from the party to Mrs. Dunne's house—"

"Which I told you about. I had dinner with Dr. Clark," he countered.

"Even if that's true, how do I know you aren't seeing a woman there? Everyone knows that house is really a brothel!"

He squeezed her hands. "Ammie, you should trust me." His voice took on a stern note. "All our lives there will be times when we must be apart. I might be working, attending conferences or visiting friends. My wife must believe in my marital vow of fidelity."

She wanted to believe him but she knew how he'd spent yesterday afternoon. She looked up into his eyes. "Tell me, Brendan. Tell me if you love another woman. Please don't lie to me."

He raised her right hand to his mouth, kissing the white knuckles. "Ammie, you're the only woman I love."

Furious, she pulled her hands away. "I don't believe you!"

"What do you mean?" He gripped her shoulders. "I haven't looked at another woman since I met you. What reason do you have to distrust me?"

She couldn't answer, caught in a trap of her own making. How could she bring up his relationship with a French prostitute unless she confessed that she was Genevieve? And if she revealed that, he'd despise her.

But maybe there was a way. "I heard...I heard you are involved with a woman at Mrs. Dunne's house."

His eyebrows rose. "You *heard*? Who would say such a thing?"

Wishing she'd never spoken, she said, "You know how it is with gossip."

"Gossip is worthless. I give you my word, Ammie. *You are the only woman I love.*"

"I don't believe you!"

His eyes blazed with anger. "If you don't trust me, how can we wed?"

"Perhaps we shouldn't wed! Perhaps Mother was right!" She looked away from the hurt that leapt up in his gaze.

"Mother was right about what?" he demanded.

She dug her nails into her palm, hoping the pain would keep her from bursting into tears. "I was wrong to accept your proposal."

"You don't mean that!"

She blinked hard. "I'll show you how much I mean it." Ignoring the agony in her heart, she stripped off her engagement ring and thrust it toward him. "Here! Take it!"

* * * * *

Women of her class didn't cry on the streetcar. The effort to hold the tears back made Amaryllis feel as though her face was frozen.

Her hand felt empty without her precious engagement ring. But not as empty and forlorn as her heart.

The remembrance of Brendan's stricken face brought a fresh wave of pain. Yet when she'd walked past him and left the clinic, he hadn't tried to stop her.

Jane let her in the front door. "Is something wrong, miss?" the maid asked.

Amaryllis shook her head and dashed into the parlor. Collapsing on the horsehair sofa, she burst into tears. What had she done? How could she possibly go on without Brendan in her life?

She'd made a terrible mistake, disguising herself and tempting Brendan beyond his ability to resist. But he'd succumbed to temptation. Why couldn't he have remained faithful?

God help her, no matter what he'd done, she still loved him.

She cried until her mother, probably alerted by Jane, hurried into the room. "Amaryllis, what is causing this regrettable display? Look at your eyes, red as a pincushion! Don't you remember that Father's law partner is coming for dinner tonight?"

"Mother..." She desperately craved a word of sympathy. Barely able to speak, she raised her empty hand. "My engagement is over."

Her mother drew in a quick breath. A look of unholy glee passed over her face. Without another word to her distraught daughter, she fell to her knees and turned her face toward Heaven. "Thank you, dear Lord!"

* * * * *

She was a terrible, wicked girl. Amaryllis knew it for certain now. She'd broken the engagement but she couldn't stay away from Brendan.

She was as bad as an opium addict. Except instead of a drug, she was addicted to his touch, his kisses. His lovemaking.

She was addicted to *him*.

That's why she'd packed a bag and left a note for her mother, saying she was visiting her sister Lily in Buffalo for the weekend. She didn't care if the transparent lie was exposed. This was her last chance to be with her beloved.

She wished she'd eloped with him when he'd asked her, before she'd ever posed as Genevieve.

When she stepped off the streetcar, she saw him at the corner, watching for her—

No, watching for *Genevieve*.

She put a false smile on her face, despite the heartache centering in her chest. "*Bonsoir*, Brendan. I came as I promised."

"I'm so glad." He gave her a quick kiss and took possession of her arm. "Come to the end of the train, pretty girl. I have a surprise for you."

How could he be so cheerful? There was an air of barely suppressed excitement about him that added to her pain. His engagement had been broken off barely twenty-four hours ago, yet he was on his way to New York City with a prostitute.

Clearly Amaryllis Gardner meant nothing to him.

How could she love him with all her heart and soul when he didn't care?

She gasped when he led her to a private railroad car at the end of the long, white-sided train that went to New York City daily. Why was he going to such lengths to impress a woman like Genevieve?

Inside, she was momentarily distracted by the elegance of the interior. The car was furnished with revolving velvet chairs, a table covered with a lace cloth and dark burgundy curtains that hid the outside from view. She blushed when she noticed the berth that pulled down into a bed.

"It is all *très belle*—beautiful," she said.

Capturing her hand, he sank down into a chair and pulled her into his lap. "Nothing but the best for my darling."

If only she could be Amaryllis now, not this French whore who had somehow captured his heart. His kiss was both tender and possessive—the kiss of a man in love. Helpless to stop herself, she wrapped her arms around his neck and returned his ardor with desperate fervor. Her pussy tingled, already eager for the passionate thrusts of his cock.

She would enjoy this weekend for all she was worth, even though her heart was breaking. His kiss made her feel hot and cold and dizzy. Lightheaded even…or was that because—

Brendan held her false curls aloft. "We don't need this silly wig anymore, do we, Ammie?" He tossed it into the corner.

Astonished, all she could do was gape at him.

He caressed her cheek. "Did you really think I didn't know my own fiancée?" His arm tightened around her waist.

Her mouth was still open in surprise. He took advantage of that to kiss her again.

"When did you find out?" she demanded when she could speak.

"I suspected as soon as I heard your voice at dinner. Although I admit you do a French accent beautifully." Putting his warm palm on her pelvis, he added, "Your pretty curls down here didn't match the curls on your head, sweetheart. That's when I knew for sure."

She pressed her face against his waistcoat, remembering everything they'd done in Mrs. Dunne's brothel. How had she dared? Wearing that wig had made her behave in the most wanton way possible.

He tilted her chin up so that her eyes met his. "Don't be embarrassed," he said, the sincerity of his voice utterly convincing. "I'm the luckiest man on earth to have a sensual woman like you."

"Really, Bren?" Relief flooded her.

"Really and truly. I love you, Ammie." With a distinct emphasis, he added, "And I trust you."

She understood his implication. "I was wrong to distrust you." She would never do so again. Holding his gaze, she said, "Brendan, I love and trust you with all my heart."

He kissed the tops of her breasts with obvious delight.

She sighed with joy, wondering how soon they could open the bed-berth.

With a jolt, the train began to move.

Looking up from her breasts, he smiled the smile she loved the most, the one with an enticing hint of wickedness. "Looking forward to New York City?"

"Oh, Bren." Her heart was about to burst from pure happiness. "But—but how can we? We can't possibly have an illicit weekend together if I'm not in disguise. Someone we know might see us!"

Before he could reply, a knock sounded on the car's outside door. Amaryllis looked up, expecting the first-class porter.

Reverend Choate from the First Unitarian Church entered, a Bible in his hand. Beaming, he greeted them. "Good afternoon! Are you ready?"

Confused, Amaryllis leapt to her feet. Her gaze flashed from the reverend back to her fiancé.

Brendan's smile widened. "Illicit weekend? Don't be foolish, sweetheart." Raising her hand to his lips, he kissed it. "We're eloping."

HAVING IT ALL

Desiree Holt

Dedication

To all the musicians who made Delphi Productions a success, this one's for you. Thanks, guys, for ten great years. You are all Mac Fontana.

And thank you to all the bands, the roadies, the club owners, the concert promoters who enriched my life and gave me a greater understanding of the music and entertainment industry. Without you there would be no Mac Fontanas.

Author Note

All the lyrics in the story were written by the author and are not copyrighted by anyone else.

The Hotel Vistana exists only in the author's imagination.

"Having It All"

When I think of all the dreams we had, the wishes that we shared

The kisses in the moonlight, the symbols that we cared

I wonder why I took those dreams and let us drift apart

'Cause the fame and glory couldn't fill the empty in my heart.

I lie awake at night and miss the softness of your touch

Knowing life without you doesn't matter very much

But with you here beside me, as my lover, my wife

Darlin', there's one thing that's certain in life

I'd be having it all.

—words and music by Mac Fontana

Chapter One

ꞩ

Daisy Giles flipped down the sun visor in her brother's SUV and checked her makeup for what was probably the tenth time. Satisfied that she'd done as good a job as possible, she blew out a breath and sat back in the passenger seat. She didn't know why she was so nervous. It was just a dinner.

Right. With a man who broke my heart. A man I've hated for ten years. A man who has a lot to make up for.

A man who, even now, she wasn't sure she was ready to see after all the pain and all the years.

Her brother, Jimmy, reached over and squeezed her hand. "Relax, kiddo. You look great."

She fiddled with the purse resting in her lap. "I don't know why I care anyway," she told him. "How did I let you talk me into this?"

"You're an event planner, right? He wants you to plan an event for him."

"Plan an event." She snapped and unsnapped the clasp of her purse. "Yeah, right. Like I'm the only one around."

"Daisy." His voice was calm and matter-of-fact. "You and Mac haven't seen each other in ten years. The way you parted was terrible and I think it's left a cloud on both your lives. I can't speak for you but Mac's regretted it every minute of every day of his life since then."

"So you say," she retorted.

"Who's in a better position to know than I am?"

Which was true. Mac Fontana had left town without her but *with* his band and with her brother Jimmy as his manager. Mac, who had a voice like golden honey, and Jimmy, who had a steel-trap mind and a knack for always knowing which deal to make, had ridden the glory train together to the top of the heap. Now Mac was an icon of country rock music, wealthy beyond anything they'd imagined when the two of them used to daydream under the big tree in her backyard. And like herself, he had a short unhappy marriage in his history book.

"You're right." Her fingers moved restlessly, smoothing the fabric of her dress. "But some pain never goes away. This just seems so...so..."

"So what? He knows he did a terrible thing, but you never gave him a chance to make amends."

"Make amends?" Her voice almost squeaked. "How can you make amends for destroying trust? For falling into bed naked with three equally naked groupies, drunk out of your mind? And when your girlfriend comes into your room to celebrate your success with you, just lying there with a goofy grin?"

"He was just a kid, Daisy," Jimmy reminded her. "It was a crazy, stupid, immature thing to do. A kid getting his first big taste of success. And it's haunted him every day since then."

"He got married, didn't he?" she snorted. "He couldn't have missed me that much."

"Hello pot, kettle calling." He wheeled around a corner. "I seem to remember you doing the same thing."

That was true. In an effort to wipe Mac Fontana's imprint from her mind and body, she'd married a man so completely opposite from Mac that she'd had nothing in common with him. And when the tiny spark of the mediocre sex had worn off, they'd discovered they didn't even like each other. It had been over and done in six months.

"Anyway, you never answered his letters or emails, or took his phone calls," he pointed out. "Besides, it didn't last as long as water in the sun."

"I don't know, Jimmy. Ten years is a long time. A lot of gold records. A lot of heady success. A lot of women. Why should I believe he even wants me or cares about me after all that?"

"Not as many women as you think, Daisy." He slid a glance at her. "Honey, he's more nervous about this than you are. I promise you. And you're under no obligation for anything. He just wants to have dinner with you and talk."

"About hiring me," she said carefully.

"About hiring you," he agreed.

"In his suite," she pointed out.

Despite what she hoped was a firm grip on herself, her mind drifted back to a night when the Texas stars had been brighter than diamonds in a black velvet sky. A special night that she'd thought at the time was the beginning of forever for them.

"I love you, Daisy," Mac murmured, his lips a gentle pressure against hers.

"I love you, too."

"I love your eyes, your mouth, your skin." His nimble fingers skittered over her breasts, barely touching her nipples.

They were in his apartment, lying in the rumpled bed, about to mess it up even more. The latest country rock music played softly on the bedside radio. Sweat-slicked from their wild orgasms, they held each other as they caught their breath and let their heart rate slow down to something approaching normal. But already the heat was building again between them, threatening to consume them as they rode the hard edge of sexual excitement.

Mac closed his lips over one taut nipple, sucking it into the wet cavern of his mouth, his tongue sweeping across the beaded tip. His hand closed over the other breast, the plump nipple pressed into the center of his palm.

"I love to taste you," he told her, releasing the nipple and trailing his lips between her breasts to her navel. "Every bit of you. Feel my cock inside your tight little cunt. God, it's like a wet fist gripping me as if you'll never let me go. Can you believe I'm already hard for you again? Touch me, Daisy."

Her fingers closed over his thick cock, loving the feel of the velvet skin over the hardness beneath. When her thumb brushed across the head she felt a drop of semen already perched on the slit.

"I love to feel it," she said in a soft voice. "In my hand, and in my body."

"Everywhere in your body?" His eyes boring into hers were hot with desire.

No, she thought, not desire. Lust. The same thing she was feeling for him. And she knew what he was asking.

She wet her lips with the tip of her tongue and let out a breath. "Everywhere."

His fingers played with the curls on her mound., then slid down and back, to touch the tiny hole of her anus.

"Roll over, Daisy flower. Let me touch it all."

"Mac…"

"You want it, darlin', just as much as I do. You know it. It's the most intimate way a man and woman can make love." He traced the cleft of her buttocks before returning to the rosy opening. "This tiny hole right here. Tonight it's mine, Daisy. And that means you'll never be anyone else's. Right?"

She nodded, barely able to breathe as the thrill of the dark forbidden raced through her. "Just yours."

"I love you, Daisy flower," he told her again. "You know that, right?"

"And I love you," she breathed, her heart beating like a wild thing.

"You know we'll always be together."

"I wouldn't want this with you if I didn't."

He bent and showered the globes of her ass with butterfly kisses before lifting her to her hands and knees. She sensed his body move to the side, then he was back, between her thighs.

The gel was cool on the tight ring of muscle, his finger slipping into her rectum and massaging the substance into her hot tissues. A second finger joined it and he scissored them to relax and soften the walls of that hot, dark tunnel. Daisy wiggled her ass at him. And his fingers plunged deeper before pulling back out.

She heard the tearing of the foil, the snap of the latex being rolled onto his cock, felt the pressure of the head at the tiny opening. Would it fit? Could she take it?

The thickness of his shaft pressed into her, burning at first and she tried to draw back.

"Breathe in and out, darlin'," he told her. "Deep, slow breaths."

She did as he asked, and with each exhalation he pushed himself in a little deeper, until at last the full length of him was inside her. Stretching her. Filling her. Oh, God. The pain became pleasure and heat raced over her body. Her blood pounded in her ears.

His hands locked onto her hips supporting her, as he began a slow in and out rhythm.

"Play with yourself, Daisy. I've got you. Tug on that little clit and slide your fingers inside that pussy. Come on, darlin', do it."

Soon her fingers were keeping pace with the stroke of his shaft in and out of her ass, and the throbbing of the pulse deep in her womb was like a jungle drum gone wild.

She felt it starting, rolling up from inside her. Mac increased the pace of his strokes, faster and faster, hands gripping her tightly.

"Now, Daisy," he shouted. "Come for me now."

And she tipped right over the edge with him, the orgasm gripping her like a hurricane, tossing her about with the force of a cyclone. Every muscle clenched, every part of her convulsed, as the muscles of her rectum clamped down on his pulsing cock. She rocked back against him as he spurted into the latex reservoir again and again. At last she collapsed forward, Mac on top of her, his chest glued to her back, their lungs rasping like saws.

She had no idea how long they lay there before Mac finally lifted himself, pulled out and rolled over. Daisy was as weak as a kitten, and she had no idea where Mac found the strength to take care of the condom, then dig around for his handkerchief and clean her with infinite tenderness. Then he pulled her into his arms, holding her against his chest that was still echoing with his heartbeat.

"I'll love you forever, Daisy. Forever."

"Daisy, did you hear me?"

She shook herself, realizing she'd been so wrapped up in her memories she hadn't heard what Jimmy was saying.

"What?" She blinked her eyes. "I'm sorry. My mind was wandering."

"No kidding. I said, 'Better his suite than in a crowded dining room, with the whole world looking on and paparazzi lurking in every corner.'"

She couldn't take issue with that argument.

"We're here," he told her, turning on his signal light and pulling into the Vistana's circular drive. He leaned over and kissed her on the cheek.

"Go get 'em, kiddo. And remember. No pressure. He just wants to talk. Oh, and he's in the penthouse suite. Someone will take you up there."

Great. How many people were involved in this, anyway?

An emotional cocktail of leftover anger and hurt with a healthy dose of nervous anxiety made her slightly unsteady on her legs as she made her way through the crowds in the lobby to the elevators. A dark-haired woman in a navy suit stood next to the one at the far end, the one Jimmy had told her to take.

"Miss Giles?"

Daisy waited for a smirk to break out on the woman's face but instead she just gave a quiet smile and held out her hand.

"I'm Portia. I'll key the elevator for you."

She slid a keycard into a slot next to the elevator door, and when the doors separated with a quiet swoosh, she stepped into the car, holding the door open with one hand. Swiping the card in a slot next to the word Penthouse, she stepped back out into the waiting area.

"Enjoy your evening, ma'am."

Before Daisy could say a word, the doors closed and the car rose soundlessly. She wasn't sure if she wanted it to hurry or take forever. While she was agonizing time ran out and the smooth glide upward ended. With another swoosh the doors opened to the penthouse foyer, and Mac Fontana stood waiting for her.

Sex personified, that's all she could think. Age had been far too kind to him. The boyish frame had filled out, and a navy silk shirt and soft jeans showed off the well-defined muscles and broad shoulders that tapered to a narrow waist. Legs that went on forever ended in custom-tooled navy leather boots.

The smooth, boyish face she remembered was now a mature landscape, square-jawed with sharp planes and angles. Stamped by the passage of time. Tiny lines framed the full lips and bracketed the silver eyes watching her from under thick lashes. His black hair was still shoulder length, only now it sported a hundred-dollar trim and was artfully layered.

His presence, the overwhelming maleness of him, the raw power that made him so successful on stage, made her dizzy, and for a moment she felt lightheaded.

"Hello, darlin'."

That honeyed voice had deepened and had a richness that came only with age and experience. It sent shivers skittering along her spine and made every pulse in her body thump so loudly she was sure he could hear them. And she knew without a doubt that despite all the anger and aguish, ten years and a mistake of a marriage, she was and always would be desperately in love with Mac Fontana.

Great. Just great. She knew this was a bad idea. For a fleeting moment she was gripped by a desire to turn and flee, to get as far away from this man as possible. Clinging to her anger was better than dealing with the mixture of emotions swirling through her.

She swallowed, a difficult task with a mouth as dry as the desert. "Hello, Mac."

He took her hand and slivers of heat traveled up her arm and shot through her body. "Thank you for coming, Daisy. Please come in."

I hate him. I still hate him. I just need to keep remembering that.

She let him lead her into the suite's huge step-down living room. Off to the right was the dining room and beyond carved double doors what she was sure was the master bedroom. Her eyes widened at the sight of every surface covered with vases holding huge arrangements of daisies.

"A little too much, huh?"

Was that a tremor in his voice? Uncertainty from the great Mac Fontana?

Don't go there, Daisy. It's just another part of the trap.

Her heart bumped her ribs. "They're lovely, Mac. You didn't have to get quite so many, though."

He shoved his hands in his pockets. "I decided to go for too much rather than too little."

She looked around, glancing into the dining room. "I thought we were having dinner? Or was that just an excuse to get me up here?" She couldn't help the bitterness that crept into her voice.

The anger roared to the forefront again. Did he think she was just going to fall into bed with him after all these years? She'd given him the ultimate in trust and he'd trampled on it like an elephant. Left her heart open and bleeding. That wasn't something easily forgotten.

Mac shook his head. "This isn't a scam, Daisy, if that's what you're thinking. They'll bring dinner up as soon as I call. I thought maybe we could have a drink first. Kind of ease into things."

"Ease into what? Jimmy said you wanted to hire me to plan an event. How much easing does that take?"

"As I do. And we'll get to it. But all in good time."

She tried to tug her hand away from his but his grip was firm. Not hard, just...solid. And damn it, his familiar scent wrapped itself around her. Her body, reacting like Pavlov's dog, responded to the nearness of him, nipples hardening, pussy gushing, muscles clenching.

No! I can't do this.

Once again he seemed to read her mind. Turning her around to face him, he fastened his dark gaze on her face. "It's still there, you know, darlin'. Nothing's happened to make it go away."

"Mac, I—"

"I want to kiss you, Daisy. Just a kiss. Nothing's going to happen here that you don't want, and that's a promise. But I think I'll die if I don't get just a little taste of you."

And this was the very reason she hadn't wanted to come. Mac was absolutely right. Neither all the anguish she'd been hoarding, nor ten years of separation had diminished one bit of the powerful attraction between them. There was absolutely no way she could turn away from this kiss. She wanted it as much as he did. Maybe more.

"I can't." She pulled her hand away. "I just can't. How can you possibly think you can wipe away what you did with a kiss and a fancy dinner? You betrayed me, Mac," she cried. "In the worst way. Does it even bother you?"

The muscles in his face tightened. "Damn right it does. I was a stupid, foolish kid. That's no excuse, just an explanation. But I threw away the best thing that ever happened to me. I know what I did wrong. But Daisy, I'm begging you for another chance here."

"Oh, Mac." The pain in her heart rose up from its hiding place and stabbed her like a sword, opening the wound all over again.

"Please, Daisy. I know we can't go back to the beginning, but can we find a new place to start? I swear to you, I'll never hurt you again. I'd only be hurting myself." He reached for her hand again. "Just one kiss, darlin'. Then if you want to you can walk right out of here."

Wordlessly, still fighting the emotions within herself, she went into his arms and he lowered his mouth to hers. His lips still felt like rough satin and he tasted like every bit of sin in the world. Tentatively he tickled the seam of her mouth with the tip of his tongue, and just as tentatively she opened for him.

And she was lost, just as she'd known she would be.

The moment his tongue swept inside, the tip dancing over every inch of the wet surface, she moaned and pressed herself against him. She expected him to move his hands over her, to reach for her breasts, to touch her in the familiar way she'd missed all this time. Instead he held her body gently against him, her hardened nipples feeling the roughness of his chest hair through the silk of his shirt, and the thick outline of his cock pressed against her throbbing mound. She felt glued to him as if she could never break away.

He was as good as his word. Just a kiss. But that kiss was more intense than any fucking they'd ever done. It drew from her very core, plundered her, swallowed her, until there was no part of her body that wasn't on fire. It went on for a very long time, tongues touching and twisting, lips moving this way and that. Her mouth felt swollen and her breath was trapped in her throat, and still the kiss went on.

All she could do was hang on for dear life.

When he lifted his head they were both breathing hard and his silver eyes had darkened to smoke. She could feel his heart beating in time with hers. For the longest time he just stared into her eyes, holding her with his gaze, hot need flaring in the liquid silver.

Oh sweet heaven, how can I do this?

Then he stepped back.

"Why don't I get us a drink? Jimmy says you hang out with the wine elite but still prefer bourbon. That right?"

An unsteady laugh burst from her lips. "You've been quizzing Jimmy on my likes and dislikes?"

One corner of his mouth kicked up. "Just wanted to get it right. So what's your pleasure?"

Wine. Absolutely. Nothing from the past.

"Bourbon," popped out of her mouth. "Lots of ice, splash of water."

He moved to the bar and she went to stand by the floor-to-ceiling window, staring at downtown San Antonio. She needed to put some space between them or this would turn into a disaster. She'd thought she could do this with cool objectivity, but it was obvious she'd been out of her mind. All the pain she'd clung to all this time couldn't blunt her fierce desire for him or the strong emotional pull that knocked down her carefully constructed defenses.

She nearly jumped out of her skin when Mac's warm fingers touched her shoulder.

"Sorry." He brushed a kiss against her bare shoulder so light she thought she might have imagined it. "Your drink, darlin'."

She took the cut crystal tumbler from him and sipped at the smooth blend, feeling its warmth trail all the way to the pit of her stomach.

Mac stood next to her, not touching her, looking out at the night with her as they sipped their drinks. Daisy could feel electricity crackling in the air around them.

"Don't overthink this, Daisy. Let's just see what happens, okay? It's taken me all these years to get my head on straight. To know that if you gave me another chance I wouldn't fuck it up. We'll go real slow here."

He turned and pressed something in his hand. A remote. Soft music, something slow and bluesy, filled the room. She tried to resist when he reached for the glass she was holding, then uncurled her fingers from it. He put both drinks on a low table and held out his arms to her.

"Dance with me, Daisy. We always danced like we were one body. Remember?"

Oh, yeah. She remembered very well. Too well. Alarm bells were clanging in her brain but latent need overrode them. She fitted her body to his in the old familiar way, and they began to move slowly.

One hand rested at the base of her spine, just above the curve of her ass. The other held one of hers folded against his chest. He tucked her head into the curve of his shoulder, putting his mouth right at her ear. His warm breath tickled her and moisture flooded her again. At this rate she'd be dripping on the floor.

She felt the muscles of his thighs as they moved, flexing against the softness of her own. They moved as one person, bodies fitted together like the pieces of a puzzle, and a sharp shaft of memory speared her—the glide of his cock into her, filling and stretching her until the broad head bumped against her womb. She could almost feel it now, causing a flood of heat to suffuse her.

From the sudden pulsing movement of his shaft she knew he had to be thinking the same thing, or something close to it. Remembering the sensations of mouths and fingers, the deepness of penetration, the swelling of desire until they crested and the earthquake took them. And then they'd rest and do it all again. And again.

A soft chuckle sounded in her ear and the warmth of his breath was like a tender caress. "I don't have the same staying power I used to, darlin'. Trust me on that." He tightened his hand on her buttocks. "And it isn't from overuse. You can take my word on that, too."

One piece of music ended and another began.

"I heard Mac Fontana was still hot stuff," she said, feeling the bunch of muscles as he tensed.

"Pure media hype." He was trying for lightness in his tone, but instead she heard anger. "A product of overactive imaginations."

She noticed they had stopped moving, were simply swaying in place. His body felt so good against hers, warm and hard and familiar. And the press of his erection brought back so many memories they swamped her. For a moment she wanted to push him away. Run. Escape.

Then the impossible truth hit her. She could never run away from him, no matter where she went or how far. He was in her blood. And she realized in the same instant what tonight was all about. Not a meeting. Not conversation. Mac Fontana was courting her all over again, only this time it was with the single-minded purpose of a mature man, not an impressionable boy.

But how did she let go of the past? She wanted to hold him close and push him away at the same time.

Again, as if he knew intuitively what she was thinking, he stopped moving and put his mouth to her ear. "I have something to say, and I'd like it if you'd listen to me all the way through before chopping my head off, okay? Which, I agree, you have every right to do."

Here it comes. The big excuse. The big lie.

"I'll listen," was what she said instead.

"Shall I call for dinner first?" He gave her a lopsided grin. "Would you rather hear it on a full stomach?"

She couldn't help but smile back, even though her stomach clenched with the anticipation of what was coming. "No, that's all right."

He studied her face, searching for something, then took a deep breath and let it out.

"I want to talk about that night."

Chapter Two

ஐ

That night. Ten years ago.

She'd always broken it into two separate components—before the concert and after.

*****

Before

In their room in the hotel, plush and luxurious, they'd been like two kids high with the excitement of success. Tonight he would be the opening act for a major star at a concert before ten thousand people. The record people were in the audience. Jimmy had worked to set things up and they looked very, very good.

"I can't do it without you, darlin'."

They were lying in bed, so horny for each other they'd practically torn their clothes off in heated anticipation.

"Good," she breathed, as his hands roamed over her.

He cupped her breasts, squeezing them lightly, his thumbs toying with the nipples until they plumped and hardened. Her cunt vibrated, the juices of instant arousal coating the lips. His thumb and forefinger pinched the ripe buds, then he moved his head and his mouth captured one, sucking it into warm wetness. With his tongue he pressed it against the roof of his mouth, the tip of his tongue rolling it back and forth.

One lean leg moved between hers, his thigh pressing against the warmth of her pussy, rubbing the pouty lips as his lips pulled on her nipple. She wrapped her arms around his neck, holding him tightly, her cunt riding his thigh, feeling the length of his cock against her flesh.

When he'd sucked both nipples until the pleasure was almost painful, he moved his mouth in a line down to her navel, his tongue licking her skin, the tip swirling the indentation. She could tell how eager he was, barely restraining himself to prepare her. When he shifted position to fit himself between her thighs, he cupped her buttocks to lift her up to him and sucked at her clit the way her had her nipples.

His tongue was like a wet flame, her hot nub throbbing with insistent need. He felt her slick readiness, lapping at it once, twice.

"I can't wait," he gasped, and plunged his sheathed cock inside her with one hard plunge.

She wrapped her legs around him, clasping him to her with fierce possession and nudging her hips upward.

"Jesus, Daisy, fucking you is like sticking my cock in a wet glove. You feel better than heaven."

And then he fucked her in earnest, hips jacking in hard, fast thrusts, his penis stretching and filling her. She rode with him, moving in the rhythm her body knew so well, faster and faster, the climax rising up within her like an unstoppable earthquake. They convulsed together, bodies in tune, the hot rush of her fluids bathing him as her pussy spasmed again and again.

He collapsed on her, his heartbeat echoing hers, their sweat-slicked skin drying in the artificially cooled air. For long moments all they could concentrate on was breathing. Then he kissed her, his tongue still coated in her taste, the kiss as much a promise as a melding of mouths.

"I love you, Daisy flower," he huffed, still struggling to breathe. "You're all I want. Ever. We're going the whole way together."

*****

After

She'd worked her way through the well-wishers after the announcement of the record contract. Promoters were whispering to Jimmy about dates and percentages and marketing. The band had been higher than kites just on the adrenaline rush and carried Mac off to celebrate.

When Jimmy finally drove her back to the hotel, she'd gratefully ridden the elevator up to their floor and swiped her key card in the door, looking forward to their own private celebration.

And stopped, frozen in the doorway.

Mac in bed, an empty bottle of bourbon on the nightstand. And three naked groupies crawling all over him, adoring his body with their hands and mouths. And Mac groaning his pleasure.

She hadn't even bothered with her stuff, just called a cab and disappeared into the night. Home, to lick her wounds and suffer her pain.

*****

Now

She waited the space of a heartbeat, convinced she should leave for her own salvation. Her heart couldn't take another fracturing. But then he pulled her back into his arms and began the slow dance again, a mournful sax providing a plaintive background.

"I was such a kid, Daisy. So full of myself. So sure I had life by the balls. Strutting like a rooster in front of the band."

"It wasn't the band I found you with," she reminded him, her body still moving in tune with his.

"I had no brains, Daisy flower." The old sweet name made her heart clench. "I poured that bourbon down until I didn't even know my name. I hardly remembered the boys bringing the girls up to our room. Until I saw you in the doorway."

"You were quite a sight." She fought to keep her voice even.

"So were you. Like a pail of cold water. You were gone before I could get myself together. You wouldn't even take my calls. Answer my emails. Nothing." He sighed in her ear. "And it was no more than I deserved."

She stopped moving and forced him to look at her. "You got married."

"So did you," he pointed out. "And I'll bet your marriage was just as empty as mine." He kissed her eyelids, her cheeks, her jawline. "You're the only one who's ever lived in my heart."

She wrenched herself back to reality. "That's quite a line, Mac Fontana. Surely you have enough women at your beck and call without me. Or is this just an attempt to prove you can still crook your finger and I'll come running?"

"Never." His voice was heavy with pain. "And I've lived with that all these years."

"So what do you want of me?" she asked desperately. "Event planners are a dime a dozen."

He ran his fingers through his hair. "Jesus, I feel like a wet-behind-the-ears teenager again."

His hand trembled slightly.

Daisy raised an eyebrow. The famous, fabulous Mac Fontana nervous? The superstar who owned every stage and every audience where he performed?

"Mac, what's going on?"

He shoved his hands in his pockets, then pulled them out again. "I've got no right to say this. If you walk out of here and never come back I'll surely understand and I wouldn't blame you." He rumpled his hair again. "I had this all planned out, you know. Wine. Soft music. Dinner. Me throwing myself at your feet begging for forgiveness. But the minute I held you in my arms… Aw, Christ."

"I can't believe you're at a loss for words. Come on, just spit it out."

His eyes stared into hers. "I want to make love to you, Daisy flower. Not have sex. Not fuck you. I want to make love and show you with my body what's in my heart." His voice was unsteady. "Will you let me do that?"

Maybe if he'd come on strong, acted like the past never happened, she would have walked away. But this was a side of Mac she wasn't used to seeing. And there was no way he could fake the need and sincerity in his voice. She stood there in a puddle of indecision, her body crying, "Yes" while her brain screamed, "No". Maybe this was her chance to find out if she'd gotten him out of her system. If she finally could put it all behind her. Or maybe, as she feared all the way over here, she'd learn she couldn't walk away at all. She'd be risking everything and could end up once again with nothing.

"Remember," he told her. "Nothing happens if you don't want it to."

Then the music changed again and the seductive lyrics of "Always Mine", the song he'd written just for her, floated into the room.

"Oh, Mac," she cried. "You don't play fair."

She could have taken her purse and walked out, but the inescapable truth was she wanted this as much as he did. Otherwise she'd never have let Jimmy bring her here to begin with. All the passion she'd hidden away, all the desperate need, came to life with the explosion of a fireworks display.

He'd carried her to the bedroom, his mouth eating at hers all the way, like a man who'd been starving, until he could put her down and undress her with a touch that was almost reverent.

Now lying naked on the huge bed in the suite, watching Mac strip away his own clothing, Daisy shivered in delicious anticipation as she let her eyes take in the magnificence of his mature body. Thick curls covered the hard chest and the muscles in his arms flexed as he pulled off his clothes and tossed them aside. His stomach was flat, neither his body nor his face bearing the marks of dissolution she might have expected of someone who was a superstar.

But it was the absolutely magnificent erection rising from his groin that took her breath away. Thick and proud, the plum-colored head already darkening. Her mouth watered at the sight of it.

Everything about his body was pure temptation.

And the song drifted from the speakers in the room, the words still so familiar to her.

You're everything to me, my every dream come true

Wherever life takes me, there will still be only you

He came down next to her, rolling her toward him, his hands traveling slowly over her body.

"I always loved your breasts, you know," he murmured. "Firm yet soft, with nipples that made my mouth water every time I looked at them." He brushed a quick swipe of his tongue over each one as he held the weight of one breast in his palm. "Your nipples still look and feel like dusky flowers, such a pretty deep rose. You have no idea how many nights I've dreamed about them. Fantasized about taking them in my mouth. Like this."

He nipped one nipple with his teeth, then soothed it with his tongue, finally pressing it between his lips and teasing the edge with the tip of his tongue.

Daisy felt heat streaking right to her cunt, striking at senses already awake after a long dormant sleep, feeling the heat and wetness of him surround her. As he pulled and sucked on her hardened tip his warm breath fanned the slope of the breasts above it, another sensation piling on the others.

He took his time, giving each nipple equal treatment, one hand moving to caress the shape of her.

Fingers danced over her skin, along the curve of her hip, the swell of her buttocks, reaching into the cleft and seeking the forbidden entrance.

I sense you all around me, your touch like an April shower

The scent of you as rich and sweet as my favorite daisy flower.

"You *are* all around me," he said in his rich, soft voice, his fingers drawing patterns around the tight ring of her anus. "Wherever I am. Whatever I do. I close my eyes and you're there with me. Your memory was like a second skin. I was the biggest fucking fool in the world, Daisy flower."

You're locked in my heart, a love for all time,

And no matter what happens, you'll always be mine.

"You could at least have let me try to explain," he murmured, as he pressed his palm on the flat of her tummy, the tip of his little fingers just barely touching her clit.

"You didn't even come after me," she blurted unexpectedly, fighting the heat of his touch as it washed over her.

"Not that night," he admitted, making circles with his fingertip. "But after that…" His voice trailed off and she heard her own pain reflected in its tone. "I could have. Should have. I've been killing myself over it ever since."

She arched up to him, still fighting her feelings. All the nights she'd cried herself to sleep. All the hours of misery calling herself a fool. For believing in him. Then for not answering him. She'd missed this so much. All of it.

"I could have called you and demanded answers, too. But I trusted you with my body in the most intimate way and all I could think of was, you trashed it. Us. All of it."

"I got what I deserved," he protested. "But Jesus, Daisy. My heart's ached every day of the last ten years."

All right, I'm a fool and an idiot but I don't care. My body certainly doesn't care.

"Touch me," she breathed, her senses rocketing. "Touch me everywhere."

She let her legs fall open and his hand delved into the wetness of her slit. Silently her body begged for more. Much more.

"I feel as if I've died and gone to heaven," he said, his voice heavy with leashed desire.

His fingers played idly in her wetness, fingertips drifting over her already swollen clit then down through the slick flesh and the eager lips. She bent her knees to give him better access, knowing that despite everything this was what she wanted.

"Don't rush me." His chuckle was strained. "I've dreamed and fantasized about this for so long I don't want to skip a single thing."

His thumb and forefinger plucked at the swollen button of her clit, pulling it from its protective hood and rubbing the hotly sensitive bundle of nerves. She pushed herself into his touch, silently willing him to delve lower, deeper, but he had his own plan and was sticking to it.

As he stroked her pussy, her slick cream coating his fingers, his head bent to a nipple again. The heat of his mouth sent streaks of pleasure coursing through her breasts, the skin tightening with pleasure. His devilish tongue and clever fingers were driving her crazy, hinting of pleasures yet to come but never quite taking her there.

When he slid two lean fingers, pads roughened from guitar strings, into her waiting vagina all her internal muscles clenched down on them and she began to ride them.

"You have no idea how good this sweet little pussy feels to me." His voice was almost a growl. "Or how many nights

I've dreamed of doing just this. With you. Showing you in every way possible my love for you."

I dream of your softness, the silk of your skin,

The touch of your hand when the magic begins

The words of the song were like swords stabbing directly into her heart. He'd written them one night when they'd made love not frantically, but slowly, drawing out the pleasure, making silent vows to each other. Was that what was happening now? Was he trying to show her with his two best instruments—his body and his music—that she was still in his heart? That he'd never abuse her love again? Ever?

And then she couldn't think anymore as his fingertips rasped her sweet spot and spikes of pleasure jolted her. Slowly he moved his fingers in and out of her sheath, adding a third one as the muscles softened and expanded. Her hands gripped the sheets and her back arched, soft moans echoing from her throat.

She wanted to tell him *Hurry, hurry,* but she couldn't form any words.

Then without warning she was flying, cast into a velvet void, the climax taking her like the slow roll of breakers at the edge of the sand. Shudders rippled over her from head to toe, a soft fist shaking her gently, her cunt clenching over and over and over. Her liquid bathed his fingers, pouring into his hand.

"That's it," he murmured encouragingly, his lips like wet fire on her mouth, whispering against her own. "Come for me, darlin'. Let me feel those hot silky juices. So warm and sweet."

As the aftershocks still rocked her, he moved down between her thighs, slid his hands beneath her buttocks and lifted her to his waiting mouth. At the first lick of his tongue she jerked, and the little spasms increased in their intensity. He probed her inner walls, drinking her nectar, his fingers pressing into her hips to hold her in place.

She squirmed in his grip, held in the clutch of a pleasure almost beyond bearing. Hot and cold chased themselves over her body as he drew a remembered response from her weeping cunt. The surface of his tongue was like rough linen, and it dragged against her sensitive skin as he fucked her with steady slides in and out of her channel, driving her to yet another orgasm.

She tried to twist away from him, afraid of the intense pleasure that had her in its grip. Afraid of the whirlpool of sexual heat that swirled just out of reach. Afraid that her body would shatter completely.

He lapped and sucked and drove his stiff tongue into her again and again. When she teetered on the brink of explosion, her body strung as taut as a bow, he pinched her clit, slipped one pinkie into the tight ring of her anus and drove her over the edge. The in and out rhythm in both of her openings took her breath away and she gave herself over to the pleasure.

He was merciless, drawing every last shiver of response from her, drinking every drop of her liquid, never interrupting his attention to her clit or her anus. Finally he lowered her to the bed, her body exhausted, her breathing choppy.

He kissed his way up her body, pausing to trace wet lines around her navel, nip at her swollen nipples and finally capture her mouth with his. She tasted herself on him, a sweet-tart taste that generated a tiny thrill inside her.

In the twilight of the evening, when day gives up the sun

My heart is filled with thoughts of you, my love, my only one

And the rising moon casts beams upon your hair so thick and fine

I feel the future, see our love, and know you're always mine.

As Daisy lay on the bed, naked, wrapped in Mac's arms, the song wound down to its closing, piercing her heart with memories.

My love for you will last through time

Daisy flower, you're always mine.

Her eyes welled with tears and she buried her face against his shoulder, unable to avoid the inescapable truth. She could never cut Mac Fontana out of her life again. But could she trust him once more with her heart?

Chapter Three

ꝸ

Mac poured them fresh drinks and carried them back to the bed, then phoned down to have dinner brought up.

"Are we going to dine in the nude?" Daisy couldn't help grinning at the idea.

"The image is more than appealing," he chuckled, "but we'd never get through the meal." He disappeared through a door and returned with two thick, fluffy robes, tossing one at her. "I should be a gentleman and suggest you might want to shower first, except I want to be able to get my fill of your scent. Besides, I have big shower plans for later." He wiggled his eyebrows.

Daisy pushed herself off the bed and slipped on the robe. She could hardly help noticing Mac's thick erection that the robe barely concealed.

"We didn't…that is, you didn't…I mean…"

He cupped her face between gentle hands. "We have all night, Daisy flower. I've dreamed about pleasuring you for so long it was all I could think of. All I wanted. We are far from done yet."

"Oh, yeah?"

Impishly she reached for his thick penis, wrapping her slim fingers around it and sliding them up and down. When a pearlescent drop of pre-cum beaded at the slit, she leaned forward and licked it with her tongue, probing the slit as she did so. Her other hand reached between his thighs to cup the sac heavy with his testicles.

He sucked in his breath. "Jesus, Daisy. Dinner will be here in a minute."

"Then maybe I should hurry," she teased, lightly raking her fingernails over the skin covered with soft, downy hair. But as she bent to take him in her mouth the doorbell to the suite rang.

"I hope the waiter doesn't look below my waist," he said with a wry grin.

It was obvious Mac had gone to a great deal of trouble arranging the meal. When he opened the door a waiter wheeled in a large room service cart. Daisy watched as the waiter arranged crystal candlesticks on the dining table, fitted tapers into them and lit them. At once the scent of vanilla floated into the air.

Next came crystal wine goblets and a cooler filled with ice, in which nestled Daisy's favorite wine. Water was poured into cut crystal tumblers, and the matching pitcher sat near Mac's place on a padded trivet. Shrimp cocktails were set precisely on china plates, the balance of the meal in covered dishes in the kitchen. Daisy noted that, obviously according to instruction, she and Mac would be sitting side by side.

At last the waiter was finished, Mac slipped a folded bill into his hand and he bowed his way out deferentially.

"You really put a lot of thought into this," Daisy commented.

He pulled her close, threading his fingers through her hair and pressing her head to his hard chest, where she could hear the thudding of his heart. "I wanted it to be just right." He cleared his throat. "I wanted this whole evening to be just right."

Was that a touch of nervousness she heard again in his voice? Surely not. This was a man who owned every stage on which he appeared. Her throat tightened with unexpected emotion.

He cleared his throat and took her hand, leading her to her chair. "Do me a favor?"

She cocked her head. "Depends on what it is."

"Take your arms out of the robe and eat naked."

Her face heated. "You're kidding."

"Not a bit. Here, I'll do it, too." As soon as he was seated he untied his robe and shrugged it off, letting it crumple behind him on the chair.

Daisy's eyes were drawn at once to his magnificent cock, mesmerized as Mac folded his hand around it and lightly stroked himself. How was she supposed to think of food?

Dinner was an erotic act in itself. They sat at the marble dining table with the heat of their bodies warming the air. Mac speared each fresh shrimp from the small bowl of ice and fed them to her, his eyes heating as he watched her even white teeth bite them. A muscle in his jaw flexed as he watched her chew slowly.

No bourbon with dinner. Instead he poured her favorite white wine—Jimmy had obviously been coaching him—and after each bite of food he held the goblet for her to sip. Then he dribbled a little on the top of her breasts and bent his head to lick away the drops. Her nipples beaded instantly, remembering the hot feel of his mouth on them.

His muscular thigh pressed against hers, rubbing against it with the tiniest of movements. She shifted in her chair as the pulse throbbed deep inside her womb and her cream soaked into the robe beneath her. Mac smiled at her, part angel, part devil, knowing exactly what he was doing to her.

The steak he'd ordered was tender and rare, the way they'd both always liked it. As he'd done with the shrimp, Mac sliced it himself, feeding one bite to her, then one to himself. She couldn't take her eyes off him as he chewed. The subtle play of muscles in his jaw, the flex of his throat convulsing as he swallowed. When he licked the juice of the meat from his lips with a slow swipe of his tongue it reminded her of the expert way he'd tongue-fucked her and she couldn't restrain a shiver. The light in Mac's eyes told her he knew exactly what she was thinking.

And all the time the music played softly in the background. Mac had switched back to the soft blues, all instrumental, slow and seductive, another assault on her senses. The music he'd selected was from a CD she used to play when they were in his truck together, one more sign that he'd kept every memory of her tucked away in his heart.

The thought made tears well in her eyes and she forcibly blinked them away.

By the time they finished the steak she was squirming in her chair. Sliding her hand across his thigh beneath the table, she found Mac's hard cock and closed her hand over it. Her cunt pulsed as her fingers gripped the hard shaft.

Mac gave her a heated glance. "Careful, darlin'," he warned. "We don't want the rocket to launch too soon."

She smiled at him. "Tell me you don't like it and I'll stop."

"Don't like it? Are you serious?" He closed his fingers over hers, but when he looked at her his face was dead serious. "Not only do I love it, I don't want anyone but you ever touching me again. And I mean ever. That's a vow, Daisy, as well as a promise."

Her heart tripped in pleasurable expectation. It was all too obvious that if Mac wasn't the man in her life there wouldn't be anyone. She wanted so much to believe him. Needed to believe him. To let go of the pain after all these years and have what he'd promised her so long ago. What they'd promised each other.

She blinked away her thoughts. "So what's for dessert?"

He cupped her chin with his warm hand, one corner of his mouth hitching up in a grin. "Remember the fantasy we always talked about, Daisy flower?"

"Fantasy?" Drowning in his eyes she felt her brain take a leave of absence again.

"You know. *The* fantasy? Come on, Daisy. We only had one we always joked about. What we'd do some day?"

"What we'd do?"

The memory flashed at her from wherever she'd hidden it, the night she and Mac had gone on a picnic. He was leaving the next day to cut the demo in Austin. Jimmy had found a backer to put up the money and they were like two kids at Christmas, riding high on excitement. They'd talked about their dreams of the future all the way through the meal. When every crumb of food was gone and they'd finished the bottle of wine Mac had brought, he pulled her against him and kissed her, eating every inch of her mouth.

"You know what I'd love to do, Daisy flower?"

"What?" she asked breathlessly.

"I'd like to cover you with chocolate syrup and whipped cream and eat up every inch of you."

Oh, yes, now it all came back, but she needed to tease him a little. She ran the tip of her tongue along the seam of her lips and watched Mac's eyes darken.

"Yeah, you know what I'm talking about, don't you, darlin'? Just hold that thought for a minute."

Mac pushed his chair back and walked into the kitchen of the suite with his easy, loose-hipped gait. When he came back his eyes gleamed with mischief and he was holding a giant bottle of chocolate syrup and a huge can of whipped cream. And the devil's own light shone in his eyes.

"Are you game?" he grinned.

"That was so long ago. I can hardly believe you remembered it all this time."

"You'd be amazed at what's stayed in my mind," he told her. "Every word, every movement, every moment of intimacy." He cupped her chin and tilted it up, his eyes dark with emotion. "I threw it away in an instant of immature stupidity. I don't plan to do it again. Come on. Let's be kids again. The magic's still there, Daisy flower. You feel it, too. I know you do."

She couldn't argue with him. She'd felt it from the minute she'd stepped through the door into the suite. And fought a losing battle with it.

Then he scooped her up from the chair and carried her back into the bedroom, juggling the cream and syrup. He picked up the remote for the music system and clicked it again. The notes of "All I Want is You", one of the last songs he wrote when they were still together, burst from the speakers.

Again she felt tears threatening, but Mac leaned his head down and licked them away. "No tears, darlin'. Tonight we start the rest of our lives. Together."

* * * * *

She stood by the bed trembling with a mixture of anticipation and arousal, watching as Mac fetched a stack of towels from the mammoth bathroom and covered the sheet with them.

"I ordered plenty extra," he grinned, a slight tremor in his voice. "I didn't want to be caught short."

"How did you know we'd even get this far?" Her voice was shaking, too. They were taking a big step into the past here.

All traces of humor left his face, replaced by a quick slash of optimism. "I didn't. I just hoped. A lot. And prayed."

Somehow those simple words touched her more than the most lavish apology. Mac could fake a lot of things, but not what she heard in his voice. That came from the heart, knocking down more bricks in the wall she'd built around herself.

"I've been dreaming about this for a long, long time," he told her, his voice heavy with desire. "Ever since that night we joked about it."

Frissons of excitement raced over Daisy's skin as Mac knelt on the bed next to her, upended the syrup bottle and like an artist, outlined her breasts, her nipples, her navel and the crease of thigh and hip. With his tongue he slowly lapped up every warm drop of the sweet sauce, placing sucking, open-mouthed kisses over her navel and her nipples.

Every place he touched her leaped to life, like tiny fireworks exploding inside and out. She knew she was wet again, her body craving him. Needing him.

I dream of the gentle touch of your hand

The sweetness of your lips, I do.

The feel of your body, the scent of your hair

All I want is you.

Daisy felt emotion welling up within her, pulling at her, Mac's deep voice invading her senses like a drug, and she gave herself over to the decadence of the chocolate and his mouth on her skin. When he'd licked up every drop he repeated the process, his breathing heavy as his mouth moved over her.

Daisy felt the pulse at the hollow of her throat beating so hard she was sure it would jump through her skin. With each touch of his mouth, licks of flame raced over her body and a fresh rush of liquid seeped from her cunt.

Mac shifted to kneel between her legs, bending them so her feet were flat on the sheets, and dripped the syrup the length of her slit. When he placed his mouth on her, mingling the syrup and her juices with his tongue, little thunderbolts shot straight from her womb to the rest of her body.

His tongue was a wicked thing, teasing, tasting, lapping, coaxing. The tiny orgasm caught her by surprise, rippling through the walls of her pussy, heat washing over her like a warm blanket. Tremors rumbled over her in wave after wave as Mac's tongue plunged and lapped, now flicking at her clit, now thrusting stiffly inside her.

Daisy thought for sure she'd been transported to another plane where she'd be caught on the crest of pleasure forever, but Mac gently eased her down, kissing every inch of her sex, warm hands caressing her thighs and hips. When he looked up at her his face was a shiny mixture of chocolate and her juices.

"You taste like heaven," he said. "You always did."

Daisy lay panting beneath his gaze, heart stumbling, pulse racing.

And his cock had not yet been inside her.

How would she hang onto her sanity when that finally happened?

"Daisy?" he mumbled, his lips brushing the inside of her thighs.

"Mmm?" She was in the grip of an incredible lassitude.

"Remember what else we talked about? With the whipped cream?"

Click!

She remembered it as if he'd said it only a moment ago.

"Yes," she breathed.

"I want to do that. Now."

She nodded, words escaping her.

"Really? You'll let me do it?"

Was that another tremor in his voice? The fact that he was unsure of himself knocked down another barrier, another piece of her armor.

She nodded again. "Yes," she whispered, her pussy fluttering at the thought. It had been another one of those "Wouldn't it be sexy to do this?" things they'd fantasized about.

"Hold on, darlin'. I'll be right back."

She laid there, eyes closed, blanking her mind and giving herself over to the moment. In what seemed like only seconds she heard Mac return, heard the sound of something clinking against glass, felt him kneel between her thighs again. She squealed when something cold landed on the curls covering her mound and her eyes popped open.

Mac held up the can of whipped cream in one hand and a razor in the other. "Still okay with this? I sure do want to see your sweet little mound naked as the day you were born."

She wet her lips and whispered, "Yes."

She felt the kiss of the razor as it swept over her tender skin in one smooth stroke. Heard it clink against the glass bowl as Mac rinsed it. With every caress of the blade Mac's breathing grew heavier. When he reached the labia, pinching each side lightly between thumb and forefinger to pull the skin taut, she didn't know which of them was more aroused. On edge. Sexually charged.

And the song kept playing, its seductive lyrics beckoning.

The sun on your hair, the curve of your lips

Haunt my dreams each night.

Mac tossed the razor into the little bowl and cleaned her gently with a soft cloth. Then he covered every inch of newly bared skin with whipped cream, bent his head and slowly licked it up. His tongue caressed each spot lovingly, lapped at the cream then kissed the exposed skin.

Daisy fisted her hands in the covers, strung tight on the rope of desire, each flick of his tongue heating her blood and speeding her pulse until she could feel it pounding in her ears. What had originally been the wild idea of two kids had turned into a sensuous tease. If Mac didn't get to the main act soon she thought for sure she'd explode.

She hitched her hips at him and the rumble of his low laugh vibrated through every cell in her body. By the time he'd eaten up every swirl of whipped cream, Daisy was in a highly inflamed state of arousal. Mac had teased and tormented her body to a fever pitch and her heart was slamming against her ribs.

He set the bowl aside, reached down and lifted her up. "I think it's time for that shower now."

Lifting her easily in his arms, he carried her into the biggest bathroom Daisy had ever seen. The shower was as big as the whole bathroom in her condo.

Mac opened the door and reached in to turn on the water. Instantly fine spray misted from a dozen jets in the walls and ceiling. When he set her inside she felt as if she'd stepped into a soft, warm waterfall. Vapor surrounded her like a sensual blanket. She leaned her head back and let it cascade over her.

"Make sure there's room for me, too." Mac's deep voice broke into her fog and his hands slid around to cup her breasts.

"I think we could hold a dance in here," she joked.

"Only if it's a dance for two." His rough satin lips brushed the side of her neck and his tongue licked the drops of water on her skin.

A tiny shiver raced over her body.

Mac reached for a full bottle of shower gel sitting on a shelf, a bouquet of flowers etched on the front, and poured some into his hand. At Daisy's questioning look, he grinned. "I wanted to be prepared for anything. Everything."

He turned her facing away from him and pulled her against his naked body. His soapy hands slid over her shoulders, massing her breasts and moving to the soft roundness of her tummy. She hummed her pleasure as his hands moved lightly over her skin, washing away the sugary concoction on her skin and rubbing in the scented gel.

When his hands moved to the newly shaved flesh of her cunt, she automatically widened her stance to give him better access.

"I don't think a single week has passed in ten years that I haven't dreamed about this," he murmured, his long fingers stroking her up and down. "Touching your bare skin, feeling your juices slick on my fingers. In my heart I knew…I truly knew…you'd never do this with another man." Two fingers pressed her slit between them. "Right, darlin'?"

"No one but you."

She heard her words slur, as if the chocolate had been a narcotic seeping into her through her pores. She had never, ever felt so totally unwound, yet at the same time hanging on the edge of ecstasy. And she meant what she said. Despite what had happened, the men she'd had relationships with had never come anywhere near as close to touching her inner core, unleashing her fantasies, as Mac Fontana.

Two fingers slid into her waiting sheath and she flexed her inner muscles around them. Her arms reached back and she clasped her fingers behind Mac's neck, anchoring herself to him as she rode the penetration. His thumb brushing her clit stirred fires inside her that threatened to erupt at any moment.

"Easy," he crooned, slipping his fingers out. "I've hardly finished lathering you."

She swallowed a groan as he removed her hands, then bent down to attend to her feet, her ankles, her legs. When his soapy hands brushed the inside of her thighs the fires sparked a little higher.

But when he stood up, she abruptly turned around and grabbed the bottle of gel from him. "My turn," she told him with a wicked grin.

Just as he had done for her, she covered every inch of him with the scented liquid. It had been so long since she'd touched him, had the freedom to roam her hands over his long, lean body, she felt like a starving guest at a banquet. She began at his broad shoulders then skated her hands over his hard chest, threading her fingers through the thick curls and rubbing the flat dark nipples until he growled and grabbed her wrists.

"You're playing with dynamite, Daisy flower. We don't want it to go off too soon, do we?"

She stood on tiptoe to press her lips against his, the tip of her tongue licking the lingering flavor of whipped cream. "Are you saying we've only got one explosion to count on? That doesn't sound like the Mac Fontana I knew."

He brought her hands up to kiss them, then released them. "This one is even better, darlin'. Have at it."

Her fingers played across the rock-hard muscles of his abdomen, twirling the lather into his navel, then combing her fingers through the dark nest of pubic hair. Lifting her eyes to his, she let her hand glide down onto his cock, wrapping her fingers around it, skimming them along the velvet covering of the hard shaft. It leaped in her grip at once, the vein pulsing against her hand.

Mac's eyes darkened and a flush stained his cheekbones. His hands smoothed up her arms to her shoulders. "Put your mouth on it, Daisy. Please. Let me feel those soft lips around it, that warm wetness sucking it in."

Placing the bottle of gel on the shelf, Daisy reached up to the showerhead, moving it around to rinse him off. Then she dropped to her knees, cradling Mac's shaft in both hands, and danced her tongue across the plum-colored head. Already a thick bead of moisture had gathered at the slit and she lapped it up, licking her lips as she swallowed the taste of him. When she dipped her tongue into the slit Mac's hands tightened on her shoulder.

"Jesus, Daisy." His voice was thick and gravelly.

"Mm, good," she laughed as she slid her mouth over the length of him.

She tilted her head back so she could suck him farther into her throat and one hand reached between his thighs to cradle his balls. The delightful taste that had been the young Mac Fontana was now a rich, ripe essence. How could she ever have thought she could live without this? Certainly not now, when he was roaring through her veins, embedding himself in her system.

She hadn't forgotten the rhythm he liked, the way he wanted her to move her mouth on him, use her tongue to elicit the extra response. Or how he liked her to cup his balls, fondle the pleated skin, lightly rake her nails over it. As he swelled within her mouth his hips began to rock back and forth and guttural sounds rolled from his throat. Daisy was lost in the act, focused only on pulling him to the crest of the wave of pleasure.

Harder and harder she sucked, her hand loving in concert with her mouth, her fingers rolling and rubbing his balls. Then she remembered what always tipped him over the edge. Her hand stole backward to the cleft of his buttocks and one finger pressed against his anus.

That was all it took. His entire body tensed, clenched, and thick spurts of semen jetted against the roof of her mouth and the back of her throat. His big body shuddered and she milked him as hard as she could, squeezing with her fingers and pressing hard against the opening to his rectum. As the last of the ejaculate filled her mouth his body shuddered and a hoarse shout burst from his throat.

At last Daisy pulled her lips back until Mac's penis lay in her hand, not fully erect but far from limp. It took a lot more than one orgasm, no matter how powerful, to wring all the power from this organ. She knew before long he would be hard and fully erect and ready to go again. Just the recollection of how it used to be was enough to set her on fire again.

Mac lifted her to her feet and kissed her, long and slow, pulling the taste of himself from her mouth. "*That's* what's been haunting my dreams. Every time I thought of it I got so hard it was painful. I wanted you so badly. You can't begin to imagine how much."

Then he turned her to face the shower wall and pressed her hands against the cool tiles, while the mist fell all around her. "Your back, darlin'." His voice was low and smooth. "We can't forget your back, now can we?"

He kneaded her muscles, smoothing the gel over her skin, his fingers working their way down into the cleft of her buttocks. She shivered as the tip of one finger traveled up and down, rubbing her anus with each pass. Her legs quivered and nearly buckled when he slipped one finger into that tight, dark hole.

"We need a bed, darlin'," he purred. "And right now."

He pressed his body against hers, his cock so quickly erect again and branding her thigh. Setting aside the gel, he turned her around under the cloud of mist until all the lather was gone from her body. Lifting her to stand outside the shower, he dried her tenderly with a fluffy towel from the warming bar.

Then, pressing his lips to her forehead, he carried her into the bedroom, swept away the towels he'd left there and placed her carefully on the crisp cotton sheets. Stretching out beside her, he moved his hand over her, mapping every inch of her body he could reach.

When his mouth claimed hers it was with such hunger and need it shocked Daisy. All the playfulness of the early part of the evening, the erotic teasing of the meal and the courting with memories and music—all of it faded behind a craving that had as much to do with emotional starvation as with physical desire. Drinking from her mouth, his tongue savoring every inch of it, his lips branding hers, he was telling her better than words ever could how desperately he wanted her in his life. How much he regretted his stupid, juvenile mistake that had cost them ten years of their lives.

He kissed her for so long she was dizzy with longing, every pulse point in her body throbbing. When he slid one leg between hers, she let her own fall wide apart. Without taking his mouth from hers, Mac rolled over to cradle himself between her thighs, bracing himself on his forearms.

Daisy wound her arms around his neck and held him tighter, the last vestige of bitterness, the last piece of armor around her heart fading away. The lyrics of "All I Want is You" were drifting out into the room again.

When it's late at night and I'm all alone, and I think of the love I lost

The empty shell my life's become is the never-ending cost

I'd give it all back tomorrow if we could start anew

Because the truth I can't deny is all I want is you.

The song evoked memories both emotional and erotic. They didn't need foreplay. The whole night had been one long episode of foreplay. She was wet and ready and Mac was hard and pulsing. Lifting his head from hers, he rolled on a condom and slid into her with one long stroke, seating himself to the balls. As he stretched her and filled her, tears leaked from her eyes and her heart tumbled over. As his cock filled her pussy, he filled a place inside her that had been empty for far too long.

He held her like that, kissing away the tears, his eyes telling her what he wanted. What he needed. Waiting for her to let him know if she felt the same way.

She took as deep a breath as she could and stepped off the edge of the cliff. "I love you, Mac."

It shocked her to see his eyes fill with tears, to feel them dripping onto her cheek.

"God, Daisy. I love you more than my life. I swear I'll never, ever do anything to damage that again."

And then he began to move, a long, slow rhythm, unhurried even though she could feel the tension in his body. He set the pace in and out of her pussy in unhurried glides, until in desperation she wrapped her legs around him and dug her heels into the small of his back. She thrust her hips higher to take him even deeper and the tip of his cock bumped her womb.

"More," she moaned, trying to set the pace.

"Don't rush me," he gasped. "I've been waiting a long time for this."

In and out, a steady motion that seared her flesh and ignited her nerves. With each thrust forward she felt his sac slapping against her buttocks. Every time he pulled back, until only the tip of his cock was embedded in her, it was sheer torture. Her breasts felt tight and stretched, her nipples tingled and every inch of her skin felt as if it was on fire. And still he kept up the same rhythm, in and out, never hurrying, his eyes locked on hers like magnets.

When he began to increase the tempo she matched his pace with her own, pushing against him, using her legs still locked around his waist. As he moved faster and faster, hips pistoning and rolling, he reached between them to find the hot button of her clit and rubbed it between thumb and forefinger.

"Mac," she cried, so close to the edge she could feel her body gathering to take the plunge. "Mac, please."

Sweat covered their bodies, enhancing the sound of flesh slapping against flesh. His cock swelled within the grasp of her pussy, jerking against the slickness of her inner walls.

"Please, please, please," she begged, struggling for the release he held just out of her reach. "Now, Mac. Now."

With a final pinch of her clit he thrust hard and fast, taking her over the edge. Spasms rippled over her entire body, shaking her as she flew apart. Her inner muscles milked the hard shaft plunging inside her, and her juices poured around him as the orgasm shook her with its incredible force.

She threw her head back to scream at the moment of intense release, and Mac captured her mouth and swallowed her cries. His tongue probed and touched, fucking her mouth as his cock was fucking her cunt, and it shoved her from one plane of ecstasy to another without space between to catch her breath. The next climax ripped through her without warning as Mac drove into her harder and faster.

She could barely breathe and her body was shaking like an aspen in the wind. When she was sure she could take no more, the muscles of his back tensed beneath her fingers and she knew he was close.

"Come now," she screamed against his lips.

Her body convulsed around him one last time as he stroked one, two, three times, and his shaft pulsed inside her, filling the latex reservoir with spurt after spurt of semen. He threw his head back, the muscles in his neck corded, his big body shaking, and screamed her name.

"Daisy!"

And then he collapsed forward and the only sound in the room was their tortured breathing as they drew air into their oxygen-deprived lungs. Daisy's heart was thudding like a diesel engine, but then she wasn't sure if it was hers or Mac's she felt hammering her chest. Or both of them.

Feeling the artificially cooled air drying the sweat on their skin, leaving goose bumps in its place, Mac reluctantly withdrew from her body and staggered to the bathroom to dispose of the condom. Climbing back into bed and pulling up the covers, he wrapped Daisy in his arms tight against him so her head was tucked into his neck and her soft hands were pressed against the mat of hair on his chest.

His hand stroked the damp curls of her hair and he feathered light kisses across her brow.

"I love you, Daisy. You're my heart. Without you I'm lost."

"I love you, too, Mac."

She snuggled tighter to his body and they drifted off to sleep. Daisy's last thought was that the magic was still there. It had never left them, just gotten derailed for a while, but now the train was back on track.

* * * * *

Daisy opened her eyes and blinked in the unexpected light. The drapes on the huge window were wide open and the sun was streaming in. She sat up and stretched, the covers falling to her waist.

"Now that's a sight I want to wake up to every morning," Mac drawled.

She looked around and saw him sitting in the big armchair near the bed. He was wearing boxers and holding his guitar. He'd carried several of the vases into the bedroom and daisies bloomed everywhere. Daisy swallowed a smile. He sure was pulling out all the stops.

"I showered already," he told her. "If you want one you'd better get crackin'. I ordered breakfast. Or you can wait until after we eat."

"What are you doing with your guitar?"

"Polishing up my new song. It's called 'Having It All'. Want to hear a little of it?"

"Yes. Of course I do." She leaned back against the pillows, still naked from the waist up.

"You look like sin and temptation." Mac grinned at her, "I'll have a hell of a time concentrating on the song."

He wrenched his eyes away from her, struck two chords on the guitar and began to sing in his warm, deep voice that had melted a million hearts.

When I think of all the dreams we had, the wishes that we shared

The kisses in the moonlight, the symbols that we cared

I wonder why I took those dreams and let us drift apart

'Cause the fame and glory couldn't fill the empty in my heart.

I lie awake at night and miss the softness of your touch

Knowing life without you doesn't matter very much

But with you here beside me, as my lover, my wife

Darlin', there's one thing that's certain in life

I'd be having it all.

Tears gathered behind her eyelids and her heart clenched as if a fist had grabbed it. "Oh, Mac," was all she could say.

He put the guitar down and came over to the bed. Very precisely he kissed each protruding nipple, skimmed her collarbone, then brushed his lips against hers.

"The song says it all, Daisy. Life without you just hasn't been worth a damn.

"You'll never know how much I regret what happened. All the years we wasted because of it. I was an idiot, Daisy. A stupid fool. If you didn't want me I couldn't blame you."

"Not want you?" Now the tears were running down her cheeks. "My life has been nothing without you. I want it all with you, Mac. Everything. All the things we dreamed of so long ago."

"I'd give it all up tomorrow if that was the only way I could have you back."

"You know I'd never ask that of you," she told him. "Just give me your heart, Mac. That's all I want."

"You've got it, Daisy flower. And my promise I'll always be faithful to you." He leaned forward and brushed his lips over hers. "You know, I told Jimmy I wanted to meet with you so you could plan a special event," he reminded her.

"And what was that all about, anyway?"

He took one of her small hands in his and kissed each knuckle, then gave her what she called the famous Mac Fontana look. Only this one wasn't for anyone but her.

"Our wedding. I want you to plan our wedding. Please say you'll marry me, Daisy. Be my wife. I can't do it anymore without you."

"Are you absolutely sure this is what you want?"

"God, how can you even ask? This is *all* I want." His voice was thick with emotion. "This is everything."

Daisy threw her arms around him and pressed her body to his. "Then yes, yes, yes. I'll marry you. I love you."

"Soon?"

The pleading look on his face almost made her laugh. "Yes. Very soon. Whenever you want."

"As soon as you can get it together." He lightly teased one nipple. "I know you have a business to run, so if we need to live here in the city instead of at the ranch—"

She pressed her fingertips to his mouth. "Hush. Those are all details we can work out."

"Then just get this wedding together," he told her. "I don't want to waste any more time. Pick whatever date you want. I'll even change my schedule if I have to."

Now she did laugh. "I told you. I would never ask you to do that. You know that, right? We can work this out, too."

"I'm cutting back anyway," he told her, pulling her onto his lap and kissing her eyelids and her cheeks. "I can't imagine spending too many nights away from you." He moved his hand to cup her chin. "Can you take time to come to some of the concerts? Maybe even hang out in the recording studio now and then?"

"Whatever you want," she smiled. "My business is flexible and I have a great staff."

"Good, because I want you with me every possible minute." He nuzzled her cheek. "I think we should seal this deal right now, don't you?"

She was laughing again as he carried her back down to the mattress, somehow losing his boxers along the way. His fingers rubbing her cunt found her already wet and waiting. The world exploded around her, then settled, as he slid into her as if they were two halves of the same whole.

"Breakfast can wait," he murmured. "This can't."

As he began to move inside her, his arms holding her tightly, she knew exactly what he meant by having it all.

You chased away the darkness with the sunshine of your smile

You healed my heart and cleansed my soul with your very special style

And now my life's complete again, the darkness gone away

You bring me so much pleasure, with you, darlin', every day

That now I'm having it all.

HUNGRY LIKE A WOLF

Talya Bosco

ꟿ

Trademarks Acknowledgement

ꟷ

The author acknowledges the trademarked status and trademark owners of the following wordmarks mentioned in this work of fiction:

Corolla: Toyota Motor Corporation

Chapter One

ꟾ

I looked behind me once more. He was back there, I knew he was. But he wouldn't show himself. He wanted to scare me. And was doing a damn good job of it, too.

A branch cracked. Shit! He was closer than I thought. The growl sent shivers up my spine, urging me to run as fast as I could. It wasn't the smartest thing I'd ever done, but dammit, there was no way I going to hang around and let him catch me.

I ran through the trees, weaving in and out, ducking under branches, hoping I would make it, that I could get away. I knew if I could reach the cabin, I'd be safe.

Pausing long enough to figure out where I was, I breathed a sigh of relief. Just around the cluster of boulders on my left was the clearing. Once there, it was one hundred yards to the cabin. The length of a football field. I could make it. I had to make it.

With a deep breath and a last surge of energy, I made for the boulders, darting out into the clearing and around the cabin. Seventy-five yards, fifty. I was almost there. Almost to—

"Oof."

A heavy, furry body hit me from behind, knocking me to my stomach. Hot breath spilled across my neck as a long tongue licked me from the nape of my neck to my ear. The wolf edged my hair aside and sniffed. His front paws were on either side of my head, and I could feel his back paws bracketing my thighs. I couldn't move.

Trapped, like the prey I was.

"Get off, you big lug."

"Woof."

I laughed.

"Okay, okay, you caught me fair and square, now let me up."

His weight pressed down and I inhaled sharply as he sniffed again. Then the voice. "You think I'm gonna give in that easily?" Warmth grew deep in my belly as I heard his voice. It didn't matter where we were or what we were doing, I grew wet every time.

"You won. You can let me up." I tried to raise myself up by my arms, and promptly came into contact with hard human male flesh. Naked human male flesh. And from the feel of the cock pressing into my ass, a highly aroused naked male. My pussy clenched.

"Nope. I like you where you are." He nipped at my earlobe and worked his way down my neck with little bites, each one sending a shock through me straight to my core. He knew how to get me every time.

"We can't." I tried to be reasonable. To exert some control over the situation.

"Why not? We're in the middle of nowhere, it's late at night. No one here to see us. And I, for one, am horny as hell."

"But the cabin—bed." My token protest was lost in the sound of my t-shirt ripping in half. His tongue licked straight down my spine and back up again, shivers spreading out from the contact. The cool breeze against the wetness of my skin raised goose bumps up and down my body. Strong hands turned me over, and he removed the rest of my shirt.

Finally I got to look at him. The bright light of the moon shone on us in the clearing, allowing me to see his body in all its glory. His brown hair and deep chocolate eyes appeared almost black, but I could see the glitter of intent in those dark orbs of his. His body was sculpted like a god's and I practically drooled as I remembered he was all mine.

"Mine," he growled as though he could read my mind, before his head came down and took my lips in a fierce kiss. He tasted of something wild and free, a man I could never tame, and would never want to. His tongue swiped against mine, darting, thrusting, teasing as he tasted me. My hands wrapped around his back, holding him closer, letting his body heat warm me as nothing else could. He spread kisses on my chin, jawline, neck, down to my breast. I wasn't wearing a bra, I knew he didn't like them, so he had unfettered access to my chest as he grasped a nipple with his teeth and bit. I moaned, and he cupped a breast in each hand as he continued to suck and nip, alternating, back and forth.

"More. I want more." I thrust my hips at him, urging him to get a move on, to give me what I wanted. My pussy was dripping, my jeans soaked through. They say one of the reasons some women enjoy BDSM is the lack of control, the element of fear. Tonight I believed it. I was as horny as I could ever remember being.

He pulled back and smiled at me. I growled. His chuckle followed him as he worked his way down my body, kissing and licking my stomach, to where my jeans began. In an instant he had the rest of my clothes off, and I was spread out naked before him.

He resumed his position and lowered his head down to the apex of my legs. Once there, he stopped to look at me once again. He buried his nose in my curls and inhaled deeply, growling a sound of pleasure. His fingers opened my lips and down he went. He had told me time and time again that he loved eating pussy more than anything, and I had come to believe him, because he would do it for hours if I let him. He licked from anus to clit, where he ran his tongue around the little nub of nerves.

My hips bucked, trying to get more in his mouth, but his other arm held me down, keeping me where he wanted. My skin flushed as blood ran to the surface, the light breeze of the mountain air like another lover's caress. Another lick, and then another, all while avoiding the one spot I craved his touch.

His hand moved down, and he inserted a long, slender finger into my pussy. It filled me, momentarily quenching my ache for something inside me. But it wasn't enough. I was breathing heavy, the tension building higher with each stroke and lick.

"What do you want from me, woman?" His question was accompanied by a thrust of his finger. He joined another to the first and thrust again as he growled, "What do you want? Tell me."

"You." My breath came out on a gasp as I told him what I wanted, what I needed from him. "I want you to suck me. Suck my clit then fuck me. Hard." I wanted to come. I needed to come.

With that he moved to my clit and sucked it hard into his mouth, nipping at it with his teeth as he rammed all four of his fingers in at once, twisting, turning them, stretching me as I screamed my first climax of the night.

He allowed me a moment to calm down and then quickly moved back and picked me up to carry me to the boulder at the side of the cabin. He set me on my feet and positioned my body facing it, away from him. Gently he pushed me down until I was leaning on my hands, bent over, my ass where he wanted it.

"I love you in this position. I can fuck you so hard I feel like I am gonna come out the other side. I want to ram inside you until the sun comes up."

His words sent liquid rushing down my thighs as I pictured what he was promising. I knew he could do it too. Weres had incredible stamina, and if he came, he could be hard again in less than five minutes. He stroked my back, down to my ass, and then pinched my cheeks, tapping one of them lightly. I whimpered in anticipation.

"Oh no, I have a better idea first." He grabbed me by the hips and pulled back, turning me around to face him. "Down on your knees. Now."

I was so excited I could barely stand. He was so rarely this demanding, this authoritative and it made me quiver with desire. I dropped to my knees in the soft grass, eager for what I knew he would want. He stepped close and waved his cock in front of my face. "Suck me off. Make me come hard. And if you do a good job, I'll give you want you want."

I opened my mouth before he was even done ordering me. I loved the taste of his cock. A manly wild taste that sent my pussy muscles into contractions. He always tasted clean and masculine and sucking him off was a pleasure. He was thick and long but somehow fit perfectly in my mouth. I reached for him with a hand, and he swiped it away. "No. Only your mouth."

I grinned. He was gonna play like that, was he? I pursed my lips in a mock pout before leaning closer to him. His cock was pointing out and up, stiff with need. My tongue touched the base of his staff, a quick dart as he inhaled sharply.

I worked my tongue around him, stroked the muscle on the underside of his penis, wrapping my tongue around it, sending wafts of my breath across his wet skin. I played with his balls, licking first one then the other, teasing them gently as I twisted my tongue around each one.

His hands wrapped in my long hair as he growled, "Suck me."

Eagerly, I obeyed. I opened my mouth wide and took as much of him as I could at first try. Relaxing my throat, I pushed my mouth down on him farther, taking more of him. I worked him hard, sucking for all I was worth, scraping gently with my teeth, massaging with my tongue.

My hands went around his legs to his ass, where I played with his cheeks. He said I couldn't touch his cock or balls, but he didn't say anything about anywhere else. I knew he wasn't a fan of anal, at least not on him, but he loved his ass to be massaged, pinched. And that's exactly what I did. I played with him until he growled, "Enough."

At the sound of his voice I stopped moving, waiting for further instruction. "Stay on my cock, but play with yourself. Pluck your nipples, fuck yourself with your hands." His skin was flushed, and his breathing hard, but I knew he wasn't ready to come. He wanted more from me than a simple little teasing of my mouth.

Regrettably, I lowered my hands, one to my breast, the other to my pussy as I spread my knees open farther and started to play with myself in concert with my sucking. I teased my nipple, flicking at the hard peak, pinching it and sending sparks soaring through my body. My other hand reached down my slit, fingers crawling inside me as my thumb went straight to my clit.

I knew what I liked, I'd done this before. Both by myself and with him. He loved when I would pleasure myself as he watched. His cock twitched as I inhaled sharply at my own actions. "Come on, babe, fuck yourself harder. I want you to scream around my cock as you suck me dry." I did as he ordered, pulled at my nipples, alternating between the two. Back and forth, twisting, pulling, tweaking.

My other hand worked in and out of my pussy, pumping me harder and harder as I grew close. His hands were back in my hair, holding my head up, supporting me as he fucked my mouth faster and faster. It grew to be too much, my breast tingling, my pussy clenching, his grunting and pumping in my mouth. Suddenly I pushed myself farther on his cock as I screamed my orgasm.

In perfect timing he shot his cum straight down my throat with his own release as he screamed my name to the stars. In one swift motion, he pulled himself out of my mouth as he dropped to his knees in front of me. His hands reached for my jaw and massaged it tenderly, making sure I suffered no ill effects. Then he took my left hand, the one I still had buried in my pussy, and brought it to his mouth.

He ran my fingers over his lips, coating them with my juices before sucking the digits in and licking them dry. The look in his eyes was gentle and loving as he tasted me. His movements erotic in their promise. I should have been sated, but suddenly I needed him again. I needed him inside me, fucking me hard like he had promised. His fingers weren't enough, my hand wasn't enough. I needed his hard, thick cock. I whimpered.

"You are incredible," he said as he once again kissed the tip of my fingers, and then leaned to kiss my lips. I tasted myself on him, and it fueled my already fever-pitch desire to an ultimate high. His musky scent drove more liquid to my crotch as my muscles spasmed around empty space.

He climbed to his feet, lifting me with him, and turned me again to the boulder. His hand went to his cock, already stirring in excitement as he stroked it. "You sure you're ready for more?"

"Yes."

"What?"

"Yes, please."

That was enough for him. He bent me over and spread my legs open as he played with my ass. He massaged my cheeks much as I had done his, but a wet finger rimmed my puckered hole. Pressure, and then his digit slid inside centimeter by centimeter. It filled me just enough as he twisted the finger, pressing against my walls. I moaned, pushing my ass back toward him, wanting even more. He moved his cock into my wet pussy, my muscles clamping around him as he slid all the way in. His finger still in my ass, his cock in my pussy, I was filled completely.

Slowly, he worked me, out with the finger, in with the cock, in with the finger, out with the cock. The dual sensation driving me closer to another orgasm. He moved harder, faster, driving me toward the edge until finally, I reached it and fell over. I screamed loudly, "Yes!" My voice shaking with sensation.

He pulled his finger out and grabbed my by the hips and started pumping me in earnest as I contracted rapidly around him. He fucked me hard and fast, just the way I wanted it, ramming into me, driving me forcefully as I supported myself against the boulder. I felt it building again, faster, stronger than before. It was right there, I could see it, feel it, just out of reach. One more, one more. I exploded.

I shattered into a million pieces as lights went off in my head, sparks shooting through my body with the orgasm. He was with me, releasing his cum as I climaxed one more time. His cum filled me hot and fast as I cried out my fulfillment. He caught me as my legs went limp. He pulled out and swung me up into his arms.

"My clothes," I murmured.

"Tomorrow, my sweet. They'll be fine 'til then. Now it's bed for you, and rest for the both of us." To bed. With him. It sounded perfect.

I woke up with a start, body tingling and alert with arousal. Fuck! That damn dream again. Oh hell, who was I kidding? It wasn't a dream, it was a memory. The last good memory I had of Ethan before everything went south. I wanted to deny it, to pretend it hadn't happened, but I knew that I wouldn't be of any use to anyone until I let it play out in its entirety.

Shit! I so did not need *this* this afternoon. I looked at the clock on the dresser. I never should have let myself take a nap. I knew better than that. But I hadn't had a good night's sleep in weeks, and had literally crashed.

I got up to walk to the shower, letting my brain play out the rest of the weekend that had changed my life. The memory didn't need my concentration, it would come all on its own.

That weekend had been blissfully incredible. We'd been dating for well over a year and were both eager for our lives to more forward. Together. That's what the weekend at the cabin had been intended to do. To see if I could accept Ethan's beast in all his forms. See if I could love the animal as well as the man.

It had been perfect. He'd changed for me the first night there, sharing the magic of his ability, trusting me with his deepest secret. My heart had been ready to burst with pleasure and love, and I'd never felt closer to anyone than I had that weekend.

By the time we were heading home Sunday morning we'd made plans for him to give up his apartment and move into my house with me. We'd been spending most of our nights together, but wanted the formality of living together officially before we took the next step of marriage.

That all changed with one phone call.

By the time we got somewhere with cell phone service again, it was almost two o'clock on Sunday. Ethan had at least five voicemail messages waiting for him.

His parents had been attacked the night before, and both of them were in intensive care, the prognosis not good. We headed straight to the hospital, but when we got there he insisted I leave him. When I tried to go in with him, he'd turned on me, blaming me for him not being there with them when he should have been.

I was too shocked to respond, so instead I took his car back to my place and waited for him.

It took him two days to come get his car. By that time both of his parents were out of danger, but he was a changed man. The loving, kind and generous man I'd grown to love was gone. Replaced by a hard, cruel one.

I had tried to talk to him, I understood why he had verbally attacked me like that, but he wouldn't participate in the conversation. All he would say was that it was over.

He left without saying anything more.

His sister Milly had told me later what had happened.

While we were away on our tryst, his pack had been attacked by a small group of werewolf hunters.

There weren't many of them in this world of reason and sanity, but there were still enough fanatics who followed the old ways of hatred and destruction. Those who believed a werewolf was evil and needed to be destroyed.

They'd somehow managed to sneak up on the pack and opened fire on one of their ritual gatherings. Ethan's mother and father were the alphas of the pack, and they'd been shot first. The rest of the pack had overwhelmed the hunters before many more of the wolves could be hurt, but the pack didn't escape without permanent damage.

Ethan's mother lost her left arm, and one of the other wolves lost his life defending his alphas. As for the hunters, well, let's say that there wasn't enough of them left to identify by the time the wolves were done with them.

Ethan blamed himself for the attack, convinced that if he had been there as the next alpha, and in charge of security, none of it would have happened.

Milly had told me he was a great protector and hunter, but even he couldn't have prevented it from happening. The hunters had been prepared. Someone from within had betrayed the pack, and as Ethan was one of the few wolves not present, and he had the most to gain if his parents died, he had been a suspect for a while. If not in the eyes of the rest of the pack, at the very least in his own eyes.

His breaking off with me had been his self-imposed punishment, according to Milly.

It made no sense to me, or any of his family. None of them blamed him in any way, but he refused to listen to reason. Instead he lived his life for the pack, making sure that not only his parents, but every single member was as safe as he could make them.

It had been almost a year, and he and his seconds had yet to find out who had betrayed the pack. It was looking as if they never would. Most of the pack had grown to believe it had been one of the wolves that had left over the years, but Milly told me that Ethan wasn't convinced of that. He knew there was still a traitor in their midst, and until he found them, he'd never let himself rest.

The rest of the pack had moved on with their lives. Although the legends were true, and they could heal almost anything, some things even the werewolves couldn't heal, so his mother learned how to do things with one hand, and seemed to have accepted her lot in life. Heather was a strong woman. She wasn't about to let the loss of one limb get her down like that.

The family had tried to keep me included in their activities as much as possible, hoping that Ethan would come around, but he made it more than difficult, staying away any time he thought I was there. After Heather got out of the hospital, I drifted away from his family and the pack. It was best for everyone involved.

Milly had been the exception. She stayed with me through thick and thin. She'd said more than once that she wasn't going to let her brother force her to lose her best friend.

The phone rang as I stepped out of the shower, pulling me out of my reverie. I quickly wrapped a towel around my body before walking into the bedroom and glancing at the caller ID. I was almost smiling as I picked up the phone.

"Hello."

"Hello, gorgeous. My ears were ringing. Were you thinking about me?"

"Nope, sorry, far from it." I had to laugh at the thought, though. Noah and Ethan couldn't be any more different if they had been born on opposite ends of the earth. Noah was fun, easygoing and the least intrusive man I'd ever met. Ethan had always been brooding and serious.

"Well then, as long as you weren't thinking of any other man, I guess I can handle it."

I sighed. "Noah."

"I know, I know. You aren't ready for anything else from me, but I won't give up, Amanda. You know how I feel about you."

"Maybe tonight isn't the best idea." I glanced at the clock again. We were supposed to meet in less than an hour for dinner and I had been looking forward to it. Until just now.

"No. I'm sorry. I promise I'll behave."

I stood there with the phone in my hand, suddenly thinking that tonight was really a bad idea.

"Amanda? You still there?"

"I'm here, Noah."

"Please. Come out to dinner with me?"

I debated it, ready to say no, but then my inner voice spoke up. I'd agreed to go out to dinner with Noah. He'd been nothing but friendly to me since I met him six months ago. He knew I'd been getting out of a relationship, and hadn't pushed me.

I liked him. I really did. Wasn't it time I gave him a chance? A real chance?

"Okay, Noah. I'll meet you at Giovanni's."

"How about you let me pick you up?"

"Sorry, I have an errand to run first. You caught me just as I was going out the door. I'll see you soon." I hung up before he could say any more. I didn't have any reason to not want him to pick me up, except for the fact I always felt better with my own transportation. More secure.

Chapter Two

ꟗ

I arrived at Giovanni's on time, and Noah was already there, as usual. He stood up when he spotted me approaching, and I saw more than one woman's gaze turn his way. He was gorgeous, over six feet tall and built like a swimmer. Bright blue eyes sparkled under the fall of blond hair that was always brushing his face, making him look much like a California surfer boy, only with class and money. His custom-made suit fit him perfectly, leaving no doubt that the man under the clothes was as incredible as the packaging promised.

"Amanda, you look exquisite this evening."

The man really was a gentleman. He never failed to be on time, or to compliment me or do any of the things that should send a woman's heart aflutter. But not mine. The spark just wasn't there. I thought maybe I could make it work, but seeing him get out of his seat, a rose in his hand and a look of adoration on his face, I realized I couldn't do it. I had to let him down now, before he got hurt.

"Noah. Thank you," I said as I took the rose from his hand. "You look gorgeous, yourself, as always."

He held out my chair for me, and sat down again after I was seated. I didn't know what to say, how to start the conversation, but it really was time for it to end. We had no future together. Thoughts ran through my mind as I tried to decide whether it would be better to tell him now or after dinner. How did you break up with someone you weren't even officially dating? Someone who didn't deserve to be hurt the way you knew you were going to hurt them.

"Noah."

"Amanda." We laughed as we both started at the same time. Before I could say anything further, though, he reached out to take my hand in his, and started again.

"Amanda, sweetheart. I know you've been burned recently, that you find it hard to trust a man again, but I want you to know I am here for you. I want to take our relationship to the next level."

My heart jumped into my throat and my breathing increased. I didn't know what to say to him. I thought I still had time, I hadn't expected this now. Even though he'd never made a secret of his feelings, I hadn't really thought they'd gotten that serious.

I opened my mouth to respond. To say something, anything, but he shook his head and squeezed my hand gently.

"Don't say anything now. I know this comes as a shock to you. But I wanted you to know that I want more from you. I know I can be everything you want, can give you everything you want in life, if only you will give me a chance."

"Noah. You know I'm not looking for that. I never promised you more than friendship."

"I know that, Amanda. But I have hope."

I shook my head. "I'm sorry, Noah, but it's not going to happen. That's what I came to tell you tonight. I can't go on like this."

"You don't mean that, Amanda." His hand tightened painfully on mine.

"Noah, you're hurting me." I tried to pull my hand away, but I couldn't get free.

"I've given you everything you asked of me. I haven't pushed you."

"I know that, and I appreciate it. But it's just not gonna work."

"Why? 'Cause you're still in love with that worthless asshole that dumped you last year?"

A felt a pang shoot through my heart at his words. Whether or not I was in love with Ethan didn't matter right now. Now all I wanted was to get free.

He pulled my hand closer to him, grasping it with both of his. "Amanda, you belong with me. If you'd only give it a chance, you'd recognize the fact. You're mine."

"I don't belong *with* or *to* anyone, Noah."

"You're wrong. You belong to me."

This was a side of Noah I'd never seen before, and it scared me. His eyes glinted with a purpose I couldn't identify, but it chilled me to the bone.

"Noah, let go. Please." For the first time, I began to worry about my safety. I knew he had an inner strength—he had to, to have made it so far in the business world, but he'd never turned it against me. And definitely not physically.

"Why? So you can run off to that bitch of a friend and whine about how mean I was?"

What the hell was he talking about? I lowered my voice, practically hissing at him. "Noah, you're creating a scene. Let me go."

Noah blinked slowly, as though coming back to himself. I tugged once again and managed to get my hand free. Not because I was suddenly stronger, but he had obviously loosened his grip.

I stood up, my chair jumping back on the carpet. "I don't know what's gotten into you, Noah, but I'm sorry. This is goodbye."

"Amanda, wait!" He stood and reached as though to grab for me again, and then he pulled his hand back. "You don't understand. I can give you what you want. I can deliver all your dreams to you."

My gaze ran across his face. All my dreams delivered? What was he talking about? My heart jumped in my chest when I recognized the sheen of devotion on his face. His eyes seemed to have gone wild with obsession.

I didn't know who this man was, but he wasn't the man I had grown fond of over the last few months. I wondered how much of what I had seen was a mask, because I knew without a doubt that this, here, was his true face. And it was frightening.

"Goodbye, Noah." I turned and walked out as fast as I could without running, fear making me shake on my heels. I wanted nothing more than to get away from him and his sudden transformation. When I made it to my car, I opened the door and quickly sat inside, locking it behind me. I started the engine and winced as I squealed out of the parking lot.

*****

"Where the hell did you learn how to drive?"

The voice penetrated before the words did. My body responded eagerly, more aware and alive than it had been in months. Ethan. I made the connection before I was completely turned around to see him at the end of my driveway getting out of his own car, fuming mad. What the hell was he doing here?

"What the hell are you doing here?"

"Where the fuck did you learn to drive?" He repeated his question as he strode up the driveway toward me, totally ignoring my own question. Of course, I couldn't expect any different from the man he had become.

I turned and walked toward my front door, answering him as I walked up the steps. "You know, I don't think I owe you any explanations at all. If you don't like the way I drive then don't follow me around town."

I unlocked the door and stepped over the threshold, prepared to turn around and slam the door in his face. I wasn't prepared for his damn werewolf speed, though, and by the time I finished turning, he'd already pushed his way into the house.

I sighed, exhausted. I hadn't seen him in almost a year and here he was, literally pushing his way back into my life, keeping tabs on me like I was one of his puppies.

How the hell had he even known? He'd been avoiding me since we broke up, I knew he had.

"How did you even see me?" I cringed as I thought of how I had probably been driving through town. I'd been freaked by Noah going all aggressive like that, that I hadn't been paying as much attention as I should have to the road. I'd been on autopilot. A thought occurred to me. "Are you keeping tabs on me? Were you watching me?"

"Why the hell would I do that?"

A feeling ran deep through my stomach. How would he have known what I was doing, how I was driving? It wasn't like I was the only person in town with a blue Corolla. He would have had to see me, not just my car. And in order for him to have seen me get into the car, he had to have been there, at the restaurant.

I know I hadn't seen his car at the restaurant or even following me on the way home. So how on earth did he know how I was driving?

I narrowed my eyes. "How did you know how I was driving, Ethan? Are you having me followed?"

"What the hell are you talking about?" He practically snarled at me, but he turned away and walked into my living room. That clinched it. He never could lie to me face-to-face.

"You bastard. You *have* been keeping tabs on me."

I watched him, his back to me, and saw it tighten before he turned to face me.

"You forget, Amanda, I broke up with you months ago. What do I care what you're doing or who you're doing it with."

"I don't know, Ethan. What *do* you care?"

Missy's assurances that Ethan really did care about me ran through my head. His family's repeated attempts to get us back together, his brother telling me that I needed to give him more time, that he would come around.

Were they right? Did they know something I didn't know? I looked at Ethan, really looked at him, and his appearance tugged at my heartstrings.

He was still the most gorgeous man I'd ever known. At six-feet six-inches, and with brown eyes and shoulder-length brown hair around that hard chiseled face that made him look like a cuddly teddy bear to me, but to others, they gave him an appearance of a man who knew what he wanted in life and went for it. There was no doubt when you looked at him that he was the alpha in any group he roamed in, wolves or not.

But there were circles under his eyes and his permanently tanned skin looked almost ashen. He hadn't lost any weight, but there was something missing, as well as an additional hardness that hadn't been there before.

My heart broke seeing him like this.

Against my will, I went to him, all anger gone in an instant. The love for him I had convinced myself was dead and buried flamed back to life.

"I'm sorry, Ethan. I'm sorry that you weren't there to protect your family. I'm sorry you haven't found the people responsible. I'm sorry it's tearing you up inside." As I spoke, I wrapped my arms around his waist, squeezing him tight.

He didn't fight me. Didn't move at all for a moment. And then his arms went around me and pulled me in tight, his head burying against my shoulder as he let out a harsh breath.

"I'm so tired, Amanda. I can't do it anymore."

"I know, Ethan, I know." I held him in my arms for a moment like that, comforting him like I knew he hadn't been comforted in a while. It was warm, him in my arms again, the way we were meant to be. I felt like I was home again, but I knew it wouldn't last. He wouldn't let me comfort him for long, so I decided to enjoy it while I could.

Surprisingly, he didn't pull away. Instead he pulled me even tighter against him, and I felt his erection dig into my stomach.

"I need you, Amanda. I'm sorry, I know I don't deserve it, but I need you right now more than I need to breathe."

"Yes." The response was more of a whisper than anything else, but he heard it. He heard my agreement. My agreement to everything he wanted.

I knew he didn't want to make love to me. He needed to get out his frustration, anger, pain. There was no way I could say no to him, even if I wanted to. Maybe any woman would do. Maybe not.

I stepped back from him and reached for the closure on the dress. His gaze flew to my eyes, and then to my body. Heat radiated in his pupils as his breathing sped up.

I'd always loved his reaction when he saw my naked form. I was never in doubt that he found me sexy, desirable. He always let me know he wanted me. And even after all these months, that hadn't changed.

I pulled the zipper at my back down carefully then slowly let the dress pool at my feet. He'd gotten me into the habit of wearing matching undergarments, and today I had on a black push-up bra and panties. It was one of my favorite sets. It was the naughtiest one I owned, with its half cups, my breasts spilling out of the lace and satin, along with the matching thong panties. I'd needed the confidence it gave me after the dream this afternoon. It made me feel sexy.

Obviously Ethan agreed. I wasn't wearing any pantyhose, so I reached for the panties, but he stopped me.

"No, not yet."

I stood there in my heels and undergarments watching his gaze trail over my body with a heat that was palpable.

He reached for me, clasping the back of my neck and pulling me in for a kiss.

His lips were as soft and smooth as I remembered, caressing mine as he started lightly then deepened the touch. My lips parted of their own volition and he thrust his tongue in to tease mine, mimicking the motions that would happen soon enough. His other hand wrapped around my waist, making sure I was plastered against his hard body.

Heat grew in my stomach and traveled through me. My pussy moistened, knowing what was coming, and eager for it. I'd been so lonely the last year.

Ethan tore his mouth from mine and quickly kissed his way across my jaw to my neck, nipping and pinching as he went. His breathing had gone ragged, puffs of hot moist air against my skin as he explored my body.

I reached for his body, eager to feel his skin against mine. Ethan grabbed my hands when I got to the button at his neck. He pulled them away and put them behind my back without saying a word. Walking, he forced me to move backward until the back of my legs were against the couch. I sat, at his insistence, and he kneeled in front of me.

I left my hands down at my sides. He wanted to lead the show tonight, and I'd let him. He reached out and caressed my arms, my shoulders, the tops of my breasts, down my waist to my hips. He grabbed them, and pulled me hard to the edge of the couch, putting all of me in his reach.

Spreading my legs apart, he leaned in and took my breasts in his hands. He cupped them, running his thumbs over the nipples as my pulse sped up and shivers ran up and down my spine.

Anticipation built in my stomach and below. The wild look in his eyes told me he wouldn't last long. This slow exploration wasn't what he wanted. He wanted it hard and fast.

I gasped when he pinched my nipples hard. He twisted them and my head went back, my mouth open as I reached for a breath. My pussy was wet, liquid seeping onto the couch as he drove me close to the edge with just that stimulation.

When he pulled my thong to the side and thrust two fingers in, I shot over the edge with a cry of pleasure. It had been too long without him.

"I'm gonna fuck you, Amanda. Fuck you until you can't think anymore. Until *I* can't think anymore." He played with me, fucking me with his fingers, curling them up to make me shiver and moan again and again.

My hands curled against the cushions, nails digging in as I fell back. He grabbed the back of my neck and pulled me to him again, his hand wrapped in my hair. Sparks shot through me as he twisted his hand in my bun and pulled it loose, his other hand continuing its actions.

"You wear your hair down. How many times do I have to tell you that? Never up, unless I tell you to."

His growl reverberated through me as my waist-length hair fell against my body. I'd almost cut it when he broke off with me, but I couldn't do it. It was too much a part of me, despite what it meant to him.

One more kiss, hard and quick, and he pushed me back, forcing my legs open wider as he dove down to my core.

No starting slow and building up down there. No, Ethan literally dove into my pussy, thrusting his face into me as he ate me out. His fingers were still buried inside me, but his mouth, teeth, tongue were busy as well. Tasting, licking, biting me all over. He sucked my clit hard, nipping at it, flicking it with his tongue.

I tensed as I got closer and closer. The earlier orgasm was a mere hint of what was to come. Ethan knew my body like no other and knew what I needed to truly explode. One last lick, suck, thrust and I was flying over the edges of ecstasy, screaming his name, writhing on the sofa as I ground my pussy into his face.

And still he played with me, wringing more and more reactions out of me until my throat was sore and voice hoarse.

Instantly, he was inside me. I wondered briefly when he had the chance to undress, and then all thought was gone as he did what he had promised to do. He fucked me until I couldn't think anymore. Couldn't think of anything but the feel of him between my legs thrusting and pushing harder and harder, ramming his hard cock into me, driving us both to the brink of need and desire.

"Amanda! Love! Yes!" he yelled for me as we both reached our peak and collapsed against the couch. The last thing I was conscious of was him brushing the hair out of my face, sweat running down his cheeks. Or was it tears?

I woke up quickly, remembering what had happened between us. I was in my bed, naked, the faint glow of the light from the bathroom shining through the room, letting me see I was alone. He'd left me. Again.

"Fuck!" I hadn't expected any different but I had hoped. A noise from the other side of the room pulled my attention back to the bathroom. A shape was framed in the doorway, a shape very like that of a tall, sexy man.

"Ethan?"

The growl sent shivers through my body. And not the sexual kind. "Who else would it be?"

I debated mouthing off to him, but thought maybe discretion was the better part of valor and kept my mouth shut.

"How many men have you had in your bed since we broke up, Amanda?"

"Individually? Or at once?" So much for behaving myself.

"I'm sorry. That was uncalled for."

My mouth was open to respond to him, to tell him to get the hell out, to remind him that he was the bastard who broke up with me. The one who refused to give me a reason for it, wouldn't even talk about it. But then his words penetrated. My mouth snapped shut with a click of my teeth. Who the hell was this man and why was he masquerading as Ethan?

I sat up, grasping the sheet around my chest and watched him as he slowly padded across the bedroom floor to my side of the bed. His shirt was gone, and the top button of his jeans was undone. I swallowed the saliva that had built in my mouth watching him. I didn't matter we'd just had sex, I wanted him again. I'd always want him.

He sat by the bed and took my hand in his. "I'm sorry, Amanda. For everything. I never meant for you to get hurt. All I wanted was for you to be happy."

"I was happy with you." Tears suddenly clogged my throat. Where the hell was my anger? My need to yell and scream at him, to call him all kinds of names? My intention to tell him that I didn't need him and didn't love him and was glad to be rid of him?

Gone. All of it was gone.

Oh gods, I was such a sap.

"But you weren't safe." He looked out the large picture window at the front of my bedroom, staring into the darkness of the night. "I realized that weekend that I couldn't protect you the way I needed to. I had no right to bring you into my life, into possible danger like that. And I still have no right. But I couldn't stay away from you. I can't stay away."

"Ethan, what happened last year was a freak happenstance. Milly told me nothing like that has happened in over a hundred years."

He turned and looked at me, pain in his eyes. "But we still don't know who was behind it. He could still be out there, waiting for the right moment."

"You can't live your life in fear of maybes, Ethan." I wanted nothing more than to take him in my arms and comfort him, but I wasn't sure he would accept it.

"My parents told me that they're stepping down. They're making the announcement next month. Samhain is their retirement date, I guess you could say."

His sudden change of subject had me stunned for a moment.

Samhain. The Wiccan New Year. Not all werewolves were pagan, but most of Ethan's pack were. They always had been, according to Missy. As far back as their pack kept records, and that was at least a few hundred years.

I swallowed hard. "Are they demanding you take a mate?" Most packs were run by alpha pairs, much like real wolves, but different in some very important ways. Missy told me that alpha pairs tended to mate for life. Ethan hadn't mentioned that part when we'd talked about a future together, but then how many people don't think they were going to be together forever when they make plans to get married?

"We haven't discussed it."

I breathed a sigh of relief. Although why, I didn't know. It wasn't like he was asking me to come back to him. And even if he was, I wasn't sure I would go back to him. Even if I apparently had forgiven him, he'd hurt me incredibly when he deserted me like that. I couldn't deal with that kind of pain again.

"So where does that leave us?" I had to ask. I didn't think he'd come here tonight for a reconciliation, but if he hadn't, I had no idea why he'd stayed. I knew when I gave myself to him earlier tonight that I was a safety net, a security blanket. A place where he could let himself go for a while.

He opened his mouth to respond but the ringing of the phone stopped him. Like idiots we stared at it as though it were a living thing we were worried might strike out. When the answering machine clicked on, I jumped.

"Amanda, it's me." It was Noah. Shit, I had forgotten all about earlier tonight. "I'm sorry about tonight, Amanda, but you have to realize how much I love you. How I would do anything for you. Please, don't let tonight be the deciding factor, my love. I'm coming over, I have something for you. If you aren't there, I'll wait 'til you get home."

I reached for the phone quickly, my hand hitting it and knocking it out of its cradle. Ethan glared and me and got up from the bed while I tried to answer. "Noah, no, it's me. No, don't come over. I-I'm not feeling well."

"I'm coming over to take care of you. You know that's all I want to do."

"No!" I cringed at my own volume. "No, really. I'm okay. Don't— " The sound of a dial tone met my ears. Shit. I hung up the phone and reached for my robe at the end of the bed.

"So is that why you let me make love to you? You and your present boyfriend had a tiff?"

"He's not my boyfriend, Ethan."

"You could have fooled me. He was declaring his love for you pretty clearly."

I glared at him, angry all over again. "Fine. What he is or is not to me is none of your damn business, is it? Remember, you're the one who left. Like you said earlier, what should you care what I've been doing or who I've been doing it with." I jerked my robe on, covering my now cold and shaking body.

I tied the belt before looking back at him. "Oh, and by the way, what we did earlier was by no means making love. It was plain old fucking."

"You got that right. Making love takes emotion."

I could feel the pain in my heart like a physical wound. I thought we'd been on the way to something good. I would never learn, would I?

"Fine. Great. You got what you came for. You got your rocks off. You can go home and tell all your wolf buddies I gave it up to you one more time. But that's the last time you'll ever get anything from me."

I pushed past him and started down the back stairs. I needed a drink, and I needed him out of my house and my life. Maybe that way I could start trying to forget him all over again.

I reached the kitchen and walked straight to the teakettle. Unfortunately tea was the strongest drink I had in the house. At least it would help me calm down. Sometimes I really wished I was a drinker.

After turning on the stove, I turned around to get one of my mugs and jumped at the silhouette of a large man against the French doors. A small screech escaped my throat and the figure moved into the spray of light from the kitchen.

Noah! What the hell was he doing back here? I told him not to come, and even if I hadn't, what the hell was he doing at the back door? And how the hell had he gotten here so quickly?

Chapter Three

ꙮ

I opened the glass doors with a frown. Noah had a bouquet of roses in his hand and a smile on his face. "Sweetheart, I know you told me not to come, but I was worried about—"

His voice stopped and I didn't have to turn around to see that Ethan had come down the stairs behind me. Probably still disheveled, leaving no doubt as to what we'd been doing.

Noah sniffed at me before a look of disgust and anger crossed his face. It was so full of hatred and rage that it made the look from earlier tonight seem downright friendly. I took a step back.

He looked at the flowers in his hand and tossed them on the ground outside. "Well, I guess I won't be needing those, will I?"

"Smithton." Ethan's voice was colder than I'd ever heard it.

"I see you and your little bitch are back together, Daniels. How'd you manage that? I thought Amanda had more sense than to go back to you after the way you'd treated her."

Ethan knew Noah? What was this? Noah hadn't said anything about knowing him in all the time we'd been together.

Wait. Little bitch? Did he just call me a bitch?

"Noah, Ethan, what's going on?" I backed up until I stood closer to Ethan than Noah.

"Didn't your new lover tell you he's a member of my pack, Amanda?"

"He's a werewolf? No. That can't be." I shook my head. Missy would have told me when she met him.

But she hadn't ever met him. Noah always seemed to manage to avoid any activity with any of my friends. All of our dates had been just the two of us.

Noah smiled, showing way too much teeth. "Sorry, lover. He's right. I'm one of his wolves."

"But then why—wha—how?" I didn't know what I was trying to ask. None of it made any sense to me.

Ethan walked down the last few steps and into the kitchen proper. "He did it to weaken me. He knew without you I wouldn't be at full strength, and it would make it so much easier for him to take over."

I shook my head. "What the hell are you two talking about?"

Noah shook his head. "What the love of your life there didn't tell you is that the two of you are a bonded pair, my love."

I looked back and forth between the two of them, more confused than ever. "Ethan?"

Ethan didn't answer me. Instead, it was Noah again. "Some of our alpha males have the ability to tell when they meet their other half. Their bond mate. When Ethan met you, he knew you were the one for him. He put a 'do not touch' sign on you. Metaphysically, of course. The two of you were destined to be together."

Destined? I didn't think so. "No, that's not possible. If that had been true, we'd never have broken up."

"Perhaps destined isn't the right word. It isn't a guarantee, my love, just a push in the right direction."

"How'd you find out, Smithton?"

"Please, you were worse than a lovesick puppy after you two broke up. It didn't take a genius to figure it out."

"Wait," I interrupted. "If he and I are destined to be together, why are you here? What do you want?"

Ethan's voice was harsh and cold. "Smithton thinks to make himself the new alpha, don't you, Noah?"

Noah smiled the smile I'd seen too much tonight.

"By mating with you, he would break the cycle and prevent us from getting back together. It would give him enough power to take over the pack without another fight."

"How the hell would sleeping with me give him power?"

"Tsk tsk, Ethan, you really should have taught her better than this. The least you could have done was prepare her."

I looked back at Ethan. "What is he saying, Ethan?"

Ethan took his eyes off Noah and looked at me for a long minute before responding. "I told you that the stories of us changing humans with a bite or a scratch were untrue, but that if you wanted, there was a way to make you one of the pack."

I nodded slowly, remembering. We'd never gone into more detail. I figured I had plenty of time to decide.

"Well, it's by magic. At our mating ceremony we dedicate ourselves to the well-being of the pack and each other. There's a complete ritual, but what it boils down to is powerful magic binds our souls and energy together.

"That's why the most successful packs are the ones with a bound alpha male and female. The power of their love, the strength of their commitment is enough to help their pack weather almost any storm."

"You are his one true love, Amanda. If I had managed to seduce you away from him, I wouldn't have had to face him in open battle."

Horror filled me at the thought of what he meant. "You're the one who turned in the pack. You're the one who got Gerry killed."

Noah bowed. "Guilty as charged. Your lover boy was supposed to be there. No one other than his family knew he'd made other plans. Plans to be with his mate. Gerry got in the way when the hunters tried to do what they were hired to do."

"Gerry was doing his job by protecting my parents." Ethan grabbed at my shoulders, and tugged me back toward him. But I was too angry and hurt to let him. Instead I pulled away and positioned myself as far away from the two of them as I could get and still be in the kitchen.

"He was doing your job, Ethan. The one you failed at with them, and failed at with your love."

Faster than I could blink, Noah was airborne, coming straight toward me. I couldn't move, I was frozen in place. A blur crossed my line of sight, and Ethan met Noah in midflight, preventing him from getting any closer to me. They landed in a heap on my kitchen floor, wrestling with each other as though their lives depended on it.

I stood there, watching as the two of them struggled against each other. I had suspected Noah was strong, but I hadn't realized how strong until I watched Ethan's muscles ripple as he fought the other man off. I wanted to scream at them to stop, but I knew it wouldn't do any good. Nothing short of one of their deaths would end this fight.

They got to their feet locked together and one of them pushed them out the open patio door to the darkness of the night. I followed them quickly, my throat in my heart, fear for Ethan nearly blinding me to my own potential danger should he lose. I cared nothing about my own safety, only his.

Noah avoided a swing from Ethan and returned with one of his own. For a brief second their backs were to each others, and that's when I saw Noah begin to change.

I opened my mouth to warn Ethan, unsure if he had seen what Noah was doing, but realized I wasn't needed. Ethan was already in full wolf form. His change took half the time of Noah's.

The two animals went at each other viciously, but with intelligence. I could do nothing as I helplessly watched them snap and growl at each other. Noah's black wolf form clamped Ethan's front leg in his jaw and bit down. A small sound escaped me as I saw Noah's mouth come away with blood.

The fight looked evenly matched, for every strike one of them got in, the other retaliated. I felt as though it had gone on for hours, but my brain assured me it had only been a matter of minutes before Ethan had his jaw locked around the back of Noah's neck. He shook him briskly, as though giving him a chance to surrender.

Noah growled and tried to swipe once more at Ethan, obviously having no intention of surrendering despite his mortal danger. The sharp "crack" as Ethan broke Noah's neck reverberated through the backyard and into the woods beyond.

Ethan opened his mouth and dropped Noah's body to the ground before looking up at me. Even with his eyes in wolf form, I saw the fear in them. The fear of rejection, the fear that I would run away from him and his wolf side. I thought I had accepted it that night at the cabin, but I had been wrong. I hadn't even begun to see what it meant to be part of his world.

Tonight showed me more than words what I could be getting myself involved in. Was he worth it? Right now it didn't matter. Right now all I wanted to do was take him in my arms and make that pain in his eyes disappear.

I ran to him and put my arms around his furry neck and squeezed it tight, holding his head against my chest. I wasn't aware that I was crying until a long, smooth tongue licked my cheek dry. A watery giggle escaped my lips and I buried my head in his fur.

I felt him morph back to his human form and suddenly I was being held in warm, strong arms, a crooning coming from his chest to calm me down.

My voice hiccupped over my tears. "Are you all right? I saw blood."

I tried to pull back from him, to check him over, but he held me tight against him, exactly where I wanted to be.

"The shifting heals most wounds. He never really got a good nip out of me, anyway."

"Dammit, Ethan, you scared the hell out of me." I knew I should be freaking over the fact there was a dead werewolf in my backyard, but the fact that Ethan was here, safe and uninjured was the only thing I cared about.

"I'm sorry, babe."

"What are we going to do about him?" I managed to pull back from Ethan long enough to nod my head to Noah's body, now in human form. I was sure it would hit me later, but right now it wasn't real.

"I'll have the cleaners take care of it."

"So he'll just be another missing person?"

Ethan shrugged. "There isn't much else I can do, babe. If it can be made to look like something other than an animal attack, then they'll make sure the body is found. If not, then, yes, he'll be a missing person."

I nodded. I understood. Safety of the pack was first and foremost in everything he did.

I pulled myself completely out of his arms and stood up. Shakily I walked back to the kitchen and turned off the screaming teakettle. Ethan didn't offer to help. I think he knew help from him was the last thing I wanted right now.

As I prepared my tea, I was vaguely aware of him calling someone and arranging for removal of Noah's body. Panic still hadn't set in. I wondered if I were in shock, and then realized that I was perfectly fine. Ethan hadn't done anything he hadn't needed to do, nothing he hadn't done before.

Did it matter that Noah was a friend of mine? Someone I knew? Part of me thought it should, but the fact that he'd been lying to me the entire time we were together made it seem less like he'd been a friend and much more like he was a stranger. Someone out to harm not only me, but the ones I cared for.

That alone was enough to wipe away any sorrow I might have had over his death.

"Damian and the crew will be here in a few minutes." Ethan pulled the curtains over the French doors, presumably so I wouldn't have to see them when they showed up.

"Don't you have to be out there to supervise them?" I took a sip of my tea and watched him approach. He reached into the cabinet and grabbed out another mug for himself. It was the one he'd gotten for me when we'd gone on our first mini-vacation together. It had a woman on the ground with a large wolf cuddled up beside her as the two of them napped in the forest. I'd always loved that mug. I always thought the wolf wasn't really sleeping, but that he was protecting her from all the evils of the world. And that was before I knew what Ethan was.

He used to tell me that my affection for the image on the mug was one of the reasons he fell in love with me. That he knew he could trust me. Of course, he would pick that one tonight.

"They know what to do."

It took me a minute to remember what we had just been talking about. While I'd daydreamed about the mug, he'd made his tea and was now leaning against the kitchen island, facing me.

I couldn't meet his eyes. I didn't know what to say to him, so instead, I walked over to the living room and sat down on the couch. I felt him come up from behind and wasn't surprised when he sat on the ottoman in front of me. I cupped my mug, willing the heat from the tea to infuse my body and stared into space while he waited patiently for me to be ready. One point for him.

"So." It was the best I could come up with.

"So."

I smiled. Ethan had a lot of faults. Being talkative had never been one of them.

I turned and looked him in the eyes. There was still a wariness in there, the same look he'd had when he'd looked at me as a wolf. "Are you ready to tell me the truth?"

He nodded as he took a sip of his tea. "What do you want to know?"

I sighed. "Everything."

He put his tea onto the floor beside him before he began. "Everything Noah said is true—to an extent. I knew after the first time we made love that you were my destined mate. But I fell in love with you before that.

"I fell in love with your independence, your strength, your willingness to help others. I fell in love with all of that well before I ever knew what you could be to me or my pack."

I felt a warmth run through me at his words. I didn't doubt he was telling me the truth. I remembered something. "The first time we made love. It was…"

"Incredible." He nodded his head as he reached for my hand.

"I thought I'd felt something strange, as though our souls had met and joined together, but decided I was romanticizing it."

He took the mug out of my other hand, placing it beside his before he held both of my hands in his tightly. "No, you were right. They had. They recognized what we could be to each other and joined in harmony."

I shook my head. "No. That's not right. That doesn't happen."

"It does for weres, Amanda."

I wanted to point out that I wasn't a were, that I was fully human, but if he and Noah were right, then I was more than that. I had the potential for much more. "Then why? Why did you leave me? Why didn't you trust me to stand by you, no matter what?"

A stricken look flashed across his face. "Is that what you thought? That I didn't trust you to be there for me?"

I looked away. I knew what Missy had told me, and I had believed her, up to a point. But deep down I knew it had to be something about me. Some failing I wasn't aware of.

He swore. "My god, Amanda, that's the last thing I intended. I loved you more than anything or anyone in my life. I needed you more than air."

"Then why did you dump me?" I knew tears were gathering in my eyes. I could barely see him through the liquid bubbling up, ready to spill over any second. I tried to blink them away. I'd be damned if he got any more tears.

"Honey, what I told you earlier tonight is true. The reason—the only reason—I sent you away from me was because you weren't safe around me. I was afraid that whoever had arranged the attack on the pack would go after you. Enough of the pack knew we were dating that being with you put you in danger. Only my family knew about the bond, though, so I figured if we broke up, no one would know any better. Apparently I was wrong. Smithton made the connection." He grimaced. "Although given my behavior since then, it probably wasn't hard to figure out."

He shook his head. "Despite everything, I put you in danger anyway. I'm sorry, Amanda. I should have told you everything beforehand, but I was afraid for you. I didn't want to drag you into this."

I was always torn when dealing with Ethan. Part of me wanted to be mad at him for his high-handed behavior, and part of me wanted to hold tight and thank him for protecting me. "I guess you were right. He did try to get to me."

"Luckily for us, he went the seduction route." His hands tightened on mine.

"Ethan, we never did anything. I never even let him kiss me."

His sigh was visible. "I know that, Amanda. I knew it before, but the jealous beast in me kind of took over."

"And what happens if something like this comes up again? The attack on the pack. Will you push me away again?"

"I lost you once, I can't do it again. It almost killed me." He stood up and began pacing the room. "After I broke up with you, I had my men following you for the first couple months. No one was bothering you or approached you so I convinced myself I was being paranoid and I had to let you live your life. The only thing more difficult I have ever done was the actual breaking up."

He quickly sat down beside me and grabbed for my hands again. "In the past week there have been grumbles, hints something was going to happen. I used that as an excuse to put my men back on you."

"That's how you knew I was upset earlier tonight."

"Bill called me to tell me what happened. That you peeled out of the restaurant parking lot without even looking where you were going. He was worried about you." He reached to brush a curl of hair out of my face. The look on his face set my heart pitter-patting again. He could be the most gentle man when he wanted to be.

"So what about Noah's allies? If you've been hearing grumbles, then others had to be in on it."

He nodded. "I have most, if not all, of them identified. I just didn't know who the ringleader was. They'll have an option. Either swear fealty to me and the pack or leave."

"And if they refuse?"

"Pack justice."

I nodded my head this time. I knew what he meant. They wouldn't live to betray the pack again. It was cruel, but it was their way of life, it always had been.

He brought my hands to his mouth and laid a gentle kiss on them while his gaze scanned my face. I didn't know what he hoped to find, but he obviously came to a decision whatever he saw.

"I never truly let you go, Amanda. I couldn't. And I can't. Please, forgive me. Tell me you'll be mine as I want to be yours. Tell me I haven't screwed it up completely."

It was my turn to search his face. I loved him, I knew that without a doubt. And I had already forgiven him. But there was still so much unsaid.

"How do you feel about me now, Ethan? You said before that you loved me when you broke up with me. How about now?"

"I love you, Amanda. I always will. I love you with every breath I take and want to spend the rest of my life with you by my side."

"And if I choose to not join the pack? If I choose to stay human instead?"

"I love you. I'll take you any way I can get you."

"Are you sure about that? What happens when something else endangers the pack and you don't have the power you need because I wouldn't change?"

"You don't need to change to give me strength. Just having you by my side makes me a stronger man, a stronger wolf. Your love does that, not some mystical connection that only the gods understand. There are plenty of packs out there with only one of a mated alpha pair an actual were.

"I don't need you to be any different than you are now. I need you to be you. With me. Will you? Can you?"

Would I? Could I? Looking at his face, the face I loved, I knew I wanted nothing more in life than to be with him again. Whether or not I'd become a were could be decided later. Right now though, I could make the decision I needed to make.

"Yes."

The word was barely out of my mouth before he had scooped me into his arms to carry me toward the stairs.

"Wait! Where are we going?" I laughed, pulling in my legs so we could fit up the narrow stairway.

"I'm taking you to bed where I can make love to you properly."

"Ethan, shouldn't we—" I wasn't even sure what I was going to suggest. His growl of intent stopped me.

"No, we shouldn't. The only thing we should do is show how much we missed each other."

A rumble deep in my belly began as I thought of finally making love to him the way we use used to. The way I had been dreaming of for months.

Gently Ethan laid me on the bed and gave me a soft kiss before pulling away.

"What?"

"I need to clean up, love. Just one minute."

He quickly disappeared into the bathroom. Almost immediately I heard the shower running. I smiled, shaking my head. I hadn't even thought of what he'd been through in the last half hour. Shifting may help heal wounds, but it wasn't going to get him clean.

I took the time to think about everything I had learned tonight. I loved Ethan more than I could put into words, and I knew deep down that he loved me as well. This bonding stuff scared me, though, more than I had thought it would.

Would we last forever? Noah had said we were destined, but that didn't guarantee us a forever kind of love. Was our love forever?

I shook my head. No one was guaranteed that. I'd always known that, and had been willing to accept it. So why did it scare me now? I loved him more now than I had a year ago. I'd take him for as long as I could hold him.

"Why so thoughtful?"

His voice surprised me. I hadn't realized I had lain there long enough for him to finish. I looked up and my breath caught. My body reacted to him the way it always had. A craving so intense it felt as though I'd be in pain if I didn't respond to it. His torso glistened with water. Small rivulets ran from his still-wet hair down his chest, despite the fact he'd obviously run a towel through it. The towel hung low on his hips, hiding what I most wanted to see.

Words were beyond me. Instead I reached my hand out to him, asking him to come closer. To be here with me.

He came to me, grasping my hand in his and sitting beside me. When he bent down to lay a kiss on my lips it was soft and gentle, full of promise. My heart beat faster, tripping my breathing into high gear.

When he pulled back and looked at me, I felt myself get lost in his eyes, in the desire, need and love that shone out of them. How had I gotten so lucky?

His hand caressed the side of my face, warmth from his palm running through my body, bringing nerve endings to life with that brief touch.

Slowly his hand worked its way down my face to my torso, caressing me all the way, until he reached the tie of my robe and tugged at it, spreading the material wide to stare at my body.

"I love your body. It's perfect." His words were a whisper as one hand caressed my stomach and the other cupped a breast. "I missed you so much, my love. I ache for you."

I arched into his hold, eager for him to reacquaint himself with me. His hands stroked and caressed, bringing forth a burning that I hadn't felt in way too long. Earlier had been what it was, a quick, hard fuck. This was making love. Slow, gentle love.

His hand cupped my core and he pressed against me, rubbing my mons with the heel of his palm. I groaned when he slid a finger between my wet lips, caressing my opening with the tip. My legs opened wider, begging him silently for more.

He brought his head down to my breast to take a nipple into his mouth. He rolled it between his lips, sucking at it gently, pulling me into him as though the rest of my body were connected through an invisible string.

First one, then a second finger slid into me and a small orgasm rolled over my body at the contact.

"You're always so responsive to me. I love the way your skin flushes when I touch you. Gods, I love you." He left my breast to kiss his way down my body, licking and nipping as he went, heat chasing all thoughts away, replacing them with need, desire, love.

"I love you, Ethan." I tugged him back up to my face to kiss him. I knew where he was headed, but I was wet enough, ready enough. "Take me now, please."

"But—"

I kissed him again, silencing his protest. "Later. Right now I want you. Inside me, loving me."

His smile melted my heart. "I'm always loving you."

He slid inside me smoothly, my body opening for him as my walls hugged him tight. Small fireworks of excitement went off in the back of my head once he was fully seated. I loved this man, and making love to him completed me like nothing else ever had.

Ethan proceeded to make love to me, thrusting in and pulling out all the while his arms wrapped around me, his eyes locked onto mine. He took it slow, and we enjoyed what we had found anew.

My orgasm built from where we were joined, each move pushing me harder and faster toward the precipice as my body heated. Finally, when it hit me, I was overwhelmed with sensations. My body exploded with love for this man. The only man in the world for me.

We came together, yelling to the heavens as we shook from our orgasms. "I love you, Amanda." He stared at me, brushing my sweaty hair from my eyes. "Will you marry me?"

I searched his face much as he did mine. I saw his love for me, he need to protect me, his desire for my body, all in his look. I'd never felt so cherished in my life. My answer was easy.

RESISTING REED

Kristin Daniels

ജ

Trademarks Acknowledgement

The author acknowledges the trademarked status and trademark owners of the following wordmarks mentioned in this work of fiction:

Armani: GA Modefine S.A.

Cristal Champagne: Champagne Louis Roederer Corp.

Glenlivet: The Glenlivet Distillers Limited

Chapter One

ꕥ

Sonja Lunsford raised her glass of champagne in a celebratory toast. "Here's to you, Marilee. You finally lost that extra two hundred pounds."

Marilee's flute met her friend's with a singsong clink. "And who would have thought it would only take one of Chicago's priciest lawyers to do it?"

"Well, I say good riddance." Sonja took a delicate sip of Cristal. "Any lawyer who can get rid of all that extra weight with a divorce settlement as good as yours is worth any price."

"Amen." Marilee Reynolds leaned back in the patio chair and lifted her face to the sun. "You can't imagine how wonderful it feels to finally be rid of the lying bastard."

Sonja's festive tone changed to melancholy remembrance. "Oh yes, I can. You're forgetting all the stories I'd told you about my first husband. He was just as bad as your Peter, worse actually."

Marilee studied her friend and mentor, recalling her stories of fear and abuse. At least Peter never raised his hand to her.

"I was so young, only twenty-two when I got pregnant. And way too trusting." Sonja took a deep breath and smiled. "But it's all in the past now, and I'm not one to dwell. Besides, I ended up with the best part of him when it was all said and done."

Reed. Sonja's pride and joy.

Sonja picked up a strawberry from a plate on the table. "I'm just thankful Everett wanted to adopt Reed when we got married. He was so little at the time, lost. Everett molded him into the man he is today."

And what a man he turned out to be. Six foot two of nothing but pure male sensuality.

Oh, God.

Heaven help Marilee if her best friend ever found out how she truly felt about her son.

He showed up in her dreams, a recollection of that night so long ago. In her sleep they had continued where reality hadn't, and it never failed to wake her with an intolerable need. The way his tongue plunged deep inside her while his cock slid in and out of her mouth left her awake and aching. She would often end up reaching for her vibrator to try to imitate his actions. And damn, if that wasn't a poor substitute for the real thing.

Marilee cleared her throat and ran her hands through her long hair. "It's been ages since I've seen him. How does he like living in the city again?"

Sonja took another sip of the champagne. "From what he tells me, he's enjoying it. You know, it took Everett a year to talk him into coming home and taking the VP position. To this day, I still don't know why Reed waited so long to agree. It's a wonderful opportunity for him."

Marilee knew why.

She could still recall the incident as if it were yesterday.

The tingle on the back of her neck told her he was watching her. She spotted him standing with Sonja and Everett, and when they locked eyes from opposite sides of the large hall, a wave of heated regret blazed through her. He crossed the room toward her, his dark eyes assessing, making her feel exposed. He looked decadent in his tuxedo, tall and imposing. But it was his lips that drew her in, the fullness of them so kissable. It would take every ounce of willpower to beg him not to.

Oh, God, to lose herself in his arms, in his touch.

Her marriage was in shambles, she'd come to that realization months ago. But just because her husband was unfaithful wasn't an excuse for her to do the same. She'd taken a vow, one that meant something to her.

As he headed straight for her, the lust in his expression shocked her. Warmth from his fiery stare spread through her body. Would she be able to do it? Could she tell him to leave her alone?

She broke eye contact and turned away. Put her back to the one man who could make her lose control.

She sensed him behind her before his hand caressed her leg, the gentle touch burning through the silk of her emerald evening gown, rising higher…

"This dress is killing me, Marilee." he whispered. A sultry breath brushed her neck, the heat from his tongue searing as he slowly ran it along the edge of her ear.

"Reed, don't. Please. It's not right…"

"What's not right, Marilee?" His hand ran up her thigh, coming between their bodies to cup her ass. He slid his fingers along the crease, the only barrier was her silk dress which dampened as he delved deeper.

"This. This is not right…"

But it felt so good. Reed standing mere inches behind her, whispering to her, caressing her in places that ached for his touch.

"Do you want me here, Mar? Could you handle my cock pounding into this tight hole? Driving you insane from the painful pleasure you would get?"

It was wrong, so wrong.

"Don't. Somebody will see you…"

"I don't mind people watching."

She turned around and sucked in her breath at the devilish grin on his lips. "I do, Reed. I'm married, and you're…you're…"

"I'm what, Marilee?"

"Actually, he just bought a waterfront condo."

The words snapped her back to their conversation. She shifted in her chair, conscious of the fact her breathing had become erratic as the hardness of her nipples poked against the lace of her bra.

Sonja shot straight up in her chair and grasped her hand. "Mar! You could decorate his new place. It would be perfect for you, get you back into the working world again. Get you out from under the shadow of that son of a bitch you divorced."

Caught off guard by her friend's job offer, Marilee didn't know what to say. To work again would be wonderful. Peter made her stop years before, said it made him look like an unfit husband. She sighed to herself. Her career was just one of the many things her prick of an ex-husband had taken from her.

But to work with Reed? Her mind went into overdrive. The dampness between her legs warned her it would be a bad idea. She could never betray her friendship with Sonja that way.

"Um... I don't know, Sonja. I've got my own place to redo and—"

"No, Mar, I won't take no for an answer. The poor boy doesn't have a decent decorating bone in his body. You *have* to do it."

Poor boy? Yeah, I don't think so. The *boy*, now thirty, held the vice president position of Lunsford Manufacturing. God, would she be able to handle standing next to him, showing him fabric samples, all the while the scent of his cologne driving her insane? Touching his fingers as she handed him a square of tile, rubbing against his muscular arm as they looked through Oriental rugs together?

Wanton. That's what she was. She could feel her body's reaction to the thought of being close to him, the swelling of her breasts and the twitch of her clit. What kind of woman lusts after her friend's son, especially one eleven years younger?

Even as she asked herself the question, her mind taunted.

You do, Marilee, you do.

Reed Lunsford snatched up the papers on the table as he walked through the kitchen of his mother's home. A vision in sapphire blue silk sitting at the patio table caught his eye as he glanced out the door. Marilee Reynolds. Here. Now.

Damn.

He wanted to give her time to get used to the idea he'd come back. It had only been a month. He closed his eyes and sighed. It'd been the longest month of his life…

He purposely hadn't attended his mother's social functions and stayed at the office long past normal hours, trying to lessen the chance of running into her. It had worked until now. She was here and he couldn't stay away from her any longer, no matter how badly she wanted him to.

He opened his eyes and once again settled his gaze on her. She was beautiful as ever. Five years hadn't changed her much. Her hair might be longer, but her curvy body remained just as tempting. Pressure formed in his chest, a cinch tightening around his heart.

He stood in the doorway, staring at her. The bronze tone of her skin complemented the chestnut of her hair, the golden earrings dangling from her earlobes shimmered in the sunlight. She sat with her head resting on the top of the chair cushion, gazing at the sky, one slender leg crossed over the other. The short skirt she wore created a teasing shadow at the apex of her toned thighs, a barest hint of what lay underneath.

Her beauty was simple, elegant even. If it had only been her looks that had first drawn him, staying away would have been easier. Her energy snared him. The way she went after anything and everything with such fervor. But as he watched her, he noticed something missing. Her eyes looked sad, haunted. The spark he so loved in her was gone.

He wanted to be the one to put the shine back in her eyes. If she would only let him.

"Stay away, Reed. Please…just leave me be."

She had walked away from him five years ago. He could've talked her out of it, pushed harder. Why hadn't he? The confusion and arousal in her eyes before she ran told him she wanted him. Maybe as much as he wanted her.

Instead, he'd given her the space she asked for. When offered the job in New York, he'd been torn. Stay and be tormented by the one woman who could give him everything he wanted, but refused to have anything to do with him, or leave. He chose to leave.

When his mother told him Marilee finally divorced her philandering husband, he knew it was time. He finally let his parents talk him into taking the vice president position and coming back to Chicago.

Reed knew Marilee's divorce had not been a simple one. He'd heard stories about Peter Reynolds, a world-class cheater and liar. If Reed ever came across him, he would have to restrain himself to keep from killing him. He'd taken the very essence of who Marilee was, torn it to shreds and tossed her aside.

The gut punch he got when he looked at her, seeing the hollowness inside her, made him only more determined to replace everything Peter had taken from her.

Letting her push him away was no longer an option.

He turned the knob on the patio door and stepped outside. Marilee peered up as he came toward her, wide dark eyes meeting his. A small hitch in her breath sent a pulse straight through his heart and directly to his cock. His mind immediately drew up images of those eyes filled with pleasure as she lay under him while he drove fast and furious into her tight heat. Damn if she hadn't always had that effect on him.

His mother rose from her chair as he neared the table. "Reed, what are you doing here at this time of day?" she said, placing a kiss on his cheek.

"Hi, Mom. I stopped in to pick up some paperwork I left here." He turned and focused a fervid gaze on Marilee.

"You remember Marilee Reynolds, right?" Sonja asked, returning to her chair.

"Of course." He leaned across the table holding out his hand to her. "It's been a while. How have you been, Marilee?"

She placed her hand in his. The warmth of it, the slight quiver of trepidation sent an electrified pulse straight to his groin.

"Reed." A beautiful flush came across her cheeks. "I've been…fine. Thanks."

Withdrawing her hand, she leaned back into her chair, her eyes never leaving his.

"Good," he said. "Very good."

"I was just telling Mar you bought a condo along the lakefront," Sonja stated. "I also told her it would be a great idea to have her decorate it for you."

Reed took the seat opposite from his mother, next to Marilee and tented his pants, trying to conceal his hardening cock. "I think it sounds like a wonderful idea."

A phone rang in the house and his mother stood once again. "Excuse me, Mar, I've been waiting for a call all morning. I won't be more than a few minutes." She turned to him as she headed toward the house. "Keep her company for me, will you, Reed?"

"Absolutely, Mother." He leaned slightly toward Marilee, and with a lowered voice said, "You couldn't drag me away now."

Chapter Two

ꟸ

Marilee was in trouble. Big trouble that started with a capital R. His face held the unmistakable expression of a man determined to get what he wanted. And it surprised her to realize he still wanted *her*. She figured in five years, any feelings he may have had for her would be gone, even if her desires for him hadn't lessened.

"Really, Reed. You look like a little boy that just got a puppy for Christmas," Marilee teased, hoping she sounded more in control than she actually felt.

"Do I?" A sinful smile spread on his tan face.

She reached for the champagne bottle and poured herself a glass of liquid courage. "Yes." She settled back against the cushion, taking a healthy sip of the sparkling wine. "You do."

"Maybe I'm just excited at the idea of you decorating my condo."

Marilee laughed. "I haven't said I would."

He leaned close, so close that the spicy fragrance of his Armani cologne and the golden specks in his dark brown irises wreaked havoc on her already faltering willpower. "Hmmm... You're right. But," he said, "I think you will."

Holding the glass, she stood and moved a few feet away to the edge of the pool. She needed clean air, hell, any air. He seemed to take up so much space with his six-foot-two height and broad chest. So much so, that when he was near, she couldn't catch her breath.

Needing to take control of the situation, Marilee squared her shoulders and put on what she hoped was a casual expression. Her body, on the other hand, had a different idea.

The pulse pounding between her legs, the tightness of her nipples and the way they rubbed against the silk of her blouse, were almost enough to make her beg him to fuck her, to hell with any misgivings she had.

"How was New York?" she managed.

Reed stood. "Small talk, Marilee?" He sidestepped the table until he positioned himself in front of her. "Okay, I can do small talk."

He took her glass and set it on a bench next to the pool. Turning back, he placed his palm on her arm, stroking gently up and down, sending a jolt of pleasure through her.

"New York was good." He placed his thumb on her chin and lifted her face to his gaze. "But, you know, I would much rather skip the polite conversation."

She should've known it was coming, and moved before he had the chance to lower his lips to hers.

The touch was soft, soothing. His hand never left her face, his eyes never looked away. "I missed you, Mar. I missed seeing the heat in your eyes whenever I looked at you. Do you have any idea what that did to me? What it still does to me?"

Reed's hand slid to her cheek and his thumb rubbed gentle circles in the flesh it found there. Every instinct told her to run, get away from him before she lost control and did something she would regret.

But her body wouldn't move. She stood there, awash with passion at the longing in his dark eyes. It would take nothing for her to rise on her toes, wrap her arms around his neck and lose herself in his warmth.

Oh, God. How could she? Doing that could destroy the treasured friendship she had with Sonja, not to mention what it could do to Marilee herself. She'd fumbled around in a fragile state of mind most of the time since her separation from Peter, unsure of what to do or where to go next in her life.

Why would Reed want her? She didn't feel as if she were anything special. A man with his looks, his charm and charisma could have anyone he wanted.

"Reed. What do you want from me?" she asked, closing her eyes.

He shifted closer, his arm wrapping around her, pressing his chest into hers, the hardness of his erection into her lower stomach. "It's not what *I* want, Marilee. It's what I can give you. It's all about what I *want* to give to you." His mouth lowered to her neck, lips nipping, licking. The juices spilling from her soaked through her panties.

She reveled in his touch, the feel of his mouth on her skin. He brought his hand between their bodies, the back of his fingers running over the hard tip of her nipple. She grabbed his biceps as she let out a small moan.

And that seemed to be all the enticement he needed. His mouth came down on hers, hard and consuming. His tongue warred with hers, fighting for supremacy. Flipping his hand, he palmed her breast before bringing his fingers to the center. He pinched her nipple through her blouse, hard enough to send waves of pleasure straight through her body.

He broke the kiss and moved his mouth to her jaw, biting and sucking along its edge. "Damn, baby." He spoke in a voice so low, so guttural, she almost didn't recognize it.

"Reed," Marilee whispered as she eased her head to the side, giving him greater access, knowing she shouldn't, but not caring. She was drowning in him, losing herself to the sheer power of his touch.

His hands seemed to be all over her body. Warm on her breast, low on her ass as he squeezed, moving closer to her core.

It was too good, and she knew it. There was no way it would stay like this. They were so different, there were too many years spread between them.

Somehow, somewhere, reason came back to her. "No, Reed," she said as she pushed him back. She groaned at what he could do to her, what she wanted him to do. He was here. This was real, not a dream. "You know I can't do this. It's…it's…"

"Don't say it's not right, Mar." He stepped closer, eyes filled with heat, following her as she backed farther away from him. "Don't say it, because you and I both know this *is* right. Nothing has ever felt so right to me. Or you."

"How can you say that? What is *this*, anyway?" She motioned back and forth between them. "There is nothing here between the two of us except a physical attraction."

God, I am such a liar.

"Why are you so angry?" he smirked. "Because you know what I'm saying is true?"

Damn it. He was picking a fight with her and from the looks of the bulge in his pants, enjoying every minute of it. "I'm not going to argue with you about this, Reed."

"What is there to argue about?" He stopped her with a gentle hand on her elbow.

She averted her gaze, shaking her head. Grasping both of her hands in his, he brought them to his chest and spread her palms over his heart. Her breath hitched at the fast-paced thumping within.

"Feel this, Marilee. *This* is what you do to me." She stared at her hands, unable to take her eyes off her fingers splayed across his hard muscles. "Look at me," he said and her eyes rose to meet his, stopping first on his swollen lips. "This is not just a physical attraction. Although believe me, I would like nothing more than to take you away somewhere and lose myself in your body for days on end."

The thought had her spinning. "Reed."

"I'm talking about what's inside." His finger skimmed between her breasts, a slow lazy touch that drove her crazy. "You have a beautiful spirit, sweetheart, but somewhere along the way, you've decided to hide it." His eyes were full of sincerity and warmth flowed through her so strongly she was sure she would melt. "Let me be the one to help you find it again."

She tried to move back but he held her hands tightly against his chest. "You're smothering me, Reed. This is too fast…"

"No, Mar. It's not. I've waited five years. I'm not inclined to wait any longer."

She shot him a look of surprise. "I can't. Your mother… She's my closest friend."

"Let me worry about Mom. Besides, I know for a fact that as *her* closest friend, all she wants is for you to be happy." He lowered his lips to her ear and whispered, "I can make you very happy."

She tried again to remove herself from his grip, to no avail. He was killing her, breaking her down. "It's not *just* that, Reed." she said. "I'm… Oh, God."

"What?" he said, releasing her hands, only to bring his to her arms, his thumbs swirling on her shoulders.

"I'm forty-one, you know," she blurted out.

"Yes, I know."

"I'm a divorced, forty-one-year-old woman." She gave him a look tinged with humor. "That alone should have you running for the hills."

A chuckle sprang from his throat. "It'd take more than that to keep me away now, Mar. Mom told me a little about your divorce. No, it's okay," he said as she cringed. "One thing's for sure, he never deserved you. And he better pray that he never comes anywhere near me, because if he does… Well, let's just say it wouldn't be pleasant."

She offered up a small smile.

"And as for your age…" he stopped when she sighed loudly. "Marilee, is that what you're worried about? Our age difference?" He drew her closer, his strong hands kneading the muscles of her back that began to tighten. She knew the touch was meant to be reassuring, but for her it renewed the flames building inside her. "Ah, sweetheart, that would never be an issue for me. Why should it be one for you?"

"Because it is," she admitted before pushing him back. "It's a major issue with me."

"Why?"

Yes, Marilee, why?

He didn't give her a chance to answer. "You know what they say, Mar. Forty is the new thirty."

She smiled despite herself. "What does that make you, then? Twenty all over again?"

"Nope, I get to stay right here at thirty. But you know," he turned with her in his arm and led her back to the patio table, "I'm much more mature than I let on. So what do you say we split the difference and call each other thirty-five?"

She sat back down in her chair as he took the seat next to her. "You're impossible." *Yeah, impossibly handsome, impossibly delectable.*

He tucked a stray strand of hair behind her ear, ran a finger along her jaw and in a lowered voice said, "And you're beautiful."

She felt her face flush with embarrassment. It had been years since anyone had told her that. She had to admit she didn't look bad for being forty-one, but beautiful? No, she didn't think so.

Reed's eyes searched hers and he sighed heavily. "Damn. That bastard took that from you too, didn't he?"

Chapter Three

ℵ

Reed threw his keys on the table as he closed the door behind him. In the three days since he'd seen Marilee, he'd called only twice, the last time leaving a message asking her to meet him here at his condo. He wasn't sure if she would show. He wasn't sure he hadn't completely scared her off.

He'd kicked himself at least a thousand times over the last couple days for pushing, for moving so fast at the pool. It was as if something took over his mind, an incredible need to touch every inch of her, to show her what it felt like to be loved by him.

He wasn't an easy lover. He could be demanding and his sexual tastes often went to the extreme. But it was different with Marilee. He wanted to slow down, take her on a physical journey through the most pleasurable acts he could think of. And there were many, many he could think of.

He turned the corner and entered the living room, stopping to take in the sparsely furnished condo. Damn, he really did need some help. The only items he'd brought back with him from New York were a dark brown leather couch which he'd pushed up against the wall, an oversized mirror propped up in the corner and a bookcase filled with his favorite books. The bedroom was just as bad—a king-size bed, and a lone dresser. Like his mother had said, he was a decorating disaster.

He headed into the kitchen and poured himself a healthy amount of twelve-year-old scotch. The liquid burned a trail down to his stomach. He blew out a breath at the fiery sensation, desperate for the alcohol to take the edge off his sexual frustration. It was either this or going for a ten-mile run. He figured the scotch would do the job quicker.

As he took another sip, the intercom buzzed. He glanced at his watch as he went to answer it. If it was Marilee, she was early. He pushed the button. "Lunsford."

"Reed?"

The recognition of her voice made his pulse increase and his cock twitch.

"Marilee. Come on up, second floor, two-oh-three." He stood there for a moment, hand on the wall, head lowered, trying to regain his control.

The knock on the door was so quiet, he was sure had he not been standing right next to it, he wouldn't have heard it. He breathed deeply and turned the knob.

As he opened the door, his heart lurched into his throat. *God, she's gorgeous.* A vision in a pink sundress, her dark hair pulled back in a simple ponytail, giving him full view of her slender neck. His eyes lowered along the formfitting dress, taking in the fullness of her breasts, the curve of her waist as it gave way to her slim hips. The dress was short, ending just below her thighs, showing off her tan legs and ending with her cute pink polished toes in a pair of high heels.

"Well, don't I get the feeling I've just been devoured?" She smiled as his eyes moved upward and met hers.

He took her hand and led her into his home. "No, sweetheart, that was just a look. A damn good look," he admitted, moving his hand to her lower back and leading her into the living room. "Believe me, when I devour you, you'll know it. And it won't feel like that."

"Oh… Really?" she grinned, walking farther into the condo.

The question sent a shot of lust throughout his body, but at the same time gave him a sense of something different in her.

She stopped once she reached the living room. "Wow," she said, looking around, dropping her purse on the end of the couch.

"Yeah, it's a little sparse."

"Sparse is an understatement, Reed. This is a clean slate."

"Well, then," he said as he sat and leaned back on the couch, arms spread wide along the top cushions. "Have at it."

She moved to the middle of the room, focusing on him. "Have at what, exactly?" Her eyes lowered to his crotch, hands going to her hips as she sucked in her bottom lip between her teeth. "Was that an invitation, Reed?"

His cock instantly hardened. What the hell was going on with her? This wasn't the Marilee from three days ago. And as much as he would like to see how this would play out, he felt compelled to stop it. He made no secret of the fact he wanted her, and he knew, deep down, she wanted him too.

But not like this. No games.

He bent forward, elbows on his knees, hands clasped together between them. "What's up here, Marilee?"

She looked startled, if not just a bit embarrassed. Crossing her arms over her chest, she lowered her head as she drew in a deep breath. "Too much, huh?" She chuckled softly and turned her back to him. "I'm sorry, Reed."

He rose slowly, came up behind her and put his arms around her waist. She shook within his arms and he sensed her nervousness. "Sorry for what?"

Her arms fanned out from her sides. "This. God, I just made a complete ass out of myself, didn't I?"

He grabbed her hands and wrapped them around her body, encompassing her in his arms. He nuzzled her ear and whispered, "Not at all." He pressed her against him, and the quick intake of breath told him she could feel his rock hard erection at her lower back. "It was actually very hot. You're very hot."

"Then why..." she started. "I thought that's what you wanted."

"I want *you*, Marilee. All of you." He placed a gentle kiss on her shoulder. "That wasn't you, baby."

"I don't know how to do this, Reed."

"Do what? You don't have to *do* anything, Mar," he said, moving his lips upward and brushing them along her temple. "Just be who you are."

Her head fell against his shoulder. "I don't know who that is anymore," she quietly said.

He spun her in his arms and gazed into her sad eyes. The tightness in his chest went up another notch. "Let me be the one to show you, then."

She felt like a fool. A damned old fool. Making the decision to come to his condo hadn't been easy. She'd gone back and forth in her mind, reasoning it out. In the end, though, it came down to how he made her feel. Sexy. Desired. Wanted.

She'd thrown all caution to the wind and finally, for once in her life, she did something because *she* wanted to. This was *her* life, her one and only chance to live it the way she wanted. She'd resolved to not let the fear of what people thought about her dictate her decisions any longer. Not Sonja, not anyone.

And now she'd made a spectacle of herself. She couldn't help but laugh. "How in the world are you going to show me who I am?"

The edge of Reed's lips lifted as he cupped her face in his large hands. "Do you trust me, Mar?"

"Trust you? Reed, what..."

"It's an easy question. Either you trust me, or you don't."

She looked in his eyes and knew she did. "Yes, I trust you. But—"

He didn't let her finish. "Do you want me?" His eyes darkened as they bounced from her eyes to her lips and back again.

"Reed…"

"A simple yes or no will do."

Marilee squeezed her eyes shut and sighed. "You're killing me here." She opened them and was struck immediately by the lust on his face. Or was that something else? Something more? "Yes, Reed, I want you. God help me, I do. As much as it may complicate both of our lives, I do want you."

"No complications. If you trust me and want me, everything else will fall into place."

He kissed her, slowly at first, then more demanding. She moaned softly in his mouth, feeling the incredible heat from his kiss move straight through her body to settle between her legs. She reveled in the throbbing, the wetness. An intense desire coursed through her, and she raised herself on her toes to deepen the kiss.

"Good God Almighty." His breath came in short gasps as he settled his forehead onto hers. "What you do to me, woman."

She smiled at the comment, thrilled with the knowledge she did this to him.

"Come here, I want to show you something." He grabbed her hand and positioned her in front of the huge full-length mirror in the corner.

"What?"

Moving her to face her reflection, he stood behind her, running his hands along her arms. Lowering his mouth to her ear, he whispered, "I want to show you what I see whenever I look at you, Marilee." He slowly lowered the zipper at the back of her dress. "I want you to watch yourself come apart for me and I want you to watch what it does to me when you do."

Every nerve ending tingled, every touch felt enhanced. His fingers feathered along her shoulders, tickling as he slipped the fabric over them. The hard points of her braless nipples brushed along the soft linen of her dress as he lowered it.

"Stand still, sweetheart," he said as she started to raise her arms. "Let me take care of it. I want to show you how good this can be. Just feel it."

"Reed." She closed her eyes, unable to look at herself in the mirror.

"Easy, now. Open your eyes, sweetheart. Keep them open." It wasn't a request. Her clit reacted to the demand.

She did as he commanded, staring at the reflection, trying to recognize the woman staring back. Her cheeks were flushed, her breathing short pants. She didn't know this person, this lust-filled woman she saw before her.

He lowered her dress to her waist, and brought his hands up to cup her full breasts. "So pretty," he said, his voice low.

The heat from his hands was incredible. She let out a small moan, unable to take her eyes from his hands in the mirror. He kneaded one breast while his fingers found her nipple on the other. She hissed as he squeezed, the pain quickly turning to pleasure.

"Like that, do you, baby?" he said, meeting her gaze in the reflection, the darkness of his eyes startling.

She watched as he kissed her neck, biting and then licking. He pushed her sundress over her hips, letting it fall to the floor.

"Step out," he ordered. She complied, and he nudged the fabric to the side.

Standing there in front of him, with just a thong and high heels on, had to be one of the most erotic moments in her life. His heated gaze raked up and down her body as his hands settled on her hips.

"You are the most beautiful woman I've ever seen, Marilee." He sucked in a couple deep breaths as she stared at him. "To me, this is paradise."

The honesty in his face, the caring along with raw sexuality in his eyes, mesmerized her.

"God, Reed. I don't know if I can take this."

A crooked smile formed on his lips as he raised a hand to the edge of her panties. "Sure you can. This is only the beginning."

His finger delved behind the pink triangle, teasing the curls he found there. With his other hand, he lifted her arms up behind her to wrap around his neck. "Leave them there, Mar. Hold your hands together and don't let go."

The position made her breasts rise and she arched into his hand as he brought it to her nipple, rolling the little pink nub between his thumb and finger.

She closed her eyes and moaned, couldn't help it, as his finger slid farther down, touching her clitoris.

"Your eyes. Keep them open, Mar. I want you to watch this."

She shook her head. "I can't."

"Yes you can. Open them."

The sternness of his voice left her no choice but to do as he said. She forced them open just as he thrust two fingers deep inside her. "Oh God!" she cried.

"Damn, you're wet. So wet and ready for me." he breathed in her ear. "And I'll take you. You'll feel my cock soon, baby. But first I want you to come for me, come for you. I want you to watch as you fall over the edge, knowing I'm right here holding on to you."

He pulled his fingers out of her vagina and ran one over her clit, circling it slowly. She cried out again.

Focused on the movement under her panties, she realized she did want to watch. Wanted to see everything he was doing to her. "Off. Take them off me."

She thought she heard him say "fuck me" as his fingers left her body and yanked on the thin edges of her thong. The material gave way and she stood in front of him now in only her high heels, arms raised around his neck. She'd never seen herself look so sexy. "Again. Touch me again."

"Jesus," he said. He gripped her thighs, pulling one back as the fingers on his other hand once again entered her. Once, twice, three times he slid them in and withdrew—slowly, torturously—before returning his attention to her clit.

"Reed, I can feel it. I'm so close…"

"I know, sweetheart. Let go," he said as her eyes rose from his ministrations to meet his. The dark depths sucked her in as her orgasm ripped over her. Her knees buckled as a brightness surrounded her vision.

"Oh, Reed!"

"I've got you."

Leaving her clit, his fingers plunged deep inside her, the contractions there milking them. She was powerless now to keep her eyes open any longer. Closing them, she dropped her head back on his shoulder as she cried out, riding wave after wave of pleasure.

His fingers pressed her cheek, turning her head as his mouth came down on hers, stifling her cries. The pure savagery of the kiss startled her.

Warring tongues, rasping breaths and soft moans. That was all she knew. He stopped the torturous motions, and cupped her there, the warmth of his palm firm, pressing her back into his cock and she felt the wetness of his release.

As she started to come down, he pulled her arms from his neck and turned her to face him, never letting go of her mouth. Tucking his arm under her knees, he picked her up and carried her to the couch, sitting with her on his lap.

"You okay?" He kissed her gently, soft lips all over her face as he cradled her in his strong arms, holding her close.

She tucked her head under his chin and placed a hand over his pounding heart. "I don't know if I'll ever be *okay* again."

Chapter Four

ꕥ

As Reed sat on the couch holding Marilee, all he could think about was the beautiful expression on her face in the mirror as she climaxed. Passion mixed with trust. A very powerful combination.

She shifted in his arms, lifted her head and looked at him. The smile on her face made his heart jump.

He loved her.

It didn't come as a shock to him, he'd felt this way for years. And he knew, given the chance, together they could overcome any hurdles in their way. All he knew was he wanted her in his life. In his home. In his bed. Forever.

"Hmmm. You're wearing way too many clothes."

He chuckled and kissed her nose. "Yeah, I think you're right. What do you say we remedy that?" he said, laying her back on the couch, twisting to press himself between her spread legs as he kissed her.

"Well, isn't *this* cozy?"

The sound of his mother's voice made his overheated blood run cold. He jumped up, confusion mixed with anger battling in his head. He stood in front of Marilee, hiding her nakedness from his mother's nasty glare.

"Mom? What the fuck…! How did you get in here? Haven't you ever heard of fucking knocking?"

"I have keys, Reed. You gave them to me yourself." Her eyes blazed, sending daggers straight through him and into Marilee.

"I gave them to you to use for emergency purposes! Not so you can waltz in here whenever you felt like it!"

Marilee pressed her forehead to his back, whispering "*Oh, God*" over and over. He bent over, grabbed her dress and handed it to her. She stepped into it, quickly covering herself.

"So, how long have you two been hiding this from me?" Sonja asked as she slowly moved farther into the room.

"Mom, seriously. Get the fuck out. Now."

Sonja's eyes snapped to his. "Don't talk to me that way, Reed. I'm still your mother."

"And as my mother, this has nothing to do with you. My private life has nothing to do with you."

"It does when it involves a woman who for fourteen years, I *thought* was my best friend."

Marilee zipped up the back of her dress and came out from behind Reed to stand next to him. "Sonja, please. Just listen to us. Really…it's not what it looks like."

Sonja laughed. "Oh no, Mar. I think it was definitely what it looked like."

Reed wanted to punch something. Damn it, if this wasn't the exact thing Marilee told him she'd been worried about. Just perfect.

He put his arm around Marilee's waist. "It's none of your business, Mom."

Marilee shifted closer. "So much for hoping we could act our ages and deal with this like adults."

Sonja sniggered. "Act our ages? Seems to me you've not taken anyone's age into consideration, especially my son's!"

Fuck. Two for two.

Marilee stood straight, pushed her shoulders back and faced Sonja head-on. "I know you're shocked and hurt right now, Sonja, and I'm sorry about that, but…"

Sonja got right up into Mar's face. "You're damn right I'm hurt. But more than that, Marilee, I'm angry." She grabbed Marilee's arm above her elbow in a strangle hold. "He's my *son*! How could you?"

Reed stepped forward and Marilee held up her free hand to stop him. She gave him a look so filled with confidence and love, it nearly made his resolve snap. He held up both hands and sent her a *Go for it* look.

Marilee turned back to his mother. "Let go of me, Sonja."

Sonja threw Marilee's arm out from her grip and turned her back on both of them. She rubbed her forehead as she let out a sarcastic chuckle. "Fourteen years we've been friends, Marilee. Fourteen goddamn years! You're the closest friend I've ever had," she said, turning back. "I've told you things no one else on this earth knows. And this is what you do to me? This is what one friend does to another? Lies and sneaks around?"

Marilee's voice took on her own angry tone. "I haven't been sneaking around, Sonja. And I never lied to you. The only person I *ever* lied to was myself." She pressed a fist to the center of her chest, and took a deep breath. "The first time I saw Reed in the last five years was three days ago—at your house. And when you suggested I decorate this place… It just gave me a shove in the direction I wanted to go anyway."

Sonja's eyes widened, looking from Marilee to Reed and back. Her mouth opened, then closed. Opened again. "So this is my fault? I walk in to see my son sprawled all over your sweaty, naked body, and it's *my* fault?"

"Enough." Reed's voice cut like a knife through the swirling heated air surrounding the three of them. "Jesus, Mom, that's fucking enough."

Marilee's anguish was clearly painted on her face as she touched her fingers to his. "I think I'd better go. I seem to have done enough damage for one day."

"No. Don't," he said.

She stooped and picked up the scrap of pink satin that at one time had been her panties and shoved them in her purse.

Reed held on to her hand. "Stay, please." He was ready to beg, and damn, he'd never begged for anything in his life.

She shook her head. "No. If I stay, things will be said out of anger, things that can't be taken back." She turned to Sonja. "I really hoped you'd understand. There is no blame here. Reed and I have done nothing wrong." Marilee looked at him and whispered, "I truly believe that."

She headed for the door, Reed close on her heels. She stopped and settled a warm hand on his cheek. "I'm okay. Just give me a little space, all right?" A sad smile fell on her lips. "You are an amazing man, Reed Lunsford. I'd be lying if I said I didn't want you in my life." She placed a gentle kiss on his lips, and his gut wrenched. "I just need some time to think...about everything."

"I'll get rid of Mom and come with you..."

She shook her head again. "No. Stay here, talk with her."

God, this was all falling apart. "Damn it, Marilee. At least let me come by your house later..."

She smiled. "You're nothing if not persistent, Reed. But no, don't. I'll call you when I'm ready." She kissed him again and walked out the door.

And that was it. The hottest night of his life, gone up in fucking flames.

* * * * *

Marilee drove home in record time. Mentally and physically drained, she trudged up the few steps to her front door and entered her house. All she wanted was a hot bath and a glass of wine. And to forget about the confrontation with Sonja. It wasn't likely to happen, but damn if she didn't wish she could. Seeing the hurt on her closest friend's face had broken her heart. And to know that she was the cause of it...well, it was more than she wanted to deal with right now.

She could only hope and pray that in time Sonja would come to understand, hell, even embrace the fact she wanted to be with her son.

In the kitchen, she poured a glass of Shiraz and made her way upstairs. The huge tub in the master bath beckoned and she set the tap to run the hottest water she could stand. As she lowered the zipper of her dress, all thoughts rewound to earlier in the evening, and to Reed. She'd never had anyone take that kind of care with her, to please just her. Her sex life, if it could be said she even had one, had been the pits. Peter preferred to have sex with anyone but her, but on the odd occasion when they were together, it was always straight missionary—wham, bam, thank you ma'am. He never took her enjoyment or pleasure into consideration. And before him, there were only two others, with pretty much the same outcome.

There was something about Reed, though. He cared. Honestly cared about her. She thought back to before he left, or rather, before she made him leave. They would sit for hours in Sonja's kitchen, debating this and questioning each other about that. He valued her opinion, had sought it out on several occasions. That's more than she could say about any other man she'd ever been with, or known for that matter.

Marilee slid into the tub, rested her head on a bath pillow and took a slow sip of the wine. Her free hand caressed her body, slow, smooth movements, doing her best to imitate how Reed had touched her earlier. Despite everything that had gone on, she was still on fire for him. The altercation with Sonja hadn't lessened her physical need for him. Being confronted only confirmed what she had suspected all along. She loved him. She loved Reed Lunsford. And she deeply hoped he loved her, too.

Sighing, she settled deeper into the tub, feeling the tension release from her shoulders. The heat from the water turned her skin a deep pink, and the tips of her taut nipples cherry red. She pinched one, rolling it between her fingers.

Setting her wine on the edge of the tub, she teased the skin over her stomach, then reached between her legs and stroked her still-swollen labia. Sliding one finger along the slit, she swirled it around her clit before delving deeper. She closed her eyes, reliving. This is what Reed had done to her. In, out, in, out, circle. Over and over again. The familiar tightening coiled inside her, the painful pleasure of the sensitivity rebuilding. She came on a deep throaty moan. "Reed, yes. *Yes!*"

"Good Lord, Marilee."

Her eyes shot open at the low, groaned words. "Oh God. *Reed.* What are you doing here?" Water splashed over the side of the tub as she righted herself.

He unbuttoned his shirt. "You shouldn't be doing that, Mar. That's my job." He unzipped his jeans.

"How did you get in here?" She flipped back and forth between being mortified and completely turned-on.

"We can discuss that later." He shrugged off the shirt, revealing a hard chest covered lightly with hair, defined pecs and a flat, toned stomach. "Which we will because, frankly, your security sucks."

"Oh. Okay," she said, stupefied, as he slid his jeans past his hips, finally setting his penis free. It stood out proudly, thick and long, from his body.

She sucked in a breath, living through visions of taking him deep in her mouth, toying with the sensitive head, swirling her tongue around and around.

His pants dropped to the floor and he stepped into the tub. He came over her, stopping mere inches from her lips. "That was the sexiest thing I've ever seen, Mar. God, I nearly came in my pants for the second time tonight, just from watching you play with yourself."

She struggled to gather her wits, a damn near impossible feat. Lord, she hated how he'd caught her off guard. "Why are you here? I told you I would call you."

He grinned, with the sexiest lift to the edge of his lip. "Do you want me to go?" He lowered his mouth to kiss the top of her breasts. "I'll go," he said, his voice muffled on her skin. "Just tell me that's what you want."

No. That was the furthest thing from what she wanted. What she wanted—no, what she needed—was right here in her arms.

"No. Don't go. Don't go anywhere. Stay right here and make love to me."

"Don't go."

"Make love to me."

Two sentences never had more impact on him. They made his cock swell to a painfully hard state, and he was positive he'd die if he didn't get inside her soon.

He kissed her deeply, the warmth of the water surrounding them, cocooning them. She arched her back, making sexy little sounds as his tongue glided into her mouth. He slid his arm under her, holding her close to his chest. The diamond-hard points of her nipples jabbed at him and her slender legs wrapped around his.

He kissed along her jaw, nipped at her earlobe before sucking the sensitive tendon on her neck.

"What happened after I left, Reed?"

He shook his head, lips brushing her shoulder. "Uh-uh. We can discuss that later." He lifted her gently and flipped them both so she was sitting on top of him. He dug his fingers into the flesh on her hips while she straddled his thighs. Her beautiful breasts were at eye level, and she gasped as he brought one nipple into his mouth, lapping at the water that dripped from it. Inching herself forward, she rubbed against the swollen length of his cock.

"Damn, baby," he breathed against her nipple. "The things I want to do to you, the pleasure I want to give." He placed gentle kisses on the underside of her breasts. "It's almost more than I can stand."

"Anything, Reed." Her legs gripped his hips in a vise hold as he sipped at her nipples. "Anything."

He stopped, lifting his hands to cup her face. Water dripped from her hair down the length of his arms. "Do you mean that, sweetheart? Do you know what you're saying? I'm not an easy lover, Marilee. I can rein it in, but…"

She stilled on his lap, placed her warm hands on his neck. "I trust you, Reed. I know you would never hurt me."

"Never."

"I don't have a lot of experience in, shall we say, the more extreme forms of lovemaking…"

"It's okay."

"But I want you—need you—to be who you are. In every facet of your life." His cock jumped beneath her. "And I want, more than anything, to be the woman you can be yourself with."

Sweet Jesus.

He'd been waiting years to hear those words fall from her lips. The realization she'd just offered up part of her soul to him only tightened the ever-present grip on his heart.

She reached between her legs and clutched his hard-on. The softness of her hands combined with the heat of the water made his balls tighten, his spine tingle.

Leaning forward, she whispered in his ear, "Take me with you, wherever you want to go. Show me what to do, tell me what you like. I'm not afraid anymore."

He raked his fingers through her chestnut hair and kissed her. It wasn't one of his gentle, nudging kisses. No, this kiss was full of all his love, all his lust and wanting. He bit her lower lip, licked to soothe it, only to do it again. The harder he nipped, the tighter she squeezed his cock as she stroked him. Perched on the edge, he had to do something before he lost all control.

"Stop," he said, holding her wrist and breathing hard. "We need to get out of this damn tub. Up." He slapped her ass to get her to move. She closed her eyes and hissed out a breath. He practically exploded at the notion of her enjoying that.

She reached for a towel as she stood in the tub.

"Fuck that," he said, picking her up and carrying her into the bedroom. "What's the point in drying off if we're only going to work up a sweat?"

She laughed, deep and throaty, as he stood her on her feet next to the bed. He pulled the sheet and comforter back, throwing them on the floor, leaving the bed bare with only the pillows on top. Sitting on the edge, he grasped her hands and drew her to him, encasing her between his knees. Lifting her hands to his shoulders, he lowered his hands and stroked gently at her wet thighs, meandering his way up until he held firmly on to each cheek of her ass.

He nuzzled her damp belly, swirling his tongue around her navel, dipping in and tasting the soapiness of the bath water. She mewled softly, every little whisper of sound going straight to his dick.

This is what he'd been waiting for, the culmination of every fantasy he'd thought up, every dream he'd dreamed.

His fingers crept along the silkiness of her ass, sliding down the crevice there, until he came to the puffy slickness between her thighs. Quickly bringing his hand to the front, he spread her lips and plunged not one, but two fingers deep inside.

Delicate fingers clutched his shoulders in a death grip, tiny nails cut into his skin. The sting made his cock harder, if that were even possible.

Curling his fingers, he pressed that spot, that perfect spot just past her silky entrance.

"Oh God," she moaned.

Juices flowed from her, coating his hand. He brought his fingers to his mouth, licking off every bit. "You're so sweet, baby. Like honey." Kneeling in front of her, he lifted one of her legs, placing her foot along the edge of the bed. "I've wanted to taste you for so long."

"Reed, I don't know if I can stand like this..."

"I've got you, sweetheart, you're not going anywhere," he said, supporting her raised leg with his shoulder. He parted her once again, his tongue slipping through her folds before spearing into her. Moaning, she grabbed at his hair, pulling slightly, making his cock throb with need as she gasped his name. He retreated bit by bit, tonguing her clit, sucking and flicking as she bucked against his face. He thrust two fingers deep inside her, slowly withdrawing, spreading her wetness back, coating her tight puckered opening.

"Oh," she gasped on an intake of breath.

"Shh, baby. It's okay," he whispered over her clit, resuming his feast on her. He slid his thumb into her drenched opening, loving the sensation as her internal walls clenched down on it. He swirled his finger, gently massaging her anus with her juices, relaxing the muscles there. A groan escaped as he breached her, the tight ring contracting around his finger.

Tilting his head up to look at her, he ordered, "Come for me, love."

His mouth returned, kissing and sucking her sex, as her orgasm overtook her. She stared down into his eyes as she came, her mouth open, moans rising from deep within her.

Damn, that's beautiful.

It was all he could do to keep from dragging her down to him and pinning her against the carpet as he plunged deep inside her. But no, this first time was going to be all about her, not about what he wanted.

Besides, he already had what he *really* wanted. Marilee. No woman had ever made him feel the way she did. And as he stood, catching her as her legs gave out, wrapping his arms around her shaky, warm body and holding her close, he realized no other woman ever would.

Hanging suspended somewhere between ecstasy and reality, Marilee barely comprehended being laid gently on the bed, a pillow being placed under her head and a hard body moving between her thighs. Forcing her eyes to open, she looked into the depths of Reed's, dark with arousal.

"Did I just faint?"

"*La petite mort*, my love," he smiled.

"French, right? The little death?"

"Mm hmm," he murmured, kissing her softly. "I've heard of it, but I have to say, this was my first time actually witnessing it." He pulled back and studied her. "Are you okay?"

She smiled, his kisses and the weight of his body on top of hers, his erection running roughshod over her sensitive clit, renewed the flutters in her womb. "You keep asking me that. I've never been better. That was amazing, Reed. You're amazing."

With his lashes lowered and the beginnings of a five-o'clock shadow forming on his jaw, she'd never seen him look so rugged, so sexy.

"It only gets better from here, sweetheart. You've got me all twisted up. I'm dying to be inside you, to slide in and out until you clench that tight pussy on me, sending us both over the edge."

Oh God, his words alone had her free-falling.

He dove to her neck, kissing and licking the flesh there, while his hands roamed haphazardly over her damp skin.

"I'm so close to the edge already, Mar. I need you,"

"Yes," she breathed as she wrapped her legs around his lean hips.

"Damn it. Hold that thought for one second." He pulled from her hold and jumped from the bed to disappear into the bathroom. Where was he going? But within seconds he returned, hand stuffed into to the pocket of his jeans. With a smile glued to his lips, he pulled out a strip of square gold packages.

"I brought them, you know, just in case."

She returned the smile, her insides dancing as he ripped one off the strip, opened the latex and rolled it on.

He crawled back onto the bed and settled between her thighs. Grabbing her wrists, he swept her arms above her head, clutching her hands within one of his as he yanked the pillow out from under her head with the other. Seizing her ass in his palm, he tilted her hips so her sex aligned with his rock-hard cock. He entered her with one deep thrust, a combination of pain and pleasure tearing through her as his width stretched her.

"Oh. My. God."

He withdrew at an excruciatingly slow pace, only to drive forward quickly once again.

"Heaven. Pure fucking heaven." His lips found hers, forceful and heated, as he parted them to dip his tongue inside. Being held so close, she could feel his fast-beating heart as it pounded against hers.

Amidst all the sensations swirling around her, a sudden awareness overcame her. She knew, right then, this was the place she was always meant to be, with the man she was meant to be with. No doubt, no second-guessing.

Heaven is right.

His grip on her ass tightened, digging into her, lifting her higher to meet his thrusts. He once again found that sweet spot and rasped over it again and again with the head of his heavy cock, with every stroke.

She closed her eyes as he rotated his hips, bringing pressure to her swollen clit into the mix. *Good God.* He filled her so deeply, fit against her so perfectly and made her feel incredibly treasured.

Reed's groans became louder, his breaths coming faster as his strokes increased in speed. Every nerve ending blazed, burning blue in the center of her womb and flaring out to red throughout her entire body.

"Fall with me, baby," he whispered against her lips. "I'm right here with you. Together… Ah, yes, together, forever."

His words speared through her, drove her higher, until she exploded around him. Despite the condom, she felt the heat of his release, vaguely heard them each crying out as they came together. Pleasure ripped through her very essence, dipping and settling into crevices that had been forming in her soul for years. Reed's love filled and repaired every one of them, making her whole. Complete.

He held her tightly still, his head buried against her neck, raspy breath hot on her skin. "I thought I was going to die if I didn't get inside you before. And now," he lifted his head, dark eyes staring into hers, "I think I might actually have. Died and gone to heaven."

He released her hands, withdrew from her body and rolled them both to their sides, facing each other.

"I assure you, you're alive and well, right here in my arms."

"And, God, there is no other place I would rather be." He kissed her gently. "I do have a confession, though."

Marilee sucked in a breath. "Oh?"

Reed chuckled. "Yeah, it's nothing bad, really." He leaned to her ear and whispered, "I've wanted to make love with you like that since I was sixteen."

Laughing, she pushed at his muscular shoulder. "Get out."

"It's true," he smiled. "Most guys I knew were pining after Christie Brinkley in a bikini. All I wanted was to be inside you. The thought would get me rock hard in an instant."

"At sixteen?"

"Yes, at sixteen. Love knows no age, Mar."

She stilled. "Love?" God, she wanted it, hoped it was true, knew it was possible, but to hear him say it?

Twisting so he once again lay on top her, he brought his arms under her and held on to her shoulders. "Yes, Marilee. *Love.*"

Chapter Five

ꙮ

Reed woke hours later, only to find himself alone in the bed. A moment of panic swept over him, and once again he wondered if he'd moved too fast.

He'd mentioned the word *love*, but hadn't said any more. Instead, he discarded the used condom, replaced it with a new one and kissed her senseless. Over and over, he pushed gently into her and rode wave after wave of a bliss so pure he knew the grip on his heart would never ease.

Running a hand through his hair, he got up and left the bedroom. A light shone from down the stairs and he followed it into the kitchen.

His lip quirked at what he saw. There she was, naked as the day she was born, perched on top of a stool at the center island of the kitchen. A huge bowl of cold pasta sat in front of her as she sipped a glass of red wine.

"Worked up an appetite, did you?"

She smiled as she forked the pasta. "A girl has to maintain her strength if she wants to keep up with you." She turned as he approached and held out the bite for him.

"Mm, thanks," he said, chewing the food and pouring his own glass of wine. He settled on the stool next to her, grabbed her fork and dug into the bowl.

"Worked up an appetite, did you?" she mocked, laughing.

He took a drink of the wine. After swallowing, he leaned in close and kissed her. "Yes I did. In a way I plan on continuing."

Her eyes lowered and a beautiful flush formed on her chest and rose to her cheeks. "Really, Reed. Stop teasing."

Placing a finger under her chin, he raised her gaze to his. The doubt in her eyes made his stomach clench. "I'm definitely not teasing you, Mar. I plan on continuing to make love to you as often as I possibly can." He brushed his thumb along her soft lips. "Nothing could change my mind about that."

Nodding, she took the fork back from him, spearing into the pasta and taking a small bite.

"Mar, what's wrong?"

She drew in a long sigh and tossed the fork into the bowl. "I've got to go see your mom." Rubbing her forehead, she said, "I can't leave things hanging like this."

Turning, he leaned his elbows on the island. "Mom will be fine. It's just the shock of her walking in on us."

A crooked smile crossed her lips. "At least you had clothes on. God, Reed, I wanted to crawl in a hole." She chuckled and gave him a sideways glance. "It seems to be my night for people walking in on me while in a compromising situation."

He nearly choked on a swallow of wine, but he loved her openness, her willingness to discuss anything. "I'm sorry, babe. But I have to tell you, seeing you in the tub really got to me. Watching the pleasure on your face, calling my name when you came… My cock's getting hard all over again just thinking about it."

She huffed out a breath. "Somehow, I think you could get hard from the wind blowing."

Laughing, he took another sip of wine. "I guess you could chalk that up to a major advantage of being with a younger man, hmm?"

She lifted her glass to his. "You do have a point there."

The smile on her face faded just as suddenly as it had appeared.

"What happened when I left?"

He shrugged. "Not a lot. Words were exchanged, and I left her there to come here."

"Damn it, don't do that!" She'd gone from pensive to pissed in the time it took him to reply.

"Do what?"

"Pull the 'I'm the man, and I have to protect my woman' crap. Men have been doing that to me all my life, Reed. I don't want you doing it, too. I just want to know what happened, and I want you to tell me. All of it, okay?"

Well, score one for the naked, hot-tempered woman sitting next to him. He nodded to her in assent. "You're right. I'm sorry." He took a deep breath. "She was pissed, no doubt about it. Spouted on and on about how could we do this to her, how could we treat her this way. She really doesn't get it isn't about her."

The anger was gone from her eyes now, and sadness took over. "She's hurt. You have to understand, we've told each other everything, and I mean everything, about what's going on in our lives for close to fifteen years. I know she's got to be upset I never mentioned being attracted to you."

"Why would you? No matter how close you two are, I wouldn't think that would be a subject open for discussion. Some things are better kept private."

"I know."

He shifted on the stool to face her, took her hand and intertwined his large fingers with her smaller ones. "Can I make a suggestion?"

Another one of her gorgeous smiles tugged at the corner of her mouth. "Sure."

"Give it a day or two. Let her get the anger out of her system, then go talk with her. She'll still be hurting, but when it comes to Mom, hurt is way easier to deal with than anger." He stood and came around behind her, wrapping his arms around her waist. "In the meantime, I'm sure we can think of some way to keep busy."

Lifting her arms around his neck, she angled her head to give him greater access for his kisses. "You're insatiable."

He whispered, "And you love it," before running his tongue along her ear and down to her shoulder.

Turning, she faced him, stood on a rung of the barstool and kissed him. A deep, long, meaningful kiss that spoke volumes.

He lifted under her arms, and her legs wrapped around him instantly. Carrying her to the living room, he set her on the couch and knelt between her thighs.

"Wait, hold on a second."

"Hmm, what?" he murmured, busy kissing along her shoulder down to the rise of her breast.

She pushed at his shoulders, breathless. "I want to taste you. I want to feel you in my mouth."

"Ah, God," was all he could manage as her palms ran down his chest, over his stomach, before one wrapped around his shaft. The feel of her hand alone was enough to send his head spinning.

"Please, Reed. I need this, please..."

Rising, he moved next to her on the couch. "You don't have to." Who the fuck was he kidding? He'd been dreaming about this for fourteen years. He felt like a damn teenager.

"Shh, I want to do this, I have for years." She came around and settled between his legs.

When the heat of her tongue swirled over the sensitive head of his cock, he nearly came right then.

"Damn," he groaned, hissing in a breath.

She sucked him in, taking as much of his length in her mouth as she could, her grip tightening on the rest. It was all he could do to keep from holding her head and thrusting himself into her mouth.

Plunging and stroking, tonguing, circling. She delved again and again before holding the crest at the back of her throat and swallowing. The sensation of her throat milking him made his sac tighten and his spine tingle.

"Just like that, baby. God, that's good. So good," he groaned, one hand digging into the edge of the couch as the other wrapped in her long hair.

He threw his head back on the couch cushion, so close to coming he could barely breathe.

A final swirl and a deep plunge was all it took. He shot hot semen deep into her throat, holding her head steady only by her hair, as he cried out her name.

She swallowed, taking in all he offered. Rising above him, she straddled his legs and kissed him. He could taste the saltiness of himself in her mouth, and as she slowly rubbed against his still-hard cock, all he could think about was how much he loved this woman, and how he would never be the same because of it.

* * * * *

Marilee arrived at Sonja's house late the next afternoon. Reed had offered to go with her so they could talk to his mother together, but she'd told him no. This was something she needed to do on her own.

She sat in her car in the driveway, mulling exactly what she wanted to say. The main point she wanted to get through was how much she loved Reed, and even if Sonja wasn't happy about it, she wouldn't stop seeing him. She'd spent too many years trying to please everyone else in her life and in doing so, neglected her own happiness. No more. Now it was her turn.

She left the car and walked to the front door. She stood there for a moment, taking in a few deep breaths before pushing the doorbell.

The heavy oak door opened with Everett Lunsford standing inside it. "Marilee," he said, surprise in his voice. "I didn't expect to see you here."

"Hello, Everett," she said, stepping into a familiar hug when he opened his arms. She pulled back and gave him a small smile. "Is it safe to come in?"

The distinguished gray-haired man patted her on the back and returned the smile. "I believe the worst of the storm is over. If we can ride out the rest of the rough waves, I think we'll all make it."

Marilee nodded. "Where is she?"

He indicated with a tilt of his head the back of the house. "In the sunroom." He gave her hand a squeeze and lowered his voice. "Just so you know, I think you and Reed make a great couple. I've watched that boy pine after you for years, even if his own mother didn't notice."

"Thanks. That really means a lot to me, Everett." She placed a kiss on her old friend's cheek. "Wish me luck."

Marilee headed to the rear of the home, stopping in the open doorway to the sunroom. Sonja sat at a small writing desk, pounding away at the keys on her laptop. Knocking on the glass of the open French door, Marilee took a tentative step inside. "Sonja?"

Sonja's eyes snapped upward. She leaned back in her chair and crossed her arms over her chest. "What are you doing here?"

Marilee entered the room and sat in the chair opposite Sonja. "I came so we could talk. Please," she said as Sonja shook her head. "I never meant to hurt you. I need you to understand."

Sonja stood and looked down at her. "Understand what? Understand you've seduced my only son? Understand you never said anything to me about wanting to? Yes, Marilee, *please* help me *understand*."

Shaking her head, Marilee said, "God, Sonja, it wasn't like that. I never seduced your son. I'm not going to sit here and point fingers and said who did what. The how is not important." Rising to meet with her eye to eye, she said, "It's the *why* that matters."

Sonja waved her hand back and forth and strode to a small bar in the corner of the room. "You're talking in circles, Mar." Pouring a glass of Glenlivet, she leveled an angry gaze at her. "What in the hell do you mean, it's the why that matters?"

Mar had known this wouldn't be easy. She had to remind herself to stay calm, focused. "The why is very important. Why? Because he listens to me. Why? Because he makes me feel like *I* matter. I could go on and on with a list of whys."

Irritation flashed through Sonja's eyes. "You're too old for him. God, it's like my best friend's a cradle robber, and it's my cradle."

Marilee refrained from laughing at the absurdity of the statement. "It's an eleven-year difference, Sonja, not thirty."

"Exactly. Eleven years, Mar. You're looking for something to replace what your husband couldn't give you. It's just an infatuation for Reed. If you think it's more than that, you're setting yourself up for another broken heart."

Marilee knew the words were meant to hurt her. She chose instead to ignore them, as she crossed the room and leaned on the bar. "Did you know I was responsible for him leaving five years ago? That he'd told me *then* how much he wanted me? And how I told him to leave me alone because I was married?"

Fury flushed Sonja's face. "You're lying."

A deep, heavy sigh escaped Marilee's lungs. "No, Sonja, I'm not. I've never lied to you. Don't you see? This isn't just some weekend fling between Reed and me. We've fought our feelings for each other for more than five *years*."

Sonja stared at her for a long moment before lowering her gaze to the drink in her hand.

Marilee hitched her hip on a barstool and continued. "I'm sorry I've hurt you. I'm sorry I wasn't more up front with you.

But you have to know this wasn't something I could have easily come to you with."

"You could have *tried*. You could have told me about all of this five years ago."

Marilee shook her head. "No, I couldn't." She sighed once again. "It was something I had to go through on my own. I was married, so I hid my feelings for Reed from everyone. Including myself." She huffed out a sarcastic chuckle. "Especially myself." She returned her focus to Sonja. "I couldn't have acted on those feelings then, no matter how strong they were. My vows meant something to me. So I dealt with it the best I could. Alone."

Sonja looked at Mar, a dawning of realization appearing along with tears in her eyes. "You're why he came home last month? Because you were getting divorced?"

Marilee nodded. "Yes. He told me that's why he finally decided to accept the job and work with Everett. My divorce encouraged him to come home, in hopes I would accept him now."

Sonja took a long sip of the whiskey and rubbed her forehead. "I don't know, Mar. I'm not comfortable with the thought of you and my son together."

"I know. And I hope in time, you'll come to realize how much Reed and I mean to each other." She grabbed hold of Sonja's hand. "I'm not going to stay away from him because you're uncomfortable. He makes me happy, Sonja. And that's something I've not been in a very long time."

Sonja's anger eased, the furrow in her brow lessened. "Then you should do it. Be with Reed. If it makes you both happy, then who am I to say it's not right?"

Marilee came around the bar and hugged her friend. "Thank you, Sonja. I know you don't like it, but it means the world to me that you accept it."

After a second, Sonja hugged her back. "Go. I know he's waiting for you to come back with an amazing story for him."

She pulled back. “Hell, give it some spice, tell him punches were thrown. He ought to get a kick out of that.”

Marilee laughed. “I love him, you know.”

Sonja nodded. “Yes, I know.”

Chapter Six

ൾ

Reed busied himself in Marilee's kitchen, cooking up a storm while he waited for her to return from his mother's house. He might not be able to decorate worth a damn, but give him a few pots and pans and watch out. As he tossed the last of the cut vegetables into the soup pot, keys rattled in the door. He set the burner to simmer and walked around the island to meet her at the kitchen entrance.

"Well, you're in one piece."

She smiled at him, tossing her purse on the counter. She looped her arms around his neck and kissed him. Deeply. "Let's just say it went well. Better than I expected, really."

He pulled her to him, holding on to her tightly. "And you're okay?"

Running her fingers through his hair, she nuzzled his neck. "Yes, I am." She pulled back and looked up at him. "I have a question for you, though."

He stared into the dark depths of her eyes. "Ask me anything."

"What happens in, say, twenty years? When you look over at me one day, see gray in my hair, wrinkles on my face and spots on my hands. What will you say?"

He brought his arm around her lower back, holding her close. "I'll tell you the same thing I know I'll be saying to you every day for all of those twenty years. I love you, Marilee. With everything I am, with all I'll become. I love you."

Her eyes filled.

"Your age has no bearing on my love for you, Marilee. It's the person you are on the inside I don't ever want to be without. Believe me when I tell you that."

"I do." She drew in a shaky breath. "And I love you. Oh, God, I've fought it for so long, denied myself your love and touches. Never again."

A tear escaped and he kissed it away before moving lower and covering her mouth with his.

Breaking the kiss, she whispered, "Touch me, Reed, everywhere. Show me what you like. Make me yours."

"Are you sure?" His cock nearly exploded at the prospect. "I can give you such pleasure, take you higher than you've ever been."

"I've never been more sure about anything." Heat flared in her eyes and flushed her cheeks.

He reached across the kitchen island to turn off the stove, then took her hand and led her upstairs to her bedroom. His hands shook as he unbuttoned her blouse, and he nearly laughed at his nervousness. The need to make all of her experiences perfect had him slowing, not rushing. He removed the blouse and her pretty lace bra, stopping to cup her breasts and placing a gentle kiss on each one.

"You're holding back, Reed. I can feel it."

He smiled down at her. "I don't want to scare you."

She ran her hands up his arms and down his chest, settling on his belt buckle. "You won't," she said, loosening the belt and unbuttoning his jeans. "I'm not made of porcelain, so don't treat me like I am." When she reached into his boxers and gripped him, a huge part of his resistance to show her how he truly wanted to love her slipped away.

"You're waking the animal in me, babe," he growled.

Releasing him, she pulled his shirt over his head, throwing it to the floor. She kissed his chest, tongued his nipple before moving to his shoulder to bite him there. "Let him loose. Tell him I want to play."

A low rumble escaped from his chest. He swiftly removed her shoes and pants, grabbed her bare ass and lifted her to him. Two steps forward, and he had her pinned to the wall with his body. He kissed her hard, one hand removing the rest of his clothing. Once he was naked, he gripped her hips, bent his knees and entered her in one stroke. The heat that enveloped him felt like molten lava on his cock and he tightened his jaw, fighting himself for control.

"God, Mar, you're so hot, so wet. You're gripping me like a vise." He was not slow, no longer easy. He pummeled into her, over and over again. Her juices ran from her, over his balls and down his thighs.

She gripped his shoulders, her head pressed against the wall. Moaning, gasping for breath and calling his name as she tightened on him.

"Yes, baby, yes. That's it..."

She clenched on him as she arched her back. Eyes squeezed shut, she came on a cry. "Oh God, oh...God."

He stilled, relishing each contraction. "You are so gorgeous when you do that."

She smiled, bringing her arms around his neck and laying her head on his chest. "I love it when you *make* me do that."

He carried her to the bed and laid her down, still inside her. She pulled his mouth to hers and kissed him. "You didn't come," she said when she released him.

He shook his head and kissed her again. "Hmm, not yet." Flashing one of his devilish grins at her, he said, "The night is still young, and we've got nothing but time."

Marilee knew what he wanted. She'd known since he came up behind her at the fundraiser five years ago. She'd dreamedabout it, fantasized about it, and now she wanted to live it.

"Do you remember the last time we saw each other, before you left for New York?"

He leaned on an elbow and teased her collarbone with a fingertip. "Every second of it. You, in that damn green dress. I wanted to run away with you that night." He glanced from her lips to her eyes. "Then you told me to leave you alone."

"I did. I'm sorry." She bit her lower lip and released it. "But do you remember what you said to me? What you said you wanted to do to me?"

His eyes darkened, and she could feel his cock thicken even farther inside her.

"Yeah, I do."

"Please, can we…" She started again. "I just want to…"

"Yes, Mar." He slanted his mouth over hers in a possessive kiss. "God, yes."

He slid his cock from her body, trailing kisses and nips down her neck. Moving lower, he grasped a nipple with his teeth. She groaned at the pain, the heat of it shooting straight to her womb. He continued, moving slowly, sucking here, biting there. Shifting to lie between her thighs, he began to torture her with his tongue, flicking it gently over her clit. She arched to his mouth, grabbing the sheets with her fists.

She was barely aware of him reaching in the bedside table. Suddenly two cool fingers, thick with lubricant, caressed her. As one circled and massaged her rear opening, his tongue delved into her pussy.

He licked and lapped at her juices before kneeling between her thighs. Lifting her knees, he opened her wide for him.

She felt incredibly sexy, him staring at her, and turned-on beyond belief. She'd been waiting for this for years. When he pushed a finger inside her anus, she immediately clenched it.

"Easy, now. Relax, Mar. This can feel so good, but you've got to relax, baby."

She nodded, unable to speak. Sensations flooded her as he eased his way into her body. He massaged the muscles there, coaxing them to relax and take more of him. He retreated only to return, adding a second finger. She gasped at the intrusion, but resisted the urge to clamp down. Moving his fingers in and out, he opened and closed them, stretching her.

He rose above her, kissing her neck and whispering, "Roll over, baby." His fingers slid from her body and as she flipped onto her stomach, he rolled a condom over his erection.

Positioning himself, one hand on her hip, the other underneath her, low on her belly, his thick cock pressed slowly into her. She muffled a cry into the mattress.

"Breathe, sweetheart. Don't fight me, okay? Relax and feel it." He hissed out a breath. "So tight. So sweet and tight." He lifted her to a kneeling position, angling his body over hers. "Do you feel it? That painful pleasure? It's so good, isn't it?"

Never-before-touched nerve endings exploded and pleasure whipped around her. She couldn't think, could barely breathe. She lived now just to feel.

"Take all of me. I'm nearly there, baby." He pushed farther, inch by delicate inch. "There you go, sweetheart." He began to move, gentle slides in and out. "Ah God, Mar, you're holding me so tight. I'm not going to last long…"

She heard the words, knew their meaning, but couldn't respond. When his hand moved to stroke her clit, she was gone. Her orgasm ripped through her, shattering all her senses. Spasms racked her body as her cries filled her ears.

He groaned, tightened his hand on her hip and muttered loving words against her neck as he cuddled over her back.

She drifted once again, but was aware of the warmth of his body covering hers, the heat from his breath at her ear. He rolled them to their sides, sliding from her body as he did so, but still cradling her close, pressing kisses into her hair.

Moments later, after their breathing had calmed and their skin was no longer clammy, Marilee turned to face him. She rested her hand on his cheek, placing a gentle kiss on his lips before snuggling into his arms.

"Marry me," he whispered.

She pushed back to look at him in the darkness. "What?"

"Marry me," he repeated. "I love you, Marilee. With you I've found my center, my home." He held her tight. "Please. It doesn't have to be now. Hell, it could be another five years from now. Just tell me you will, make the promise to me."

Her heart swelled, bursting from her chest. She knew what he said was true, she'd found her center in him, too. He'd helped her to heal, to push away all the failures of her past. He was her present, but more importantly, her future. "I promise. Yes, Reed. I'll marry you."

He kissed her then, a tender, heartfelt melding of their souls that completed them both.

"Perfect."

TRAPPED

Cindy Spencer Pape

Dedication

This one is for all the hardworking staff at Ellora's Cave who make it possible for my stories to find a home. So much goes on behind the scenes in getting a book from the author's mind to the readers' hands, and these folks too often go unappreciated.

And, of course, to the wonderful readers – without you, we writers would be all alone with the voices in our heads. So thank you.

Chapter One

ꟗ

"Die, bitch!"

Tabrin Jones ducked behind a bulkhead as blaster fire slammed into the wall behind her. It was only a moderate energy pulse that wouldn't puncture the hull of the ship or breach the pressure seal but it would've done a number on her unarmored skull.

Damn that thug, Thosis Dinse. She should've known he'd manage to smuggle an illegal blaster on board the inter-system shuttle. All she had was a stun-gun, paralysis cuffs and a monofilament dagger in her left boot. Nothing with any range to speak of.

Another shot cracked open a crate of apples just to her right. At least she'd run him down in the cargo hold and not out where he might start shooting around innocent passengers. Tab didn't mind putting herself at risk but the thought of accidentally shooting a noncombatant made her sick to her stomach.

"You'll never take me alive, you Keisian freak." Dinse was backing up toward the airlock leading up to the main part of the ship. The wall in here was lined with escape pods. There was always the possibility he'd take one of those and jettison himself. Tomorrow's shuttle would pick him up and hand him over to the authorities. He'd still be caught but she wouldn't get the bounty and Tab needed that money.

"Oh please," she called, throwing her voice to the left. It was an old theatre trick, one she'd learned from her magician father, but Dinse was just stupid enough to fall for it. Meanwhile she slowly eased her way around the bulkhead to the right, trying to cut him off. "Could you be a bigger cliché, you stupid fuck? Maybe ask me if I want a saucer of milk?" A lot of so-called "pure" humans got all superior just because her Keisian ancestors had added a bit of feline DNA into the mix. She was a little more limber than the average person and could see better in the dark but other than that, she was as human as anyone. It pissed her off when people couldn't see that.

She slipped around the end of the bulkhead with her stun-gun raised and ready. A few more steps, if she could keep him looking the other direction. He was a small-time counterfeiter who occasionally moonlighted as hired muscle. The bounty on the bastard was up to sixty thousand credits and that would go a long way toward her kid sister's tuition for the year. Meika wanted to be a doctor, of all things. And if that's what the kid wanted, then Tab was damn sure she was going to get it. Since their parents' deaths ten years earlier, Meika was all the family Tab had left. Tabrin was determined to provide the best education money could buy, even if it meant risking her life to capture losers like Dinse.

Just two more steps. Her bare toes moved silently across the rubberized floor. Being half-Keisian might get her kicked out of swanky society events on some planets but that feline agility sure helped when it came to sneaking up on people.

But Dinse must've had some sort of enhanced perception implant going. Right as she was about to trigger her weapon, he spun and fired the damn blaster.

Tab dived for cover but even her reflexes weren't faster than an energy pulse. Luckily for her, something else was. Out of nowhere, an enormous shape rose up and slammed her out of the path of the blast into the open hatch of an escape pod along the wall behind her.

Zeyd Vasari.

The earthy, sweaty scent of him penetrated her senses even as she was being flattened against the floor of the pod by what felt like a bullet train. What the hell was he doing here? Even in the middle of being shot at though, her body responded to his presence, softening and dampening. Her instant, instinctive reaction to the man was so embarrassing, not to mention inappropriate under the circumstances. "Son of a bitch."

"Yep. In the flesh—and hardware." He braced his weight on his arms in preparation for standing. "Now stay down, Tabby Cat. I'm armored. You're not."

"Am too." She jostled to get her knees under her. "Dinse is my collar, damn it. And don't call me that!" The nickname was so damn condescending. The worst part was she knew he only used it to get under her skin and yet it still did—just like everything else about the big Xyran bounty hunter.

There was a peal of faintly maniacal laughter behind them. She braced, expecting to hear the sound of blaster fire, even though she knew it would never penetrate the massive cyborg on top of her. His skin was probably tougher than her thin, flexible body armor, though gods help her, she worried about him anyway.

But apparently Dinse had a moment of almost comical lucidity. Instead of shooting them where they lay, he just slapped the release button for the escape pod. The hatch whooshed shut, all the console lights came on and a tinny mechanical voice announced that they were about to be jettisoned in five-four-three-two…

"No," Zeyd bellowed, leaping to his feet. He was fast but not fast enough to block the hatch and halt the sequence. Two seconds later, they felt a shudder as the pod was released from the shuttle, dropping them helplessly into space.

Slowly, Tabrin stood.

"This is all your fault," she muttered, crossing her arms and glaring up at three hundred pounds of pissed-off Xyran ex-Ranger. His indigo eyes glared down at her from his chiseled deep brown face. The straight black hair she loved to run her hands through was longer now, caught up in a tie at the nape of his neck. Zeyd's six-and-a-half-foot stature dwarfed her petite frame but she figured she'd proven on more than one occasion that she could hold her own.

"Escape completed successfully," chimed the computer voice on the pod. "Distress signal has been sent. The next scheduled ship on this route is in twenty-three point five Earth hours. Food, water and sanitary arrangements have been prepared for our Macandilar guests. Please enjoy your stay."

Tabrin and Zeyd looked at one another in horror.

"Macandilar?" His voice sounded choked, more distraught than she'd ever heard him, even in the middle of mind-blowing sex.

She inhaled deeply—or started to, then stopped. She already wanted to both kiss him for saving her and slug him for the last time they'd met. No telling what she'd be tempted to do once the gas got into her system. "At least they eat carbon-based food and drink ordinary water," she said weakly. "Plus the lav will fit us. And their air won't kill us."

Macandilar physiology was about ninety-nine percent the same as human. But that remaining one percent was a lulu.

"No." He set his jaw grimly. "Just give us the buzz of a lifetime."

"Yeah." She looked around. The pod was basically ovoid, with one small door beside the hatch that probably led to the lav. There was no real furniture, just a wide padded bench that ran around the room with storage bins above and beneath it. The soft covering of the cushions would have been sanitized just before takeoff.

Zeyd immediately moved to the console to see if he could hack into the system and change the air mix. He didn't need to say a word. Tabrin knew that was what he was up to. She could have told him not to bother. These old pods were pieces of crap, with programming so arcane, he'd never be able to find it in time, even if there was an input panel. But Zeyd was a control freak and she knew he had to try.

She shook her head and began checking the storage cabinets. First-aid kit. Handy. Blankets. Useful. Bottled water, even better. She popped the seal on one and tossed another to Zeyd before closing the bin with her foot. He caught it without even turning around. They'd always been like this, working together seamlessly, almost intuitively when they weren't at each other's throats or jumping each other's bones. The fourth bin held packaged foodstuffs. Nothing exciting but now that she thought about it she *was* kind of hungry. She'd missed lunch trying to track down Dinse's hiding place. She tossed a few snacks onto the bench then closed that bin too and sat on the end of the U-shaped bench furthest from Zeyd and the control panel.

She curled her feet under her and relaxed into the comfortable cushions. This was going to be an interesting day, no doubt about it. Macandilari were green-skinned humanoids from a world with just a slightly different atmospheric blend from most other Earth-settled planets. Their air wasn't toxic to other races but it did tend to have a somewhat narcotic effect. It wouldn't make you do anything you didn't want to do. She wouldn't start singing opera or shooting up the place. But what it did do was lower human inhibitions.

And that was a problem. Because around Zeyd Vasari, she had regrettably few inhibitions to start with.

Zeyd banged his hand on the panel. He could already feel the gas starting to work in his system, easing his concerns. So he was trapped with his occasional lover and permanent professional nemesis for the next day. So what? Why not just relax and enjoy it? He'd been following her for days, hoping for some time alone, maybe even away from the job. He really ought to just take advantage of their enforced proximity.

He sipped the water she'd tossed him and stared at the computer monitor. Absolutely no way to input code whatsoever. No question about it, he was screwed. But then, around Tabrin, that didn't necessarily have to be a bad thing.

At least she wasn't dead. His heart had damn near stopped when he'd seen that stupid son of a bitch shooting at her. His stomach still hadn't unclenched completely. Why couldn't he have fallen for a woman in a less dangerous career than his own?

"So you never did tell me what happened on Chansa Six," she asked. "I assume you got the bounty for Rackin. And what did you slip into my drink that night to make me miss the pick-up?"

Shit. And so it began. It was like this every time he ran into Tabrin Jones. He adored her and she drove him crazy. Either they were competing for bounties or fucking each other's brains out. He sat down across from her and studied her, noting with dismay the new scar across her right cheekbone. When would she quit trying to get herself killed?

Tab was a beauty, even among Kiesians, a race known for sleek bodies and delicate features. The pointed tips of her ears poked through her thick, gold-streaked tawny hair, presently hanging in a disheveled braid down her back. Her amber eyes with their vertical pupils studied him back, just as coolly.

"Just a mild tranq," he admitted. "The bounty was good. But not as good as the one you suckered me out of on Divonne." Waking up para-cuffed to the bed, naked, had not been one of his finer moments. "And I still owe you for sending that pair of transvestite hookers in after me."

"All's fair, my man," she said with a chuckle. She licked the crumbs of her nutrition bar off her fingers and Zeyd's cock leapt to attention. He couldn't help remembering that sweet, slightly rough tongue licking him like a lollipop.

Heat was starting to build up in the pod—Macandilari liked it warm. Zeyd could have turned on the cooling function of his armor but it was a whole lot easier just to pull his flexible carbon-weave tunic off over his head and kick his heavy boots into a corner. They weren't going anywhere any time soon. Might as well get comfortable.

"That's a new scar on your shoulder, Zeyd," she pointed out. "Piss off somebody's husband, or get into another bar fight?"

Was Tabrin jealous? What a thought. Not that he really was the ladies' man she liked to paint him as. He'd always been a loner. His on-again/off-again relationship with her was the longest connection he'd had in his life. He shook off the moment of thoughtfulness and answered. "Bounty had a girlfriend and she had a mono-knife." Something that might have been regret flickered in her eyes as she looked at the healed line showing at the edge of his sleeveless shirt. It ran all the way up to his neck and the wound had damn near killed him. Even with his nanotech-enhanced healing abilities, some injuries just bled out too fricking quickly. Was it possible that Tab actually cared? Something in his chest began to ache at the thought and he decided it was time to turn the tables. "How 'bout the one on your cheek?"

"Oh that?" Her laugh was forced but only someone who knew her well would ever guess. "Idiot bounty with an old-fashioned slug thrower. Took it away from him and shot him in the ass for his trouble."

She'd been shot? In the face? Damn, he didn't like the nausea that roiled in his gut at the thought. He simply didn't want to imagine a universe without Tabrin in it. "You ever think of retiring? Moving on to a job where no one's trying to kill you?"

Why the hell had he said that? Might as well just start spouting poetry if he wanted to sound like a pansy. Something about Tabrin always aroused all kinds of feelings he'd never expected to experience.

"Yeah, I've thought about it." She shrugged and took a long swallow of her water. He watched her throat work and went fully hard inside his pants. "One of these days the reflexes will start to slow down, my body will quit healing so fast. Lose my edge. But not yet. Maybe in a year or two, I'll be able to start saving up, open a bar someplace."

"A bar?"

She made a face at him. "What the hell else would I do? Go back to school at my age? Sell ladies' shoes? I'd like a place near a spaceport, not too pricey, lots of traffic. Maybe a few rooms in back for people to crash."

He could see that, he supposed. Her running the kind of place where people like them hung out. It was a pleasant image, one he could envision for himself, now that she'd brought it up. Be nice to keep in touch with the life, even if you weren't getting shot at on a regular basis. He'd made few friends over the years—growing up in the barracks, friendships had been discouraged—but those few would be nice to stay in touch with.

"What about you? Or do cyborgs live forever?"

"No, we're mortal just like you are." He was sixty-three and after eighty or so, his systems would start to slow down too. Two hundred was about max for an enhanced Xyran and that was without getting cut, kicked or blasted. Keisian lifespan was close to the same, or so he remembered from his mercenary training. He wondered how old Tab was. She looked so bloody young it always felt like he was robbing the cradle whenever he got her into bed but she'd looked just the same for all the years he'd known her.

"So what do you plan to do when you retire?" She'd drawn her knees up to her chin and wrapped her arms around them, a sure sign she was tired or feeling vulnerable, though she'd never admit it.

"Hadn't thought about it," he answered honestly, fighting to suppress the surge of protectiveness. "It's not about the money—got plenty of that. Just don't have any idea what else to do."

"Plenty of money. Figures. And you still have to screw me out of bounties." She gulped the last of her water and wiped her chin with her sleeve.

"I'd rather just screw you," he said without thinking. Damn gas was already letting his mouth run away with him. "You're the one who turned it into a competition between us, years back."

"Yeah, well, some of us do need the money," she grumbled. Then she winced. "Can't believe I said that out loud. Is it getting hot in here or is it just the stupid gas?"

"The green guys like it warm," he reminded her. "Take off your armor, Tab, I promise not to shoot you."

"Would kind of make saving my ass a little pointless, wouldn't it?" She sent him a whimsical smile. "Thanks, by the way. Though I'd rather you'd shot Dinse, that annoying little prick."

"Your ass is well worth saving. I have a lot of fond memories of those pretty little cheeks." He licked his lips, remembering the taste of her silky tan skin, the tang of her cream. Then he shifted to ease the massive pressure of his erection against the front of his pants. He liked seeing her flush, watching her chest rise and fall with shallow, rapid breaths.

"I'd believe that more if I'd woken up just once to find you still beside me. You have a nasty habit of running off while I'm asleep."

"Like you don't do the same to me, given the chance. I'm not going anywhere now, sweetheart," he growled. "Take off your armor."

He watched the struggle going on behind her eyes. She knew her resistance was lowered and Tab hated that. She hated not being in complete control, even for a millisecond. He'd never even seen her drink anything but water. Something else they had in common. Zeyd couldn't stand giving up control to anyone, which is part of why he was a lot happier as a bounty hunter than he'd ever been as a soldier.

But she wanted him. That much was a given between the two of them. Something about her set every nerve and circuit he possessed to humming and he knew that she was already wet, just from being alone here with him. He could smell her arousal from across the pod and it was taking every bit of his control not to lunge over there and rip her damn clothes right off her body.

Finally she sighed. "It's going to happen sooner or later, isn't it, Zeyd?"

"It always does, T. Even without the happy gas."

"I guess that's true." She stood and began to unbuckle the straps on her jacket. "Even when I know better, I can never seem to stop wanting you. It's like you wormed your way into my bloodstream or something."

He saw her make a face—yet another thing she hadn't meant to say out loud but Zeyd couldn't have been happier. He stood and took the two steps across the pod, replacing her hands on her clothing with his own. "Goes both ways, you know. Never been able to get you out of my system either."

He pushed the reinforced leather down her shoulders and stared at her luscious breasts, barely contained in a skimpy bra-top, the kind most women wore for swimming or working out. The peachy-pink cloth set off her creamy tan skin to perfection and was snug enough to outline her generous nipples, which were clearly on full alert.

"Gods, Tab. Been too damn long." He bent his head and sucked one of those peaks into his mouth, fabric and all.

"Ten months," she murmured, arching her back and gripping his head with both of her hands. "Two weeks. Three days."

"And about six hours, give or take time changes," he added, taking just a moment to switch to the other breast. Yeah, he'd been counting the days too, damn it. Ten and a half months was an awfully long time to go without getting laid. But lately, nobody else seemed to appeal. In the last two Earth Standard years, the only woman he'd been with was Tabrin. The rest of the time it had just been him and his fist.

She tangled one hand in his hair, yanking out the tie and running her fingers through the strands. Her other hand scrabbled at the fastening of his pants.

The pants were part of his armor, meaning they were biometrically keyed to his system. He triggered the release, then let Tabrin push them down his legs, along with his skin-hugging shorts. While she did that, he pulled his shirt off over his head.

She reached for his erection but he intercepted her hand. "First, you get naked too." He grabbed her other hand and held them over her head with one of his while he found the zipper on her pants and shoved them down to her ankles with the other. Her tiny thong panties—also that rosy peach color—were cute but now he wanted her in nothing but her skin. Finally he pushed her bra up over her breasts, freeing their weight to bounce enticingly. He let go of her hands, allowing her to tug the bra over her head, while he captured those twin globes in his hands.

"Gorgeous," he growled, bending down to feast. Her nipples were a dusky brown against her tawny skin and they tasted like heaven. He sucked first one, then the other into his mouth, unable to get enough.

"Zeyd!" She cried his name as she fisted her hands in his hair. The scent of her arousal fueled his own and he shoved her back against the cushions, pushing her down so she sprawled with her legs spread and him between them. He knelt, sitting back on his heels and draped those sleek, toned legs of hers up over his shoulders.

"Play with your nipples for me," he murmured.

She licked her fingers and used them to pinch the tips of her breasts, rolling them back and forth while he watched, growing even harder by the moment. Leaning in, he buried his nose in her pretty golden curls, just inhaling the full potency of her scent. She was drenched, her flesh plump and inviting. Pheromones hit him harder than a laser cannon and drove all thoughts of happy gas from his mind. He was drunker on Tabrin than he'd ever been on any kind of drug or drink.

Using both thumbs, he parted her wet folds. He took a moment to just gaze at her gorgeous pussy, so wet and swollen with the same desire that was shuddering through him. Her clit was a tightly furled bud, poking out as if begging for attention. First he swiped his tongue through her slit, lapping up the taste of her thick juices, then he used just the tip to tickle that pretty pink pearl.

"Fuck me, Zeyd," she cried as he felt her strong thighs clamp down on his shoulders. "Don't want to wait."

"Not until you come, sweetheart," he told her between licks. He slipped his thumbs into her channel while he went back to sucking her clit.

"Bully," she panted but he could tell she was close. Her whole body had started to quiver and her breathing was nothing more than a series of gasps. "Yes. Right there. Oh, Zeyd..."

His cock throbbed. He'd never get tired of hearing his name on her lips. He pinched with his lips at the same time as he pushed in harder with his thumbs.

She fractured, her pussy tightening around his thumbs and a rush of cream coating them as well as his chin. He licked it up, drinking as much of her as he could, like a man dying of thirst.

Finally her tremors slowed and he rose up on his knees. With her legs still up over his shoulders he pushed forward, sliding his heavy cock all the way into her twitching cunt. His implants filtered out any germs, so he couldn't catch anything or make her sick, and unless he turned them off someday, he couldn't get her pregnant. Sometimes, it was very, very good to be a cyborg.

The groan that ripped from his throat might just have been the sexiest thing Tabrin had ever heard. Knowing that she could reduce him to incoherent rumblings almost made up for the fact that she was just a quivering mass of protoplasm. Of course, even though she'd just come so hard her ears were probably bleeding, she still screamed his name when he finally shoved that long shaft up inside her.

She looked up at him, his sculpted muscles and the nipples that were a rich dark chocolate brown against his milk-chocolate chest. Stars but he was beautiful. Her pussy clamped down on his thick, hard cock and his gorgeous eyes went hazy for a second. She loved having that kind of effect on this big, strong predatory male.

How had she survived without this? Nothing had ever filled the emptiness inside her like Zeyd could. And not just because of his size. She had a vibrator even bigger than he was and it didn't do the trick. There was something about *him* that made her feel more feminine, more complete, than anything she'd ever known.

Zeyd began to move, a slow, powerful glide in and out of her drenched channel. His hands were clamped on her hips, gripping her hard enough to leave bruises. Tabrin didn't care. She'd look at those bruises, for the day or two they lasted, with pride. Especially since he obviously had his technologically boosted strength turned off. Otherwise, he'd break her in half when he came. Thank the gods that Xyran Rangers had off switches on their enhancements.

"Did you miss this, Tabrin?" He drove into her until his balls slapped against her ass. "Did you lay awake in your lonely bed and ache inside, wishing I was there?"

"Yes!" Damn it, she hadn't meant to say that. At less than half his body mass and without his nanotech toxin filters, she was a lot more affected already than he was. Another in the long list of life's little inequities.

"I did too, damn you. I'd be tracking a bounty and I'd wonder where you were, if you were on the same damn job." Another slow withdrawal. He hovered there for a moment, then powered back in, nudging her cervix with just the right pressure. "A couple of times I even took jobs because I thought you'd be in the same place, hoping to run into you."

Tab tried to reply but all that came out were incoherent whimpers. She'd sought him out too, even though she knew she shouldn't. But she didn't want to talk anymore. All she wanted to do right now was feel.

The position he had her in made it impossible for her to move, for her to touch him. The best she could do was dig her nails into the cushion and tighten her muscles around his cock. He increased his pace with a harsh gasp, letting her know he'd noticed the difference. Now instead of sliding in and out he was slamming in and out, every one of his thick muscles coiled and tense.

One hand left her hip to caress her mound, his finger unerringly finding her hyper-sensitized clit. She squealed as he rubbed it, spreading her juices around. He pressed down just a little harder and she shattered, convulsing so hard she honestly saw stars flashing in front of her eyelids. Zeyd bellowed her name, then rammed himself home. Staying deep, he exploded, filling her with wash after wash of thick, hot fluid.

They stayed still for long moments, as Tab wallowed in the long, slow aftershocks that danced through her body and Zeyd gasped for breath. Finally he eased her legs down off his shoulders and slumped down onto his heels, slipping out of her as he went. He leaned forward laying his head on her thigh and sighed.

"Ten months is too long to go without sex."

Go without? While she hadn't been with anyone since her last encounter with Zeyd, she'd certainly never imagined he'd abstained. Wrung out though she was, she managed to lift one hand off the now-shredded cushion and tangle it in his silky hair. "Yeah," she wheezed. "Too long."

Chapter Two

ꟾ

After Tabrin drifted off to sleep, Zeyd puttered around the pod for a while. First he did some tinkering with the air circulation system. Once that was done, he found pillows and blankets in the storage bins. Then he activated the mechanism that extended the bench into a platform bed, tucked a pillow under Tab's head and covered her sweat-sheened body with a layer of thin, soft fabric. Their discarded clothing he picked up and folded neatly. Sitting around naked with Tab sounded good to him. Xyrans weren't particularly hung up on nudity, especially a former soldier like himself who had lived in a barracks since he was old enough to walk.

At least they had plenty of food. The pod was stocked for up to eight Macandilari. Zeyd polished off a couple of nutrition bars and another bottle of water. He'd need all his strength to deal with Tab for twenty-three more hours. Then he quit fighting the urge to lie down beside her. He wasn't tired but he couldn't resist the urge to snuggle—an unexpected pleasure when it came to Tabrin. She snuffled daintily as he pulled her close against his chest but she settled easily, as if she belonged there. She was never this docile when awake. In fact, she'd be grumpy as a wet warthog to know how her body betrayed her in her sleep. Underneath all those carefully cultivated prickles, she really was a sweet little armful of woman.

What was he going to do about her? No matter how he tried, he couldn't seem to get her out of his system—something that had never happened to him before. When he'd seen Dinse fire that blaster at her, Zeyd's whole field of vision had gone red. He could have cheerfully twisted the fucker's head off, and relief at having saved her had slowed him down enough that he'd missed the door closing.

He even felt guilty about screwing her out of the bounty on Chansa Six. How was he to know she needed the money? And for what? There was so much about her that he wanted to know better.

A little while later, she stirred, stretched and looked up at him with her wide amber eyes. "Hey, soldier."

"Have a nice catnap?" He knew the pun would make her squirm but he couldn't resist. It was just so much fun to tease her.

"Mmm. Pillow's a little lumpy but I've slept on worse." Then she made a face and punched his stomach lightly. "Asshole. How long?"

"You were only out about an hour," he told her. "Twenty-two left of my scintillating company."

"I've survived worse." She yawned and sat up. "How about you? Anybody going to be worried if you don't check in on schedule?"

They'd never even discussed families, he realized. Hell, for all he knew she could be married. The red haze started to cloud his vision again. "Nobody," he grated. "How about you?"

"I call my sister once a week or so," she said, rummaging around for a bottle of water. "But she thinks I'm a secretary with a boss who likes to travel, so she's used to me being erratic." She opened the bottle and drained it in one long glug.

"You have a sister?" It was only slightly less unsettling than the thought of her as a secretary—which was patently absurd.

"Yeah. Meika's a great kid—smarter than anybody I know. She's twenty-five and in med school." Tabrin winced and pulled her knees up to her chin again.

"So that's why you need money," he reasoned. For now he let her keep her distance. "No parents?"

"Killed in a shuttle crash ten years ago," Tab answered. "A year later the insurance money ran out."

"And eight years ago was the first time I met you in the field." Zeyd sat up and leaned back against the wall. "How'd you get into bounty hunting?"

"A friend of a friend," she said. "I was waiting tables in a bar and he wanted someone to distract the quarry while he snuck up behind. I worked with him for a couple of years, then when he got himself killed I finished the job on my own. How about you? I know you were a Ranger. They're usually career soldiers. How'd you end up on your own?"

He shrugged. "Pissed off one too many superior officers. When it came time to re-up or retire, I took the buyout and split. Been doing this about fifteen years now." Rangers were required to serve twenty years to pay off the cost of their enhancements. Most stayed for three or four hitches, especially the ones raised in military schools or families but taking orders had never been Zeyd's strong suit.

"No family?" She'd tipped her head to the side and her posture was more relaxed now that they were talking about him.

"Nope. Father was a Ranger killed in the line when I was just a month or two old. Mother didn't want anything to do with parenthood, so she dumped me off at the base daycare and split."

"I'm sorry, Zeyd." Tabrin shook her head. "People who don't want kids shouldn't have them."

"No point in dwelling on it." He shrugged. "I managed well enough."

"Yeah, me too." She gave him a quirky grin. "You ever think about settling down, big guy? Making little cyborgs?"

Not until I met you. Despite the tongue-loosening effect of the gas, he managed not to say that out loud. "About as often as you consider having *kittens*." He threw the pillow at her head. "They wouldn't be cyborgs. No implants until you're done growing. That's one thing the Xyrans figured out early on."

"Kittens, my ass," she grumbled, throwing the pillow back. "You're such a jerk, Vasari. I'm only half-Keisian, you know. My father was from New Australia. Pure human."

"You mean a full Keisian might be even cuter than you?" A low chuckle rumbled up out of his throat. "Nah, they'd have taken over the universe by now."

Her eyes narrowed. "Take that back. I am *not* cute."

"Sorry, sweetheart. I call it like I see it. Cute, tough, meaner than hell and utterly fuckable, all at the same time."

She paused as if mulling over the implications of what he'd said. "All right. I guess that's relatively accurate. But turnabout is only fair. You're big, stubborn and pretty damn fuckable yourself."

"Oh yeah?" His body had fully recovered from their last bout and was more than ready for round two. "Care to prove that?"

She shook her head and stood. "Maybe in a minute. Right now I'm going to go check out the lav."

* * * * *

Tab made a face at her reflection in the polished steel mirror of the microscopic lavatory. She was in a whole pile of trouble here. Making sure she got whatever bounty was at stake wasn't the only reason she'd taken to slipping out on Zeyd in the middle of the night. With each successive encounter, she'd become more and more aware of him as a person, not just an available fuck-buddy. She *liked* him, damn it. And every single time it had gotten harder and harder to leave him behind and disappear into the darkness, or even worse, to wake up and find that he'd left her first. Her addiction to his touch could so easily become an obsession and she just couldn't afford that. Not now. Maybe in a year or two when Meika was finished with school. She splashed cold water on her face, refusing to let herself even think about the l-word. Not possible. Just not possible.

"Wondered if you'd gone back to sleep in there," Zeyd mumbled when she came out.

She shot him a sideways grin. "Nope. Just trying to clean up a bit in a space roughly the size of your shoe."

"Ooh, a kitty tongue-bath and I didn't get to watch?"

She rolled her eyes. "You are such an ass. Good luck fitting in there, by the way. Don't forget to duck."

"Already did." He grimaced. "About broke myself in half. Think I'm just going to hold it for the next twenty-two hours."

She sat down on the far side of what was now a platform bed and gazed at him. "So now what? Don't suppose you have a pop-up video screen in your arm, or any useful cyborg gadgets."

"Sorry. Got a few time-wasters on my personal com-link but nothing two-player. How about you?"

"Nope. I went for the most streamlined version possible. All mine does is make and receive communications. No vids. No web. No games." Every available credit went to Meika's tuition, not on extras for Tabrin's amusement.

"There was a deck of old-fashioned playing cards in one of the bins," he told her. "Underneath the video edition of the Gideon Koran-Torah-Bible. You ever play poker?"

"Once." She nodded thoughtfully. "But I'm not betting money. Not against you."

"Nope." He shook his head and his long hair fluttered around his broad shoulders. "And strip poker won't work, since we're already naked. How about favors?"

"Favors?" Her heart sped up, wondering just what he had in mind. Zeyd had always been…inventive.

"Yeah." He licked his lips. "Whoever loses the hand has to do anything the winner asks for. We can bet in terms of minutes."

Hmmm. They were trapped together anyway. She didn't really see how either of them could lose and it would pass the time. "Fine. Give me the cards. I'm not letting you deal."

He reached into one of the overhead cabinets and pulled out a thin packet she recognized as a deck of playing cards. Retro Earth games had made a comeback a few years earlier and poker was still a barroom favorite, so she knew the basics. She slit open the seal on the pack and shuffled the thin plastic sheets with their holographic images.

Meanwhile, Zeyd turned his back and rooted through his clothing. Damn but the man was almost as pretty from the back as from the front. While she shuffled she watched the play of his thick muscles under smooth chocolate-colored skin. Speaking of tongue-baths, it took all her willpower not to lean over and lick her way up and down his spine.

"Here we go." She averted her gaze as he turned, pressing buttons on his personal communications unit. Soft strains of woodwind music filled the air in the little space.

"Dakanian flutes? How very…sedate, Vasari. Had you pegged as more of a speed-plasma freak."

Zeyd shrugged. "Got that on there too. You want something different?"

Damn, did nothing faze him? "Nah. This is fine." The sound was kind of mellow and relaxing. She crossed her legs beneath her and dealt out the first hand.

* * * * *

After three hands, Tab was up eight minutes to four. Zeyd didn't really give a rip about winning. In this situation, he figured there was no way he could lose. Wasn't as if he minded being Tab's personal body slave. He couldn't help wondering what favors she would pick if she won.

"I'll see your two minutes and raise you one more." Tab grinned at him and something tightened in Zeyd's gut.

"Call." He looked down at his baby straight. Worth a shot, at this point.

Tab discarded two, while Zeyd tossed one. He dealt out the replacement cards and looked at his. Four of clubs. That gave him an eight-high straight. He waited for her to make her bet.

"Five minutes," she wagered. "Think you're up for it?"

He caught her gaze and deliberately stroked his erection with the hand that wasn't holding his cards. He'd been as hard as a titanium beam through this entire game. "Oh, sugar, I'm *up* for anything you can dish out. I'll see your five and raise you one secret."

"Secret?" She tipped her head, amber eyes wide. But she was watching him fist himself and he could smell her renewed arousal, see it in the tightening of her nipples. Oh yeah, she was ready for him again.

Zeyd nodded. "You have to tell me one personal secret you've never admitted to a single living soul."

Tabrin considered for a moment then nodded her head. "Fine. The pot's up to eight minutes and a secret." A broad grin stole across her face. "But you'll be the one telling it, big guy. Three aces."

With a chuckle he shook his head. "Sorry, Tab. This one's mine." He laid his straight down card by card. "That makes it eight minutes for you, twelve for me. And a secret."

Tab picked up the deck and started shuffling. "Loser goes first, right? Or do we just subtract the numbers and you'd have won four minutes?"

"Oh, no. I think we play them all out. Loser claims their minutes, then the winner."

"So this hand decides the winner."

"I'm ready to move on anytime you are," he growled. More than ready to end the game, he waited patiently while she shuffled and dealt them each five cards.

Hmmm. A pair of fives and four spades. Drawing to the pair was a better bet but playing things safe wasn't in his nature. "Two minutes and another secret."

Her teeth worried at her lower lip as she regarded her hand. "I'll see that and raise you another minute."

After calling her bet, Zeyd discarded the five of hearts. Tabrin dealt him one, then took three. This was looking good. Zeyd slipped his card into his hand and hissed out a breath. Nine of diamonds. That gave him a pair but not a good one. It all depended on Tab's hand now.

But bluffing was an essential skill for a bounty hunter and competition had always been a fierce component of his relationship with Tabrin. He kept his face immobile and bet. "Five minutes."

"Your five and five more."

The pot was up to thirteen minutes and a secret. Zeyd took another gamble. "I'll see that and raise you one date once we're out of here. An honest-to-goodness dinner date. In public. Winner chooses, loser pays."

She almost folded. He could see the panic in her eyes but he didn't know whether it was the threat of the expense, or the implication that their relationship would continue after they were picked up tomorrow. But her inhibitions were still a bit relaxed and he knew—or at least hoped—that on some level, she wanted them to have a genuine relationship almost as much as he did.

Instead she licked her lips. "Call."

Zeyd placed his cards face up on the cushions between them. "Pair of nines."

A small smile twitched at the corners of her lips. She fanned her cards and spread them out. "Aces. Your ass is mine, buddy-boy."

Zeyd grinned back and wiggled his eyebrows, just because it always made her laugh. "So it is. But not until after yours is mine."

Her breath caught and she darted her gaze up to his. "You don't mean..."

He'd never taken her anally but he wasn't about to start that with only twelve minutes to play. "No. Not this time, sweetheart. All I want this time is to watch you take me in your mouth." He scooped up the cards and set them on the floor. Then he picked up his com unit and set the timer before lounging back against the wall. "Think you can handle that?"

"I always have," she returned. "Couldn't come up with something more creative?"

He shook his head. "Nope. Not a single thing in the world I'd rather spend twelve minutes on."

She reached over and took his com from his hand, started the timer and set the unit aside. "Works for me." Kneeling between his legs, she took his rigid cock in her hands and lowered her head.

Just the sight of her tawny head bent over his lap was almost enough to set him off. Her long hair, free from its braid now, tickled his hips and thighs as she stroked him with her fingers. That rough little tongue licked its way from the root to the tip, circling the crown slowly before dipping in to lap up a bead of pre-cum.

"I might not last twelve minutes," he muttered. He could use his cybernetic implants to slow things down, of course, but somehow that had always seemed like cheating. When he was with Tabrin, he wanted everything that happened to be genuine.

"Oh, I'm sure you'll come up with alternatives." Her voice was low and husky, almost a purr. She slurped one of his balls into her mouth and sucked gently, then switched to the other. In between, she paused to murmur, "You taste like heaven, Zeyd. I could do this for hours."

"Feel free." His hips flexed upward as she licked her way back up along the thick vein that ridged the underside. "Any...time."

When she sucked the head of his erection into her mouth he closed his eyes and groaned. All that wet heat closing around him, her raspy tongue dabbling into his leaking slit—it was the stuff dreams were made of. Well, his dreams anyway. He'd woken up with spattered sheets more than once after dreaming of Tab.

She worked him with the intimate knowledge of longtime lovers. Hard to believe that they'd only been together a couple dozen times over the last few years. It always seemed like he'd known her all his life, loved her forever. He dreamed about that sometimes too—forever. He'd never believed in that sort of thing but something about Tabrin with her unique blend of toughness and vulnerability had him wondering if happily ever after might really be possible.

"Suck it harder, sugar." He threw his head back and clenched his stomach muscles.

Tab obeyed with flattering eagerness. Giving a soft hum, she took him deeper into her throat and swallowed, caressing his tip with the rippling muscles of her throat. She increased both suction and tempo, fisting his shaft with one hand to match her own rhythm. The other hand slipped underneath to cradle his taut, heavy sac in her palm. One finger slid forward, pressing up against his sphincter.

"Hell, yes!" The strangled moan was barely recognizable as his voice. It wouldn't be long, not now, not like this. Although it took a good bit of effort, he forced his eyes to stay open. He wanted to watch, to remind himself that this time she was really here. Not just a memory, not just a dream, but Tabrin, in all her naked glory.

He was so close. Even after coming inside her just a few hours ago, his balls felt so full they were liable to burst. Then Tab swallowed his cock just a little deeper and pushed the tip of her index finger up into his ass.

"Tabrin!" If they'd been in a building, the walls would have shaken with the force of his shout. His testicles damn near exploded from the orgasm that blasted through his body, releasing a powerful stream of semen. She swallowed repeatedly, drinking from him thirstily until he was done.

When Zeyd slumped back against the cushion, she daintily licked him clean, washed off her fingers with a sanitary wipe, then crawled up his chest to kiss him soundly on the lips.

He wrapped his arms around her and crushed her against him, loving the taste of his essence on her lips and tongue.

Finally, she curled against him in his arms. She snaked out one hand and grabbed his com unit. "You have six minutes left, big guy. What do you want to do?"

"This is good." He trailed his fingers through her hair. "I like holding you, Tab. Knowing if I fall asleep for an hour, you won't disappear on me."

"Mmm. I like that too." Her fingers traced lazy circles on his chest. "Meika only has one more year of medical school. Then maybe I can take some time off. Maybe even…a vacation…or something."

"Sounds good to me, sweetheart." He lifted her mouth for another long, sweet kiss. "Don't expect me to wait that long to have you again, though." Not going to happen. His brain was busy sorting out plans and ideas.

"I sure hope not." She nipped his chest playfully. "I still have twenty-one minutes of your services coming."

"Uh-huh." And Zeyd was looking forward to every one of them.

Chapter Three

ꟷ

"So what are you going to claim as your favor?" he asked lazily.

Tab grinned against his chest. "I haven't decided yet." Her hand trailed down his chest to cup his cock, which had nearly recovered. A few strokes from her palm and he went from half-mast to full erection. She loved the fact that she could affect him so easily, that she could literally bring this big powerful man to his knees.

"I give one hell of a backrub," he rumbled into her hair. His arm tightened around her, one hand idly fondling the crack of her ass.

"Mmm. I remember. But I'm already feeling all loose and mellow. Besides, I kind of like you like this, lying here at my mercy." She giggled and nipped him again. A germ of an idea began to form, just as the timer on his com unit chirped. Scrambling out of his arms to sit beside him, she retrieved the unit and reset it, for twenty-one minutes this time. "My turn."

"All yours, kitten. What do you want me to do?"

She licked her lips. "Just lay down, all the way, on the cushions. Hands over your head."

He cocked one eyebrow but obeyed. Tab reached for her tunic and pulled the para-cuffs out of the pocket.

"Remember Divonne?"

"No!" His dark blue eyes flashed with alarm and he jackknifed to a seated position. "Tabrin, you don't want to—"

"Yes I do, Zeyd. When I cuffed you to that bed and left you, I remember thinking what a colossal waste it was. There you were, all tied up and I couldn't stick around to enjoy it."

"Tabby..." It wasn't quite a whine. Zeyd would never sink that low but she heard the plea.

She watched his throat work as he overcame his reluctance to be dominated in any way. It would be good for Zeyd to learn to give up control once in a while, she decided. As soon as he lay back down, arms out above his head, she moved closer and clipped the flexible cuffs to his wrists, activating the neurological blocking switch. Zeyd would continue to feel everything she did to him but he wouldn't be able to move a muscle on either of his arms or legs. "Relax, lover." She kissed him on the lips, a light flutter of a touch. "I promise, it will be good."

"You're going to pay for this one, Tab," he warned. "I promise you that too."

"Oooh, I'm so frightened." She nipped his chin and tickled his ear with the tip of her tongue. "I'm on to you, Vasari. The big tough bounty-hunting cyborg is really a big, cuddly teddy bear."

"I wouldn't count on that." His tone smoldered with the assurance of retribution.

Tab laughed. She'd take whatever punishment he wanted to dish out. Meanwhile, it was her turn to play. She nibbled her way down his chest, pausing to swirl her tongue around his navel.

"I need you nice and hard, Zeyd. Think you can handle that?" Of course he could—he was already fully aroused again.

"When you're around? No problem there, sweetheart. I can keep it up for hours on end just thinking about you."

"Aww, sugar, you always say the nicest things. For that you get a bonus." She took his cock back into her mouth and rolled her tongue around it, savoring his taste. She'd go to her grave remembering that salty, bitter tang. Nothing she'd ever known even came close.

"Any time, kitten. You want to suck me off, all you have to do is ask."

"Not this time." She wiped her chin and shifted to straddle his hips. "This time it's the kitten's turn to ride."

"Well then, saddle up, cowgirl."

She chuckled as she poised his swollen tip at her soaking-wet entrance. Only with Zeyd had she ever actually laughed during sex. That element of fun was almost as heart-wrenching as his tenderness. "I'd forgotten your addiction to ancient cowboy stories."

"Spent my first twelve years on Outpost."

That explained a lot. Outpost was a Xyran protectorate but out at the edge of the galaxy where technology was sometimes hard to come by. The agricultural planet had culturally reverted to a low-tech society, using horses and cattle for a lot of the farm work instead of machinery.

She lowered herself and his eyes rolled up in his head. Tabrin closed hers for a moment too, content just to feel the smooth glide of his thick rod filling up all the emptiness inside her. By the time she rested on his hipbones, the tip of his penis was nestled up against her cervix. She wiggled her hips from side to side, enjoying the stretched fullness. They'd always been such a perfect fit.

"If you uncuffed me, I could play with those pretty nipples of yours," he coaxed. "I haven't had the chance to suck on them very much tonight. You know how much you like that. My mouth on you while you get off on my cock."

Her nipples, already taut and aching, budded up even further at his words. She did love that but she was having so much fun with him immobilized for her pleasure. Stretching her arms up over her head, she lifted her heavy breasts and swayed, giving him an eyeful. "Maybe later." Using her knees, she set up a slow glide, up and down on his rigid shaft. "After all, my twenty-one minutes has barely begun."

"Later," he said with steely intent. "I'm going to bend you over a pillow, point that cute little ass of yours up in the air and fuck you from behind until neither of us can remember our own name."

"That's supposed to be a threat?" She braced one hand on his chest and slid the other down her stomach to finger her clit. As always when Zeyd was near, the little bud was tightly furled and extremely sensitive. Her hips speeded up of their own accord and her inner muscles clenched down on Zeyd. "I can take anything you can dish out, Xyran."

"See if you still say that when I can move."

Tabrin tried to retort but she was too far gone. All that came out was a breathless mewl as she rode him hard and strummed at her clit. "Z-Z-Zeyd!"

"Come for me, Tabrin. Let me feel that pretty pussy of yours clench around my cock like a fist. I want to feel those sweet juices of yours wash over me while you scream."

And just like that, she did. It wasn't a massive explosion like the last time but a slow, rolling climax that rippled through her like waves until she fell forward, limp, onto Zeyd's chest.

"Keep moving," he grunted. His hips made tiny upward pulses, which shouldn't even have been possible with the para-cuffs. "Either keep moving or let me go. *Please.*"

She pushed herself up with both hands and moved her hips. It wasn't much but she could tell by his clenched teeth and corded neck that he was close. She squeezed him with her still-twitching inner muscles, lifted up her pelvis and brought it back down as hard as she could.

On the third stroke, Zeyd bellowed, "Yes!" and she felt the hot wet splash of him pouring into her yet again. His stamina amazed her but she couldn't help a little frisson of pride that it was her he wanted so much and so often.

Eventually she mustered the energy to reach up and disengage the cuffs. Zeyd immediately rolled her beneath him and proceeded to kiss her until she was sure she'd forgotten how to breathe.

"I'll take that backrub now," she gasped when they finally came up for air.

"Okay," he wheezed back. "As soon as I can move." His lips descended on hers again, hot and sweet and tender, all at the same time. She felt the unfamiliar prickle of tears at the corners of her eyes. Had to be the air, damn it. She couldn't, wouldn't, cry in front of Zeyd.

"One massage, coming up." In one lithe move, he rolled off her and to his feet. After pulling a box out of one of the overhead bins, he rooted through it. "I knew it. Macandilari have problems with dry skin during space travel, so they always need lotion." He tossed the box aside and came back to the cushions with a plastic tube.

Tab smiled up at him. "What do you know, he's smart as well as pretty."

His eyebrows wiggled enticingly, those thick slashes of black against his chocolate skin. "Good with my hands too."

Before he rejoined her on the platform, he grabbed two bottles of water and handed her one, helping her to a sitting position. They both drained their bottles, then Zeyd gently positioned her face down on the cushions. She heard the squirt of the lotion and then heard him rub the thick fluid between his big hands. Then those hands were warm and gentle on the muscles of her shoulders.

"Your skin is so soft, Tab, and you're so delicate to the touch. If I didn't know just how tough you are, I'd be trying to keep you wrapped up in bubble foam somewhere."

"You and what army, big guy?" It was hard to speak with her nose pressed down in a crack between two cushions. She adjusted the arrangement, giving her a wide gap for her face and then relaxed back down. Zeyd's hands kept a steady glide across her shoulders but he didn't deepen the touch until she'd settled.

"No army. Just you and me and I'd never try to tame you, to make you into anything you're not. We make a good team, sweetheart. We could try working as a pair, split the bounties instead of fighting over them."

Tab felt the tears try to start again. "It would never work, Zeyd." The short life expectancy in their profession was only one of the problems. Kiesians were unwelcome in so many places, starting with on Xyra, Zeyd's home planet. He'd be shooting himself in the foot to get hooked up openly with her.

"Just think about it. Having backup in the field wouldn't be a bad thing. And the nights between jobs would be a hell of a lot more fun."

He had her on that one. But she couldn't give in. Her heart would be broken to pieces when it was over. Even now she was having one hell of a time keeping her emotional distance. She kept her face in the pillows so he wouldn't see the moisture beading in her eyes.

Zeyd must have gotten the hint because he went back to kneading her back and shoulders with an expert touch. After a few more minutes she was so relaxed she nodded off. She awoke when the timer beeped, to find he'd moved down to her feet, which now felt as relaxed as the rest of her.

Zeyd turned it off, tossed it aside, then moved to her thighs and calves, giving them the same thorough treatment as her back. Her arms were next and then her neck and scalp. At that, Tabrin made a little sound of contentment. Zeyd could make a living at this.

"Did you just purr?" His voice was laced with fond amusement.

"No." Not really. Not much, anyway. Just one little genetic holdover from her feline DNA but it tended to freak people out, so she'd deny it to her dying breath.

"I think you did. I know you do during sex sometimes but I didn't know I could make you purr just by rubbing your back." He dropped a soft kiss on her neck and put his hands on her shoulders. "Front side now. Roll over, Tab."

"Fine." She wasn't about to argue. She settled on her back while he got more lotion from the tube and began working her shins and the fronts of her thighs.

"I have an apartment on Xyra, you know. It's small but it's got this really nice hydrotherapy tub—big enough for two. After we collar Dinse, I can take you there. We can figure out what we do next." He rubbed her belly with long slow strokes, inching ever closer to her breasts.

"Sure. That'll work. How long do you think we could be there before they ran me off with laser torches? Or is it a red-light district where Kiesians are welcome, as long as they're prostitutes?"

"Shit. I never even think about it but yeah, a lot of Xyrans think they're better than anybody else. Idiots. Still, there are plenty of planets out there where people don't give a damn. We can find one of them, camp out in a hotel for a few days."

Gods, it sounded so idyllic. She was starting to feel more than relaxed, she discovered. Her breasts were aching and her nipples pointed again. Fresh moisture gathered at her pussy, which was still swollen from the last bout. She was just plain insatiable when it came to this man. Spending that kind of time with him would be far too dangerous. It had to be the influence of the air when she heard herself whisper, "I guess that would be okay."

"Perfect," he whispered, slicking the lotion over her sensitive breasts with his palms. The slight herbal scent barely registered over the smell of sweat and sex that filled the pod. She hoped the stuff was food-grade, because as soon as he was done with the cream, he bent his head and brushed her nipple with his lips. "Beautiful." His tongue swirled around the furled peak, then he sucked it into his mouth.

"Oh, hell, Zeyd." She didn't know if she was up for another round, not really but she clutched his head to her chest, tangling her fingers in his hair. He drew on her in a slow, steady rhythm, while his other hand palmed her other breast.

Just when she thought she was about to come just from the pleasure of his mouth on her nipple, he switched to the other side. This time his hand slid down to settle at her cleft, rubbing between her wet labia. He plucked at her clit and the tension in her womb coiled again, even tighter than before. She started to whimper, gasping for air, when Zeyd stopped, pulling away abruptly.

"Roll over."

Ah. He'd said he wanted her from behind. She shifted to her stomach, settling her hips on a pillow he'd found from somewhere, so her ass was lifted up like an offering.

"I can't get enough of you," he muttered roughly as he moved between her thighs. "You're in my blood, Tabrin." His thick cock speared into her drenched pussy in one sure thrust.

"I know." She raised her hips to meet his strokes as much as the position allowed. "Just fuck me, Zeyd. Until I don't have the energy to think."

"My pleasure." They didn't speak further while he fucked her hard and fast. It was over in minutes, in a cataclysmic mutual orgasm. That left her utterly limp and wasted. Zeyd rolled her over and pulled her up against his chest. Long, content moments passed and she once again drifted off to sleep in Zeyd's arms.

*****

"You still owe me a secret, sweetheart. So what's it to be? What's one thing you've never admitted to another living soul?" They'd woken several hours later, still curled together under the thin blanket. He loved the feel of her in his arms when he woke, the foggy haze in her tawny eyes as she blinked at him.

Tab shifted uncomfortably against his chest. "You already know more about me than anyone else in the universe. Nobody else in the business knows about my sister, Vasari. Nobody."

"Settle down." He rubbed his hand up and down her back. "It's just pillow talk. I'm not going to tell anyone."

"I know." Tab pressed a kiss just to the side of his nipple. "I just don't know what else to tell you. Other than Meika, I don't have much of a life."

"Neither do I. It's a lonely business we're in, Tab. But there has to be something." He didn't know why but it mattered that he know something about her that no one else did. Even if he had to walk away from her after tomorrow, he wanted to have some link, some extra intimacy to hold onto while they were apart.

"I'm forty-one but that's not a big secret. My mother was a Keisian waitress and my father was a performing magician. They settled on Chimera, had two daughters and died in a shuttle crash right after Meika started high school. She was in one of those special programs for gifted kids and they were on their way to visit for her birthday." Her voice choked at the end of her sentence.

He hugged her close. "I'm sorry, Tab. Sounds like you really loved them."

"They were good people. Never made much money, though and Meika's school was expensive. The shuttle company settlement paid for it for a year or so. I already told you the rest."

"So you were in your thirties when your parents died. And you said you were tending bar?"

"Mmm-hmm. And sang in a band for a while. Keisian torch songs I learned from my mom. I was going to be the next intergalactic sensation."

"So what happened?"

"The usual." She shrugged, a soft, subtle movement against his skin. "I wasn't really all that good. I made an adequate living, between mixing drinks and singing for the tourists but not enough to pay for Meika's education."

"You'll have to sing for me sometime," he murmured into his hair. "But that's still not a secret."

"You never quit, do you, Zeyd?"

"Not when I really set my mind to something. And that, my dear, is something you'd do well to keep in mind."

"Fine. You want a secret? How's this?" She pulled away to sit up beside him, then took a deep breath and faced him squarely. "The first boy I ever kissed was Locan Deene, my father's apprentice, when I was thirteen. The first man I ever fucked was Falco Braz, a Grimaldian lounge singer who promised to make me famous. But the first man I ever loved-"

"Who?" Red, murderous rage warred with tenderness, swamping him in a confused haze of emotion.

"The first man I ever loved, Zeyd," she whispered, with a broken hitch in her sweet voice. "The only man I ever loved—was you."

Zeyd's throat worked. It was what he wanted to hear but the heartbreak in her voice tore at his soul. "Shhh. Tabrin. I love you too. That's no bad thing, sweetheart." He sat up and tugged her onto his lap, crushing her in his arms. "I've loved you for so long, Tab."

"But it won't work," she argued, snuggling her head into his chest.

"Why not?" he asked reasonably. "Marry me, Tab. We can work as a team for a few years, then maybe buy that bar you want." Well, sooner rather than later. He had more than enough money in the bank to pay for her sister's tuition and to buy a tavern. But he'd ease Tabrin into that idea, once she got over being afraid to simply be with him.

"M-marry you?" She went rigid in his arms, then shook her head. "Don't even joke about it, Vasari. You have no idea how much I want to hold you to that but it wouldn't be fair. We can talk about it later, after we've gotten the gas out of our systems."

Oops, time for another confession. "Yeah, about that. Remember when you fell asleep the first time?"

"Yes?"

"I managed to rewire the air circulation system and shut off the Macandilar components. By the time we got to our card game, any and all of the atmospheric happy gas was gone."

He felt her go still as she processed the information. "So everything we said, everything we did, was all genuine—not drug-induced?"

"Afraid so, sugar. When I said I love you—I meant every word."

"It will still never work. I'm only half-human and I've got a lot of baggage. You don't really want to be tied to someone like me."

"No. I don't want to be tied to someone like you. Just to you, Tabrin Jones." Words had never been his strong suit, so he struggled to find the right ones to convince her of the depth of his feelings. "I don't care what planet your parents come from or whether your pupils look the same as mine. I'm part machine—that should bother you more than your feline DNA bothers me. And if you look back in history, you know that in some times and places, I'd have been discriminated against because I have dark skin. Funny how little that matters just a thousand years later."

"You don't have to marry me, Zeyd." Tears glistened in her eyes and Zeyd had to fight the urge to punch a hole through the pod wall. "We can go away together, if you want. Enjoy the sex for as long as it lasts."

"No!" He winced at the sound of his own frustrated roar. "I don't want to just sleep with you for a while. I want to be with you for the rest of my fucking life. Why can't you get that through your head?"

She pulled away again and studied him intently. "So this isn't just about sex? You honestly want to marry me, to work as a team?"

Zeyd nodded.

Slowly, an incredulous, beautiful smile suffused Tabrin's face and she launched herself back into his arms.

"Is that a yes?" He tried to ignore the knot of fear in his stomach that she might still say no.

"It is."

Zeyd's breath left him in a whoosh.

"Vasari, looks like you've got yourself a partner—for life."

About the Authors

ꟈ

Debra Glass

Debra Glass' previous experience as a medium inspired her interest in writing Alabama ghost stories, although she's also got a passion for spine-tingling paranormal romance. Since 2002, Debra has written several books on regional folklore and has had numerous articles published in Fate Magazine and various Civil War magazines.

Now she's writing steamy erotic romance and dabbling in the paranormal with her Phantom Lovers series which features passionate and sexy ghosts who are guaranteed to keep you up at night!

Also by Debra Glass

Death by Chocolate

Gatekeeper

Restraint

Shadowkeeper

Watchkeeper

Solange Ayre

Solange Ayre, galaxy-hopping investigative journalist, also serves as a policy advisor to the United Conglomeration of Planetary Jurisdictions. She makes her home on Ayriana, her private island-republic in the West Caribbean region of Earth.

After a whirlwind childhood living in the capitals of Europe, Solange married St. Georges Ayre, one of the wealthiest men in the world. The crystal palace he bought her on Ayriana is the primary tourist attraction in the area—at least, for those who can find it. St. George's mysterious assassination is still mourned by his grieving widow.

Directly descended from King Louis XVI and Marie Antoinette, Solange graciously supports the democratic government of France and relinquishes her claim to the throne. Under no circumstances will she answer to the title "Your Highness."

In her spare time, Solange enjoys breeding and showing her prize-winning miniature dragons as well as researching and writing erotic romance.

Also by Solange Ayre

Bride Reborn

Bride's Holiday Gift

Ellora's Cavemen: Jewels of the Nile III (*anthology*)

Emerald Eyes

One Thousand Brides

Tempting Treats

Wizard's Woman

Desiree Holt

I always wonder what readers really want to know when I write one of these things. Getting to this point in my career has been an interesting journey. I've managed rock and roll bands and organized concerts. Been the only female on the sports staff of a university newspaper. Immersed myself in Nashville peddling a country singer. Lived in five different states. Married two very interesting but totally different men.

I think I must have lived in Texas in another life, because the minute I set foot on Texas soil I knew I was home. Living in Texas Hill Country gives me inspiration for more stories than I'll probably ever be able to tell, what with all the sexy cowboys who surround me and the gorgeous scenery that provides a great setting.

Each day is a new adventure for me, as my characters come to life on the pages of my current work in progress. I'm absolutely compulsive about it when I'm writing and thank all the gods and goddesses that I have such a terrific husband who encourages my writing and puts up with my obsession. As a multi-published author, I love to hear from my readers. Their input keeps my mind fresh and always hunting for new ideas.

Also by Desiree Holt

Candy Caresses

Cupid's Shaft

Diamond Lady

Double Entry

Elven Magic *with Regina Carlysle and Cindy Spencer Pape*

Emerald Green

Hot Moon Rising
Hot, Wicked and Wild
Journey to the Pearl
Letting Go
Line of Sight
Night Heat
Once Burned
Once Upon a Wedding
Teaching Molly
Touch of Magic
Where Danger Hides

Talya Bosco

Talya is an avid fan of all forms of the printed word. She has been reading for as long as she can remember and has dreamed of being an author for almost as long. On any given day, when she's not working you can find her at the computer or curled up somewhere in her house reading whatever has caught her fancy that week. She has been known to push the limits of her deadlines or go to work on little to no sleep, only so she can finish a book she is reading.

Her reading habit was the bane of her family's existence while growing up, but she has found a wonderful man that shares her evil inclination. They live quietly, reading books, playing on computers, practicing martial arts and enjoying one another's company.

Tayla feels all the reading has helped her to become a better author. She has devoted her professional life to writing fun, erotic stories that make you believe in second chances and happily-ever-afters.

Kristin Daniels

Kristin has always been a reader of romance, but it wasn't until she discovered the *erotic* romance genre that she finally figured out what had been missing from all the books she'd read before. The heat, the passion, that was it! Her love of reading (any genre, any format…really just *anything*) led to her taking a chance on writing something of her own, and she's been hooked ever since.

Kristin calls the suburbs of Chicago home, where she lives with a hero of her very own and their three great kids.

Cindy Spencer Pape

Cindy Spencer Pape has been, among other things, a banker, a teacher, and an elected politician, though she swears she got better. Her degrees are in zoology, and she currently works in environmental education, when she can fit it in around writing. She lives in southern Michigan with her husband, two teenage sons, a dog, a lizard, and various other small creatures, all of which are easier to clean up after than the three male humans.

Also by Cindy Spencer Pape

Between a Rock and a Hard-On

Djinni and the Geek

Ellora's Cavemen: Jewels of the Nile III (*anthology*)

Elven Magic *with Regina Carlysle and Desiree Holt*

One Good Man

Stone and Earth

Stone and Sea

Teach Me

Three for All

Whispers of Magic

The authors welcome comments from readers. You can find their websites and email addresses on their author bio pages at www.ellorascave.com.

Tell Us What You Think

We appreciate hearing reader opinions about our books. You can email us at Comments@EllorasCave.com.

Why an electronic book?

We live in the Information Age—an exciting time in the history of human civilization, in which technology rules supreme and continues to progress in leaps and bounds every minute of every day. For a multitude of reasons, more and more avid literary fans are opting to purchase e-books instead of paper books. The question from those not yet initiated into the world of electronic reading is simply: *Why?*

1. ***Price.*** An electronic title at Ellora's Cave Publishing and Cerridwen Press runs anywhere from 40% to 75% less than the cover price of the exact same title in paperback format. Why? Basic mathematics and cost. It is less expensive to publish an e-book (no paper and printing, no warehousing and shipping) than it is to publish a paperback, so the savings are passed along to the consumer.
2. ***Space.*** Running out of room in your house for your books? That is one worry you will never have with electronic books. For a low one-time cost, you can purchase a handheld device specifically designed for e-reading. Many e-readers have large, convenient screens for viewing. Better yet, hundreds of titles can be stored within your new library—on a single microchip. There are a variety of e-readers from different manufacturers. You can also read e-books on your PC or laptop computer. (Please note that Ellora's Cave does not endorse any specific brands.

You can check our websites at www.ellorascave.com or www.cerridwenpress.com for information we make available to new consumers.)

3. ***Mobility.*** Because your new e-library consists of only a microchip within a small, easily transportable e-reader, your entire cache of books can be taken with you wherever you go.
4. ***Personal Viewing Preferences.*** Are the words you are currently reading too small? Too large? Too... ANNOYING? Paperback books cannot be modified according to personal preferences, but e-books can.
5. ***Instant Gratification.*** Is it the middle of the night and all the bookstores near you are closed? Are you tired of waiting days, sometimes weeks, for bookstores to ship the novels you bought? Ellora's Cave Publishing sells instantaneous downloads twenty-four hours a day, seven days a week, every day of the year. Our webstore is never closed. Our e-book delivery system is 100% automated, meaning your order is filled as soon as you pay for it.

Those are a few of the top reasons why electronic books are replacing paperbacks for many avid readers.

As always, Ellora's Cave and Cerridwen Press welcome your questions and comments. We invite you to email us at Comments@ellorascave.com or write to us directly at Ellora's Cave Publishing Inc., 1056 Home Avenue, Akron, OH 44310-3502.